"YOU, ME, AND YOUR DAUGHTER ARE THE ONLY WHITES LEFT ALIVE FOR TWO HUNDRED MILES."

"Tomorrow morning," added Slocum, "we're packing up and leaving."

"The Indians won't let us leave," said Laura Duffy firmly. "One of Crazy Horse's relatives been comin' here visiting." She hung her head demurely. "He has marriage on his mind."

"Well, hell," said Slocum in a nasty tone. "Maybe you ought to just get hitched. You got a considerable dowry."

Laura laughed. "Oh, my, you must think me quite the merry widow. But no, Mr. Slocum, he isn't a bit interested in me. He wants my daughter Opal."

JAKE LOGAN
SLOCUM'S RUN

PLAYBOY
PAPERBACKS

SLOCUM'S RUN

Copyright © 1981 by Jake Logan

Cover illustration copyright © 1981 by PEI Books, Inc.

Published simultaneously in the United States and Canada by Playboy Paperbacks, New York, New York. Printed in the United
States of America. Library of Congress Catalog Card Number:
81-82165. First edition.

Books are available at quantity discounts for promotional and indus-
trial use. For further information, write to Premium Sales, Playboy
Paperbacks, 1633 Broadway, New York, New York 10019.

ISBN: 0-872-16927-8

First printing November 1981.

1

"Honor goes where honor's due," the mountain man said stubbornly.

John Slocum had rarely met a man he disagreed with so often, or liked as much. Slocum half turned in his saddle. "Now, Jim, you know that ain't true," he said, mildly enough. "Hell, some of the most honored men have been some of the worst scoundrels."

"That ain't honor," the other came back without repressing the note of triumph in his voice. It was a note not unlike the caw of a crow. "That's 'white man's honor'—what other people think of you—whether they praise you and such. It ain't the real thing, not by a long shot. The Indian—he understands honor more than we do. Why, we went ahead and honored that fellow J. P. Morgan—that fellow with the banks. Well, no Sioux would have honored him, not the way he behaved."

John Slocum had never heard of J. P. Morgan and wasn't sure the mountain man had heard much either. "Trouble with you, Jim," he said, "you got used to bein' by yourself too much. Got to figurin' your own chin music was the sweetest sound under the heavens."

"I guess the ford's safe," the older man opined.

The two riders had waited, motionless, for half an hour, above the shallow ford crossing the Heart River. Half an hour wasn't enough time to spot a Sioux warrior waiting in the alders beside the stream, but the ford was wide and well used, and they were just hours out of the fort, so they could be a little careless.

"If you weren't a little careless, a man couldn't ride anywhere." Slocum was tempted to say, but didn't because he knew the mountain man wouldn't agree with him. "Let's give her a try," Slocum said, pulling his saddle carbine out of the scabbard and across his saddle. No sense being *too* careless.

Thirty feet apart, the two men entered the ford. Two well-armed white men crosssing the Heart River ford, a few miles west of Fort Abraham Lincoln, Dakota Territory, sometime in late June or early July of 1876.

Slocum knew men who took care to scratch off every day before they lay down to sleep, so they could note Thanksgiving and Christmas and New Year's, but Slocum wasn't one of them. He knew what moon it was, whether you had enough light to hunt at night or travel. He knew where the evening star rose and set, and the indescribable swirl of the galaxy overhead was his nightly companion, but he didn't keep track of the date.

Beckwith rode the drag, his carbine in his hand with a round down the spout and twelve more in the tube under the barrel. Beckwith preferred the Henry .44 for close work, though a single-shot Sharps .69 was wrapped in the oilcloth bundle behind his saddle. He preferred the greater accuracy of the Sharps for hunting. When the Sharps was new, he'd killed plenty grizzly with it, but high in the Wind River range when there were plenty of beaver in the high streams, and a damn sight more grizzly too. Jim Beckwith had been new, too, about the same age as his present companion—early thirties at a guess.

Slocum settled the butt of his Winchester against his thigh and scanned both banks of the stream as his horse picked its own footing in the shallow water.

A bird called from the bank. Catbird, most likely, and a real one—not some Sioux buck signaling. A man couldn't ride tense day after day through Indian country. He'd crack up sure. John Slocum rode easy.

Beckwith had his long legs stuck down over the sides of his black. He used leather straps instead of stirrups because that's how he'd ridden when he'd come into the far west, with Bridger's own company back in 1845. His shirt was a single layer of buckskin, thonged down the front, flapping open. There was a single purple scar over his breastbone. Through the open shirt you could see half of it. A long-dead Crow had arrowed him right in the bone, by God, and it hurt like hell. The tip of that arrow was still in there. In cold or wet weather, it still hurt. Buckskin pants, high moccasins, no spurs. A black slouch hat to keep the sun off. He had some of his teeth left, but not the front ones. Jim Beckwith, mountain man.

Beckwith had trapped all the furbearers: mink, beaver, muskrat, weasel, fox, and wolf when he couldn't help it. He didn't like to think of himself as a wolver because that was a quantity business. But the fact was, with the slaughter of the buffalo herds, there was such a glut of wolves, a man could kill wolves until he was sick of it and sell every pelt he took.

Beckwith didn't think of himself as old either, but he was.

His younger companion was as quick an animal as ever he'd seen. A grizzly or bison or moose or elk and maybe even a good-sized buck mule deer would have more strength than Slocum. But he'd kill them all the same. Unarmed, he'd be a good match for a gray wolf in his prime, but a little outmatched by a big timber wolf. That's how Beckwith rated his companion.

Slocum wore his raven-black hair in braids shorter than Beckwith's patchy gray-blond locks. His eyes were the green of green fire opals. His face bore the marks of a great sadness. Though he hadn't spoken to Beckwith about it, Beckwith knew why. There were few enough white men on the west side of the Missouri, and they kept track of one another.

John Slocum had heard of Jim Beckwith long before the older man rode into Slocum's camp at the mouth of the Platte nine days ago.

Slocum had a coffee pot in one hand and a drawn Colt in the other and his funny green eyes flashed. Politely, the Colt was pointed away from Beckwith's middle, but not far away.

"If I get my choice, I'll take the coffee," Beckwith had drawled.

Slocum smiled. "Light, then, pilgrim," he said.

"Name's Beckwith," Jim said before sliding off his black, just to let the other know.

"John Slocum."

"You the fellow wintered up with the Blackfeet?" Beckwith asked. He untied his tin cup from his possibles bag and held it to be filled.

"The same."

Beckwith had nodded. He'd heard something of the strange white man who'd lived with the mountain Blackfeet. Heard he'd taken himself an Indian wife named Bird-Calling, and, if he recollected right, Slocum had had a child too, a son or a daughter, he didn't know which. Last spring, the smallpox took them both.

It was getting dusky, and after Beckwith grained his animals, he pulled a pint bottle from his saddlebag. It was trade whiskey, half gunpowder, half mustard, rust-colored, rust-flavored, and a hundred fifty proof. A quart of it would blind you sure, but Beckwith only had a pint and there were two of them to drink.

Talk was general at first, and as the two men discovered common acquaintances, it got particular. They drank and swapped news.

In the morning, Slocum announced his intention to travel upstream to the fort.

"Mind company?" Beckwith asked.

"There might be Indians enough for both of us," Slocum said.

Beckwith's sardonic drawl: "Seemed like I heard something about those Indians myself."

The frontier was at war, sudden and bitter. The Sioux, pushed west for two generations, had stopped against the mountains that they called the Backbone of the World, and let the white men know they intended to go no further.

In 1875, an expedition under the command of Col. G. A. Custer had found gold in the Black Hills—and publicized the discovery. In the spring a host of gold seekers hit the Bozeman Trail in a westerly direction. The Sioux killed most of them, hundreds of whites. Back in Washington, Grant's administration was in deep trouble, and the slaughter didn't help matters much. Grant went to his old friend General Sheridan and said, "Do something, Phil."

The Sioux forced the closing of Fort Tullock. The Sioux pushed the whites to the east.

"Taken by the sword, retaken by the sword." Slocum clucked quietly to his horse. They'd been pushing their horses hard. Some oats and a little corral time were in order.

"Like I was sayin' about honor," Beckwith continued as if they'd been thinking about nothing else, "the Crow have a great sense of honor."

Without meaning to, Slocum slipped into the Blackfoot tongue. "The Crow are horse stealers," he said of the Blackfeet's hereditary enemies.

Beckwith followed him into the Indian tongue with no pause. "They are not the braggarts the Blackfeet are."

And so they rode for an hour or so, quarreling quietly, like a long-married couple. When they first heard the sound, they didn't recognize it. It was no more than a rhythmic high pulse of air. Something registered, because they broke off their argument and John Slocum's right hand came to rest on the stock of his Winchester, but neither man commented. The pulse was far up-river, and if the pitch and season had been right, it might have been the pulsating call of passenger pigeons on their annual fall migration.

A whistle. "It's the steamboat," Beckwith said. He relaxed once he'd identified the sound.

"You got sharp ears for an old man," Slocum remarked.

Beckwith showed his gap teeth in a grin. "That's why I still got 'em, son. Many a warrior would look on this old pair of ears as his proudest possession."

"That steamboat sure is hootin'."

"Well, I for one am glad to hear it. It means there's

still some soldier boys at Abraham Lincoln. I'd hate to ride in and find the place crawlin' with Sioux or Cheyenne."

"There had better be soldier boys at the fort," Slocum said. Something in his voice invited the older man's query.

"You never said why you was comin' up here," Beckwith said.

"That's right. I didn't."

Beckwith shrugged. "Don't mean to pry," he said.

Nine days on the trail through Indian country create a certain comradeship. Slocum rarely spoke about his private business, but made an exception. "I'm looking for the quartermaster of the Seventh Cavalry. He sold some blankets last fall that proved inferior, and I require satisfaction."

"Uh-huh." The steam whistle, more distinguishable now, was traveling across their front, left to right, downriver presumably.

"Thought I might become a prospector," Beckwith said. "Hell, there ain't furs left to trap. Bridger has set himself up to guide rich limeys into the mountains. For sport!" Beckwith snorted. "What sport is there anyhow? Hell, it's all used up. When I came west there was so much game only a crazy man would say one day there wouldn't be none."

"Well," Slocum said, "we killed it off, you and me. Nobody but us did it. How many buffalo did you kill on your best day?"

"Two hundred sixty-four. The old Sharps got so hot from shooting I had to swab the barrel with wet rags. 'Course I was shootin' off a stand. Hell, in those days I could keep four skinners workin'."

Slocum eyed the older man sharply. "The Indians too. They're done."

Both men's eyes were glued on the point where the steam whistle was steadily hooting. "Boat's moving, all right." Beckwith said. "Goddamn this black horse. My butt's so sore, I got to sleep on my stomach tonight. I guess that damn sidewheeler isn't aground, but

I'm fooled if I see any smoke. If you think the Indian's done, you should tell old Crazy Horse about it. Or Rain-in-the-Face. Probably if they heard you say that, they'd go in on that treaty and hand over their rifles and go on the reservation like the white commissioners keep tellin' them to."

"They're done all the same," Slocum said quietly. "I ain't cheerin' the event either, Jim. There ain't nourishment out there for us and them both. Hell, it won't be long before the damn railroad's in the Black Hills."

For miles around them, the prairie was flat and green, so close to the river, green with greasy grass, purple with sage, bordered by the high prairie buttes, and only a few miles outside Fort Abraham Lincoln, the prairie was destitute of human life as the moon.

"There's the smoke." Beckwith was pointing. "Damn, will you look at that! I believe that gentlemen is putting the fire to her!"

Slocum judged the bend in the column of smoke. "She's rollin' all right."

The two men had been close as they would be. They'd been dependent on each other for their lives, and now their separate pulls made them individual. Before they had reached the outskirts of the fort, they had become apart.

Usually this time of year a couple of hundred blanket Indians camped as close to the fort as they could get. Not today. They didn't see a single tepee.

The river took a wide bend before coming into Fort Lincoln, and the riders had gained on the steamboat.

The only open gate in the low stockade was guarded by blue-uniformed recruits and a downy-cheeked corporal. "Halt!"

The steam whistle hollered as the paddlewheeler sighted home port. The sudden blare of a bugle sounded assembly.

Fort Abraham Lincoln was an older fort. It had never been abandoned, even during the Civil War when the army contracted its presence on the frontier. The houses on officers' row were elaborate two-story structures, with lawns and summer gliders and verandas. The siding was uniformly shingle. The officers' wives had planted trees. They were spindly yet, but give them another twenty years and they'd amount to something.

The downy-cheeked corporal turned to the hoot of the paddlewheeler. "That'll be the *Rosebud*," the corporal informed the two strangers. "Did you see any hostiles?" he asked them eagerly. These were the first riders to make it to the fort in a week.

"Not real close up," Slocum replied. The boy turned his attention to the noise from the river without waiting for his answer.

Over the gate, a brightly painted sign read:

FORT ABRAHAM LINCOLN
7TH CAVALRY U.S.A.

Again and again, the bugle sounded assembly, as if the bugler meant to sound the call until his lungs gave out. He stood in the center of the street, his braces flapping at his sides, his face white as porcelain.

Front doors banged open and kids' feet raced across the veranda, hurling down the broad wooden stairs, down through the picket gate. All the kids ran alone, even those who normally went together, as if, this once, privacy would protect them. Boys and a few black servants hurried down the dusty street toward the parade ground and the wharves where the steamboat hooted its crazy disconnected hoots. The cries of a desperately wounded loon, circling around an arctic pond, bleeding out life blood.

All the soldiers here were recruits, like the white-faced bugler, or had been injured. Many swung along on crutches or carried their arms in slings or wore prominent clean bandages. Like the recruits, the wounded hurried to the Missouri, their crutches swinging far out ahead of them.

Army nurses—four grubby men in dirty white shirts

and brown trousers—marched in a neat block. These unkempt men marching in perfect military unison spooked John Slocum a little.

The two riders had slowed their mounts, so they rode the crowd the way a canoe rides rapids, holding back with logs and jetsam racing by in the rush of white water.

The bugle was still working on assembly, but apparently the bugler had forgotten the last part of the call because he blew the first three notes over and over again, ignoring the four notes that closed the call.

The parade ground was shallow, squeezed between the river and the bulk of the big houses on officers' row.

The sidewheeler was a one-stacker, irregular in shape, as if someone had blurred its shallow sharp lines.

"The *Rosebud,*" Beckwith identified the craft.

The *Rosebud* was the workhorse sidewheeler for the army on the upper Missouri. Earlier in the spring, her sister ship, the *Judith,* had caught a snag on the Yellowstone bar and done so much damage that when the men roped her off, the bottom came right out of her. The *Rosebud* did double duty now.

The far side of the river was miles and miles of great plains. The far side had a few huge buttes, but not as many as the west bank. The north winds scoured this part of the prairie, and beside the short, stubby, tenacious greasewood and alders, the overloaded *Rosebud* stood out like the last remnant of man's hopes.

"God Almighty," John Slocum said slowly. Without thinking, he removed his hat, and Beckwith followed his gesture.

Naturally, the commanding officer's home was the largest on the post, and it bordered the parade ground. On fine days, the officers' ladies sat on its wide porch, sipping tea or lemonade as the sweating soldiers drilled under their husbands' eyes.

Women marched across the porch, led by a short,

dark-haired woman in front. She walked alone like a shepherd leading a flock, and the others, twenty of them, followed side by side in a column.

Many grieved and a few were carried between two stronger sisters, but Mrs. George Armstrong Custer—Libby Custer—was dry-eyed and firm-stepped as she led the wives of the Seventh Cavalry onto the parade ground.

When the Seventh Cavalry rode out of Fort Abraham Lincoln—a month previous—Colonel Custer led with Tom Custer, his dashing brother, at his side. A brother-in-law, Walter Reed, was a lieutenant under Keogh, and Autie Reed, a young man he'd raised like his own son, rode at his other stirrup.

The Custer Clan, they called them.

The Custer wives marched behind Libby Custer, followed by the others, by rank.

There were more enlisted wives and laundresses than officers' wives because it was thought unseemly for a lady to follow her husband on the rigors of a western campaign, though a dozen or so—following Libby Custer's precedent—had followed their men through Kansas, against the Washita, and up the Missouri. Today was one of the days in their life.

The *Rosebud* was wide beamed, and shallow. Except for the pilot's cabin in the rear, the deck space was given up entirely to cargo. A single six-pound swivel gun mounted on the bow was the *Rosebud*'s sole armament, and the steam engine that propelled her was uncovered against the weather.

Mounds of blue blurred the *Rosebud*'s stern lines. Soldiers against the low railings with their feet out before them. Soldiers lying on the decks. A good half dozen lying stiff in the stern under their ground sheets. Funny thing. The dead were stretched out quite comfortably—all the living gave them plenty of room, though the boat was desperately overloaded. The river was shallow now, and scrapes and bruises had sprung her planks as she lumbered downstream, and there was water in her scuppers. Pools of water filmed with the fine crimson oil of men's blood.

A low noise came from the boat, somewhere between a murmur and a moan, a blend of groans and the chatter of men who'd taken leave of their senses or been overwhelmed with fever.

The crowd on the parade ground parted for the column of ladies. As they approached the dock, two ladies fainted. They were laid gently on the ground, but none of their sisters stayed with them.

A lieutenant had one foot on the shoreside railing. He'd made a little room for himself and was shouting orders about disembarking. "Don't tip her, men. Least-hurt men, help your pals!"

Boys ran toward the fort dispensary for stretchers. The four grimy male nurses were already helping men ashore.

Ashore, the lieutenant took a second to brush his pants legs free of dust. His eyes were on the ground, while everyone else's eyes were on him. Behind his back he pulled his long cavalry gauntlets from his belt. He drew them on like armor. He marched toward the crowd, head held low. High on his horse, Slocum could see the top of the lieutenant's skull covered with fine blond hair. His forage cap was gripped tight in his right hand.

When he raised his eyes, you could see that his neatness was a function of carriage. His fine uniform was stained and soiled but hung elegantly from his shoulders. His eye sockets were sunken and the whites were shot with blood. His voice was the high-pitched squeak of a boy. "I am directed," he began. Took hold of himself. "By Colonel Major . . . Captain Benteen. Captain Benteen directed me . . ."

Now that the news had arrived, Libby Custer relaxed her stance and folded her hands demurely. One hand was gripping the other as if it had discovered its only friend.

"Colonel Custer and his command are no more," he said.

Like snow melt off a pine tree, his words fell into a dead silence. Sweat beaded the young man's forehead and his eyes slipped a few inches above everyone's head and stayed there.

"Ambushed," he said. He opened his mouth again, but no word came out. He drew in a deep breath. "Five thousand Sioux and Cheyenne warriors," he said.

Libby Custer's voice came through the lieutenant's confusion like salvation. "How many survivors, Lieutenant?" she asked. She spoke with the pleasant drawl of a woman who obeys the army wife's rules.

The lieutenant swiveled his head from side to side like a pendulum.

"Oh," Libby Custer said.

Some woman shrieked and fainted. No hand held her fall.

The lieutenant choked. The tears came to his eyes and he spoke with gritted teeth. His words were mumbled, but everyone heard them. "I am directed by Captain Benteen to inform Fort Abraham Lincoln and the secretary of war of the loss of Colonel George A. Custer and the two hundred sixty-four men of his command to overwhelming forces of Indian warriors under the command of Crazy Horse and Sitting Bull. I am directed to return to Fort Abraham Lincoln and telegraph the sad news. Many of Captain Benteen's wounded are on the *Rosebud*. Captain Benteen with Major Reno acting as rear guard set out from the Little Big Horn when we did." He broke. His eyes begged. "Are they here?" he asked. "Did they make it through?"

Again Libby Custer was the spokesman. "Lieutenant, they did not return to the fort, but, as you know, the *Rosebud* is somewhat speedier than riders across these rough plains and we must not expect Captain Benteen. Surely you can't fear they have been overwhelmed by hostiles? A full squadron. . . ." Her voice snapped as clean as a dry twig. She closed her mouth firmly. Her complexion was naturally dark, darkened more by the western sun, but the color ran right out of her face like a cup upended. She put one hand to her forehead and swayed, very slightly. When Mrs. Tom Custer reached out to steady her, she brushed her arm away curtly. "Thank you. I am quite able to fend for myself."

"It's Major Reno too. They're acting as rear guard," the lieutenant repeated stupidly.

"Excuse me, ladies," one nurse said. "If you will withdraw, we can get the wounded to the dispensary that much faster."

"Yes. Of course. Ladies!" And though she was awful pale, she spoke like a commander again, directing the women away. A tall young redhead stepped forward to take a place beside Libby Custer, where she could see and hear everything. One of the wives was ruffled at the young woman's forwardness and sniffed angrily, but if that was meant to put the redhead in her place, it failed. "Sergeant Edward Pollitz died out there, same as your man. They are one rank now, deceased, and we are one rank too, widows."

The women rearranged themselves silently, ignoring their husbands' previous status; like race spectators, they lined the path, calling out their questions.

"Are they all dead? Every one?"

"My husband was Captain Miles Keogh."

"My man, his name was Flaherty. He was one of the Wild Geese. Rode with A Troop."

"Sometimes the company surgeon stayed back. Dr. Greenbough. What of Dr. Greenbough?"

Maybe the wounded soldiers knew something, maybe not. Most of them passed by the line of women stoic as Indians running the gauntlet. Those who did know something about the fate of one man or another stopped briefly. A few of the wounded had seen the battlefield after the Sioux departed, but most had been too badly injured and had their information secondhand from the grave detail.

"Sergeant Edward Pollitz. A round, moon-faced man. His hands were scarred from his boxing days. Has anyone news of him?" The redheaded widow was full of entreaties. The lieutenant was explaining in more detail how it happened that the finest troop of cavalry in

the U.S. Army had been killed to a man. The Custer
wives hung in close because his news was for their
ears too.

Jim Beckwith stepped across the rail of the *Rosebud*
and prowled the rows of hurt and dying men, looking for familiar faces. He'd scouted for the Seventh
before and knew most of the noncoms to drink with.
He hunkered down beside a pale-faced corporal. One-
handed, he rolled up a quirly, scratched his lucifer on
the varnished bloody rail, and set it alight. He passed
it to the other man's lips. The corporal took a deep
drag and then coughed so hard it seemed his lungs
would spill out. "Thanks, Jim. You always was a
good egg."

Beckwith was facing away from the riverbank, and
the people on the bank couldn't hear the questions he
was asking. But the corporal had one of those odd
basso voices which cut through chatter like a bludgeon,
and his replies were plainly audible. On the shore, the
lieutenant answered Libby Custer's questions and, posi-
tioned midway between them, Slocum heard the two
sets of answers at once.

The lieutenant said, "There were five thousand
hostiles. Sioux. Under Sitting Bull, Crazy Horse, and
that devil Rain-in-the-Face."

The corporal said, "There were Plains Cheyenne,
Gros Ventres." At Beckwith's look of surprise, the
corporal elaborated. "Yeah, even them Quaker redskins were there, and they wasn't peaceable today.
There was Crows riding with the Cheyenne and some
Assiniboine. I never got to see their camp, but they had
the biggest pony herd I ever saw gathered on the
plains."

The lieutenant said, "Major Reno tried very hard
to come to your husband's rescue, ma'am." He ran
his hands around his hat.

"I was with Reno when they hit us, and once the
first wave crashed into us, it was near all over. Custer
was on ahead, all his bugles blowin', and then the
gunfire started and it wasn't too long before you

couldn't hear the bugles anymore. Tell the truth, I wasn't thinkin' about that, I was just fearin' for my life because they turned our flank and we was high on the bank of the Little Big Horn with hostiles between us and the good ground and such a confusion of firin' and yellin' and heat as I ever did see, and by God, the damn riverbank was crumblin' under our horses' hooves and a couple men already toppled and smashed and there wasn't anything for it but to jump into that stream and hope you could outride the bullet with your name on it. Custer? Hell, it was every man for himself, and if we hadn't dug in on the far bank of that river, we'd be just as dead as he is."

A silent John Slocum boarded the *Rosebud* and examined the wounded for one particular face: the quartermaster's.

"And what of my husband, Lieutenant?" Libby Custer said.

"Ma'am, the Indians, they . . . uh . . . treated him with great respect." He turned to Mrs. Tom Custer and said, hurriedly, "And your husband too, ma'am. Though most of the bodies were scalped, the officers were not; it was their way of showing respect."

One officer's wife said, "Oh, thank God."

One sergeant's wife said, "Oh," and fainted.

"I wish to speak to anyone who has seen the body of my husband. He was a large man and not easy to miss. Sergeant Pollitz."

The corporal asked Beckwith for a drink. Beckwith still had some of that awful damn trade whiskey, which he held to the other man's lips while the quirly smoldered between his own yellow fingers. "Rain-in-the-Face did what he promised he'd do," the corporal said. "Remember when we had him in the stockade and he swore if he ever got a chance he'd cut out Tom Custer's heart? Remember how Tom used to laugh at him and jab him through the bars with his riding crop? Well, Rain-in-the-Face cut out young Tom's heart, and some say he ate it there on the spot. The women, they cut everybody up. Cut off their scalps and their balls and gutted a few of them. They scalped the colonel, 'course they did, but he had short hair, you know, he'd cut his long yellow hair, and so they didn't recognize him. If they had recognized his body, they'd have cut it into scraps."

The lieutenant said, "Your husband died painlessly, ma'am. Probably the last of his gallant troop to . . . to . . . perish."

"Thanks for the hooch, Jim. You always were a pal. Custer didn't even make it to the top of the hill where everybody died. Somebody brained him with a war club, looked like, and somebody else shot him in the head."

John Slocum bent over one private. From the man's insignia, he belonged to the quartermasters. The man said something and Slocum ambled toward the stern.

The lieutenant continued his tale. "Yes, ma'am, a detail from Benteen's troop buried your husband's gallant men just where they had fallen. It was the heat—you understand."

For the first time, Libby Custer's composure failed her. "And your own crying need to get your tails safe," she snapped.

The lieutenant drew himself up. "Ma'am? We did everything in our power. . . ."

"Of course you did. Of course you did."

The corporal was talking to Beckwith. "I don't know how old Sitting Bull pulled it off, but he had every damn hostile tribe of Indians in the west fighting together for a change. Oh, they just plumb overwhelmed Custer. Hit him so fast and hard, his men didn't even do much damage."

"Your husband's gallant men fought to the last fiercely and honorably. . . ."

"Sitting Bull rolled them up like they was a bunch of ignorant children and cut them down before they had a chance to do more'n get down from their horses. They was dead before they knew they were fightin'. Custer wanted to repeat the trick he used against the Washita and Black Kettle. Ride into their camp and start killin' their old people and kids, and the Indians get confused and you have them then. Well, Yellow Hair forgot that Sitting Bull had heard about the Black Kettle fight too and this time the Indians was ready for it. When he charged into their damn village, they came boiling out like a dumb cow had kicked over a bee-gum."

John Slocum lost the track of what the corporal was saying. The lieutenant's voice faded too, along with Libby Custer's. He'd found the face of the man he was looking for. The quartermaster who'd sold Bird-Calling her winter blanket. He almost laughed aloud. He'd been too long silent, and his whole body vibrated with laughter, but not one sound issued from between his clenched teeth, though his lips were drawn back in a smile and a snarl. The quartermaster was probably five years older than Slocum. He must have been a crackerjack soldier. A warrant officer's rank was hard to get in the heat of wartime, and in the slow years after the war when the army shrank from Civil War size and generals like Custer were reduced to colonels, such a rank for such a young man was unusual, even rare. "You must have done somethin' special for those gold bombs on your shoulders," Slocum said, smiling so fierce his lips hurt.

The warrant officer had his head flopping against the rail, more dead than alive. His young cheeks were unlined by passion or fear or love or anger and his uncombed light brown hair ruffled briefly by the wind across the water. With a mighty shriek of escaping steam, the *Rosebud*'s captain shut down his engine. John Slocum went down on his heels before the wounded man he'd dreamed about so many nights and hated so many days. In the roar of that steam, he could have killed him right then and nobody would have noticed. The shriek died away into gasp and sputter as the last of the steam vented. Voices, drowned out by the roar, reestablished themselves. The moans, the sounds of weeping, Libby Custer's insistent questioning, and the lieutenant's evasive replies. Slocum's face was close to the quartermaster's. Spittle hung at the corners of the man's mouth. He was bundled in a blanket, and all you knew about his wounds was that he hadn't been hurt in the face. Sensing human warmth, the quartermaster opened his eyes. They were brown, the irises red and blood-flecked like the eyes of a man who'd been on a two-week bender. The pupils shrank to accommodate the sun but the eyes commenced to wander, rolling in their sockets unsettled.

"I'm here to talk about blankets," Slocum said. He'd meant to speak softly but his voice came out between his teeth as a hiss, and the man's eyes strained to focus to meet the threat facing him.

"Goddamn three-beaver blanket," Slocum said. His voice had found a neutral tone. "Brown it was, with yellow stripes."

The quartermaster blinked rapidly, but his eyes were still soft and the drool ran from the corner of his mouth.

John Slocum rocked back on his heels. He laughed once, or barked. Hard to tell which. It was a sound strange enough to rouse another desperately wounded man nearby, who said, "Quartermaster got a chest wound, friend. He ain't said much that made sense since the Yellowstone. If you're a friend of his, the best thing would be to leave him be. He's dying, but I don't think he's in bad pain."

"Uh-huh." Slocum stretched that funny grin across his face again, and the man who had spoken went quiet seeing it. "Three-beaver blanket," Slocum said. "It was so thick you would have thought it came right off the trader's stores."

The quartermaster's eyes rolled about in his head, less focused than the eyes of a steer or a ewe, and before Slocum's mind the simple tale unfolded itself, again, as it had a thousand times since last winter when he'd come back through the lowering twilight to his lodge, high in the Bitterroot where he and Bird-Calling lived with their year-old daughter they called Dove.

His snowshoes were long and narrow with turned-up toes. Hunting shoes. During the winter, game was scarce, and on this trip he'd been lucky to find a cow elk and her newborn calf, yarded up under the pines they had already eaten down to the bark. By spring, the cow and her calf would both be bones. Grazing animals never wintered well in the mountains, and those who hadn't dropped to lower country by the first heavy snowfall would be trapped until the spring sun licked their bare bones. Only wolves flourished in the high-country winter. The wolves, coyotes, small cats, and man. Slocum killed the two elk with two shots from his Winchester. He figured he'd done them a mercy. Not to mention the mercy he'd done to his own family. He'd been away on this hunting trip for two weeks, circling their lodge searching for game. He'd never meant to get this far out. It was January. They had smoked meat, fish, and jerky to last a month, but it would be March before iceout and they could travel again. Nothing to worry about, so long as John Slocum brought meat. If he failed, or fell and broke his leg, or was ambushed by Crows, he would die and his wife and child, they'd die too.

He butchered the two elk carefully, skinning them out, cooling the meat in the deep snow. In ten-below weather it wasn't hard to get the heat out of the carcass fast. He picked through the entrails for the liver, kidney, and heart. Them and the small intestines he washed with snow and wrapped individually. The livers and kidneys were fine delicacies, the hearts would make stew, and the entrails could be used for sausage casings. Though he regretted the waste, he spread the skins out for the coyotes. If he hadn't been so hurried, perhaps he could have saved the skins. There's nothing softer than elkhide for mukluks and leggings, but there was only room on Slocum's sled for the meat.

He quartered the carcass. Backhams, rack and front shoulders. He lashed the raw meat to his simple flat-bottomed toboggan, balancing the weight as best he could. It would be heavy and must be balanced.

When he put his shoulders against the lines, they stretched and cut, but held long enough to break the sled loose, and then John Slocum, hauling better than six hundred pounds of good lean meat, started back toward his lodge, his family, and his hearth fire.

He spent two nights on the trail. In the winter, towing a sled, a man can't get much distance through woods, and Slocum was thankful to make eight miles a day.

He and Bird-Calling had built their lodge against a high bank in the valley it surveyed. It was a low log affair with sod for a roof. Two windows faced the trail and the long valley. There were shutters to cover the windows when weather required, but they were glazed with oiled butcher paper that provided light but not vision for the cabin's inhabitants.

The days were short, and long shadows preceded Slocum and the sled up the slight incline of the valley he and Bird-Calling called home. In the spring he meant to trade for some Nez Percé spotted ponies. In the lush graze he'd break them and train them—trade goods to the Piegans and Bloods for the furs only they could take out of the mountain fastnesses. Slocum didn't plan to get rich—he'd never wanted that. He just hoped he and Bird-Calling could have a life together. As he leaned against the heavy lines and the sled slid along crisply behind him through the blue light and the gaudy red of the sun setting already behind the blue spruce, Slocum thought how lucky he'd been. Lucky to have lived this long when other men, braver and smarter than he, lay moldering in their graves. Lucky, when he had been so unprepared for it, to find a happiness he had long decided would forever be denied to him. Yes, this narrow valley would be fine for horses. A brush barrier would close off the valley mouth and the sides were steep, and they could sit outside their lodge in the morning and watch them graze. Perhaps Two-Medicine would help. As was the Blackfoot custom, Slocum and his new bride had separated from the main band, but not so far that they couldn't share the burdens or the fights if the Crows came after the pony herd. The main camp, a dozen lodges like Slocum's own, was on the banks of the Popo Agee, a day's walk, seven miles below them. Two-Medicine, Bird-Calling's brother, would have visited during Slocum's absence, as Slocum had asked him to, so his sister didn't get too lonely with only a baby and her cookfire to keep her attention. In the spring, Two-Medicine would help Slocum, going with him to the Nez Percé for the spotted ponies. Many of the Blackfoot were slightly put off by the tall white man who'd come among them and married such a young woman. Too often they'd seen the white men take women only to abandon them or, worse to the puritanical Indian, turn them into whores. They feared Slocum was another squawman, and were slow to change. True, he was a fine hunter, but he had fine guns too, better than any brave, and that was an advantage, any man had to concede. And true, he had fought the Crow raiders, shoulder to shoulder with his brothers, and counted coup three times on warriors of that fierce nation. And true, he could gamble like a man. But he was white, and many of the brothers could not—would not—trust a white man. Two-Medicine was his friend. Bird-Calling was his wife. Dove was his daughter. That was plenty for him.

He could almost smell the woodsmoke. In September, when the sap was well down out of the trees, he had felled mountain ash and limbed the long trunks. When the ground was snow-covered, but before it drifted, he skidded the dry wood to the lodge, where he bucked it up into a mound of firewood slightly longer than the house and as tall, protected from the weather by the lee side and canvas he'd placed over the top of it. The canvas would freeze and make a roof good enough to hold the snow off his wood supply until the wan sun warmed it in March. It was fine wood, quick to light and made a long fire. His nostrils quivered. This close to the cabin, he should smell the smoke from the hearth fire. The cabin sat, snug against the bank, shutters over the windows. And the shutters were odd, because Bird-Calling loved the light and never used the shutters unless the wind was angry enough to tear the oiled paper.

Snow between the front door and the wood pile, unbroken, a full white skin covering it. The door was closed and stayed closed, though John Slocum, with his heart in his throat, dropped the lines and was running and shouting Bird-Calling's name. His long snowshoes jumped through the snow just too slow, and his anguished cry rang in the icy stillness. "Bird-Calling! It's John!"

The snow was banked up against the door, and when he unlatched the rawhide latch, the snow rolled into the cabin on his heels.

It was dark. Cold as a troll's tomb. Only the light from the door and thin strips of light at the shutter edges. The snow that had come in on his heels was hissing across the frozen pine boards he'd laid for a floor.

A mound of blankets and furs in the corner. The rug off the floor, the bearskins they'd slapped against the walls for insulation, the robes and wraps. In one mound.

It stank. It stank of vomit, and feces and sweat. But the cabin hadn't been attacked. No sign of a Crow raiding party, and anyway, they wouldn't have left the furs. Mindlessly, almost angrily, he moved to the mound and started hurling the furs behind him, the heavy robes whipping like sails. His breath hung in front of him and his breathing was harsh as he flung the covers aside.

At the very bottom of the heap, underneath the warmest and softest of them all, he found his wife, and his girl child.

"Ahhhhhhhhh," he said. "Ahhhhhhh, Jesus." And his cry was a plea that things should not be what his eyes told him they were. Both of them were naked. The child curled into herself beside her mother, as if she had never left the womb. When Slocum reached out his hand and placed it on Dove's bare back, it was cold—

no body heat left in it. He made a sound then. It was indescribable. The child's back was covered with red pustules and broken sores. The draining of pus streaked her tiny back like little streams, frozen like tears.

And his wife's beautiful face was covered with the pustules too. Her eyes were open. Unlike the child, she was still breathing, though her ribs scarcely moved with the push of her lungs. Her breath made moisture in the air.

Her mouth opened. Though it was dead quiet, Slocum had to bend to hear what she said. She said, "Cold."

"Bird-Calling. It's John," he said. His voice didn't break though it surely wanted to.

"John?" Bent over thus, he watched her lips move as they formed his name and a sweetness crept over him as her lips tasted his name, and he knew he'd carry that sweetness with him so long as he lived. "John?"

He pulled the blanket up over her body. Her smooth dark cheeks were bright red. Red with the fever and red with the pox. He touched her forehead and it was as hot as the baby's was cold.

He didn't think her eyes saw. "John, the baby . . ."

"Yes. Dove doesn't hurt anymore." He tucked the blanket around her chin and stroked her hot forehead. He thought of getting snow to wash her face but feared the shock would kill her. He'd have to get a fire going, and soon. The blanket was a fine one, a Hudson's Bay blanket, soft and heavy wool, but it wasn't enough in an unheated cabin. Her eyes still didn't recognize him.

"Don't you move. I'll get some heat in here directly."

The woodbox beside the hearth was empty. She'd run out of wood and hadn't had the simple strength to get more. Smallpox. It was a wonder she had the strength to get under the covers with the child. The fevers were incredible.

He hurried outside, not bothering to close the door, and to his dismay it seemed warmer outside in the waning winter light. The loaded sled waited below, abandoned. He stripped the paper birch bark for tinder and laid it carefully under some dry jackpine. The wood went up with a whoosh once he touched the lucifer to it, and the fire started fighting the cold. Even before the licking flames had fully caught, he had a pot of snow melting beside the blaze to wash her. She had lain under those blankets for two or three days, he guessed, and he didn't know where the strength had come from to live for his arrival. When he came to her with a bowl of cool water in his hand, she had uncovered herself again. Eyes glassy and in another world. When he stooped over her, her lips moved. "No," she said. "Burn it."

Humoring her, he stripped the lovely three-beaver blanket off her skinny frame and tossed it into the corner. The next cover was fur. He swabbed at her forehead, cutting through the perspiration. He wrung out a clean handkerchief and dribbled water past her parched, flaking lips. She opened her mouth to his ministrations. Her tongue was shriveled and thick and her words were unclear. "Burn it," she said again. "It has slain us."

And, for a moment, her eyes were in this world and hot and feverish, but connected to his and she moved her small hand, and perhaps she thought that the tiny motion she made had conveyed her impossibly heavy hand to his because she squeezed as if she had his hand and was squeezing it. He touched her palm tenderly and squeezed back, willing his own strength to pass along their linked arms. Willing his own strength to be hers.

"John," she said again. Her eyes were bright with message. The message may have been of love or tenderness. She may have meant to ask him about Dove. But her heart stopped then and her lips fell slack and he felt her heart stop through her hand and the coldness that entered his hand from hers as her life went elsewhere. Her eyes faded last of all, glazing over, the way they will. With her eyes she loved him past her last breath.

Slocum knelt beside her, washing her face tenderly and cleaning her body where she'd fouled herself. He forgot to keep the fire going twice during the night and had to start it again. By dawn, mother and daughter were clean and dressed in their formal best—both wore buckskin dresses. He'd tried to braid their black hair in the plaits both normally wore, and had some luck with Bird-Calling, less with Dove. Dove was curled up and stiff, and to straighten her he would have had to break bones.

The next morning he carried his wife outside the lodge in his arms. He was singing the Blackfoot song of death and he had slashed his chest to free his pain, the way the Blackfeet do. After he unloaded the sled, he laid her there on a buffalo robe and her baby beside her. He wrapped them to keep them warm.

He climbed, pulling the sled behind him, into the morning sun until he reached the spot above the valley where he and Bird-Calling had first seen the valley that they wanted to be home.

From the branches of a spruce tree he suspended a platform of woven branches lashed with rawhide. He had never made such a platform before, though he had seen them where the Blackfeet buried their dead. He tied the butt ends together and made the lashings strong and accurate. Here she would rest while her spirit and Dove's took their long journey across the shadow land. He covered them in the robe and belted it at the head and feet. He lay a few of her belongings beside her: her bone comb, her bright yellow strands of beads. At her feet he placed elk meat to nourish her on her journey. Below, their home glistened and shone in the bright sun bouncing off the snow. He sang the death song again until he got hoarse. He returned to the cabin and burned it. Burned the robes, the walls, the woodpile, the few utensils they owned. He loaded the sled with elk meat and started down into the valley. Rolled across the back of the sled was the Hudson's Bay blanket. He'd never seen it in their lodge before and he meant to ask Bird-Calling's people where it had come from.

Behind him the fire took hold, roaring at the roof, making the snow cover hiss and steam. The paper

windows burned out like eyes gone blind. When the
roof fell in, Slocum was a small figure far below in the
valley, pulling the sled behind him. He never looked
back.

The dying quartermaster on the deck of the *Rosebud*
didn't want to talk about blankets. His eyes were un-
hinged and roving and his tongue flicked at the drool in
the corner of his lips.

Slocum rested easily on his heels. "And you're the
one who gave those damn blankets to the Blackfeet.
'It'll be a harsh winter,' you said. Remember? 'And
the Great White Father has taken compassion on your
suffering and provides as many fine blankets as you
might want.'"

The young quartermaster formed a word with his
mouth. The word was "Opal."

Slocum's voice was deceptively easy. "So that's how
it was," he said. "I came down off the mountain where
Two-Medicine's band was camped. Wasn't but fifteen
lodges of Blackfeet there in Two-Medicine's bunch and
it was hardly worth the trouble you Seizers took killing
them."

"Laura." For a moment the quartermaster's eyes
cleared and he knew there was a man talking to him.
His brown eyes were begging. "Mister," he said, "you
got to help. You got to help them."

Slocum nodded. "Sure," he said. "Well, like I was
sayin', when I got down to Two-Medicine's camp . . ."

"Two-Medicine?" The quartermaster was puzzled.

"Blackfoot Indian. About your age, give or take a
year. He'd be shorter'n you. Oh, and he held his arm
funny. Broke the upper arm when he was a kid."

The quartermaster was pleased. "Him. Oh, sure. I
remember him. He had a band on the Popo Agee. Came
into Fort Tullock to trade."

"And you gave him blankets. You gave him fine
Hudson's Bay blankets. Plenty for every man, woman, and child in his band. Enough so he could give
them away. You made Two-Medicine a big man, did

you know that? Hell, he gave those damn blankets away to all his kin."

A hand on Slocum's shoulder. Jim Beckwith. "Howdy, son," he said quietly. His hand flickered at the quartermaster's brown blanket. Beckwith drew it apart and clicked his tongue. "Will you look at that?" he said wonderingly. "Surprisin' he's got as far as he has. Can you see there? That's his damn spleen hanging out. That purple thing, all swollen up."

"Damn," Slocum said.

"I don't believe this pilgrim's gonna take up vertical space much longer," Beckwith said.

"Oh, well, now. Ain't that a hell of a thing."

"This is the hombre you're hunting."

"Uh-huh. Like I said. He gave my wife a defective blanket and I wanted satisfaction."

"You won't get it now. Not on this side of the shadow land." Deliberately, Beckwith kept his hand on Slocum's shoulder.

Again the quartermaster said, "Opal."

The nurses were working this side of the *Rosebud* now, separating the quick from the dead. They didn't bother with the worst-wounded, and when one examined the wounded quartermaster, he covered him again and went on to the next man.

"Please help," the quartermaster said.

The nurse was in a hurry. The next man might be saved. "I'll send the chaplain by directly," he said. Perhaps he didn't mean to be rough. Perhaps he was just in a hurry.

"There ain't much you can do about that blanket now," Beckwith said.

"Take your fucking hand off my shoulder," Slocum said.

"Sure." He did. Light as a feather in the breeze.

"Please help," the quartermaster begged. His eyes were yellow around the edges, and Slocum thought that was how he'd die, poisoned by his own body.

"You gave my people the blankets," Slocum insisted.

"They'll both be killed," he said.

"Who?"

"My little girl, Opal. My wife, Laura."

Slocum's smile wasn't good to see.

"John," Beckwith said. "Let's go ashore. I'm feelin' a little green around the gills. I never saw nothin' like this before."

"Yeah. Out there trappin' all through the war. You already told me."

"John. . . ."

Slocum raised his face to look Beckwith in the eyes. Slocum wore his smile like something inappropriate. His eyes were hard as coal chips in his head, and a funny green glint danced in them. "Jim," he said. "I suppose I got to tell you that findin' this man has been the only thing that's carried me from January until now. You see, the blankets he gave away—they were secondhand and they were supposed to be firsthand. Took me a while to get the true story, Jim. I went all around from encampment to encampment, followin' the work of this man, Jim. I rode into Two-Medicine's camp that evening and there weren't but three people to greet me, and one of them was dead before morning. We buried them. Blackfoot style, wrapped in the blankets that had killed them. Those soft three-beaver blankets that the army took off the smallpox wards in their damn hospitals. Blankets that were covered with the sweat and the smell of the dying. They brought them out west in special boxcars and nobody was allowed near those cars unless he'd already had the pox, Jim. And when the Indians came into Fort Tullock looking to trade, they let them take away as many blankets as they could carry."

"Smallpox?"

"Damn right. Smallpox. Hell, they were all dead at Two-Medicine's camp except Two-Medicine himself. He told me where he got the free blankets. He told me about a quartermaster who issued the goods that the white man meant to give away. With brown hair. A warrant officer with little gold things on his shoulder.

Warrant Officer Duffy. Of the goddamn Seventh Cavalry."

"Oh, my God," Beckwith breathed.

Slocum made a short gesture. "Now look at him. Gonna goddamn die on me. I been following him around for three damn months and I had some ideas on what I'd do when I found him. Some good ideas, too. Some of 'em were Sioux ideas and some were ideas I'd picked up from the Comancheros." Slocum spat over the side.

Beckwith didn't say anything. Nothing much to say.

"My wife . . . my daughter. . . ." The warrant officer's eyes were pleading.

Slocum cocked his head curiously. "Anything bad happening to you, pal?" he asked softly. "Anywhere it hurts especially bad? How did you come to be a blanket seller to the Indians?"

The man's jaw dropped. "Oh," he said. "That."

"So now you remember."

The man had the grace to drop his sick eyes. "How could I forget? It was orders. They said they'd have my rank if I didn't move those blankets."

"Your rank?"

"They said they'd revert me to sergeant. I'm just a brevet warrant officer."

Slocum reached out and pulled at the man's uniform shoulders. He tossed the badges of rank into the Missouri. "Don't guess your rank matters too much now," he said.

The man dropped his head. "Oh, God," he said. "I'm sorry." He raised his head again. "My wife."

"What about her?" Beckwith asked.

"Somebody has to get 'em out," the dying man begged.

"Well, where the hell are they?"

"They're on the Powder River. Just below where Mizpah Creek joins the river. They're all by themselves. Two white women. And the nearest soldiers are here in Fort Lincoln. They're surrounded by thousands of Sitting Bull's Sioux."

"That's a shame," John Slocum said softly.

Once again, Jim Beckwith put his hand on Slocum's shoulder. "John. . . . " he warned.

"Tell me about them," Slocum said. His fingers went into his shirt pocket for his tobacco pouch. Idly, he tapped the tin box of papers against his knee before he unfolded one to lay out the line of tobacco. The nurses came for the wounded man on the quartermaster's near side. Slocum rolled a perfect cylindrical tube and stuck it behind his ear. The quartermaster eyed the cigarette. "Please," he said.

Slocum's smile was easy. "Sure." He lit the cigarette and put it between the man's lips. A grateful quartermaster drew in the smoke. When he coughed, it was pretty violent. His head went back and snapped forward and he spewed his lifeblood in tiny spatters from his nose and mouth. The soaked cigarette fell to the deck, like an amputated finger.

"Waste of good tobacco," Slocum noted.

Beckwith came nearer into Slocum's vision, standing where he coudn't be ignored. "I'm sick of this," he said.

"Don't believe I asked you," Slocum replied without taking his eyes off the dying man.

"What in creation do you hope to do?" Beckwith asked.

"I'm here to get a blanket refund. I already told you that."

"He's dying. For God's sake."

Slocum nodded. "It's the least he could do."

The coughing fit had taken its toll and when the man's eyes focused again, they were weaker, moving so slow and heavy. "Our roadhouse . . ."

"Tell me about it," Slocum said.

"It's a one-story soddy. Nothing fancy. But we're close enough to the creek to draw water and wash, and there's a spring beside the soddy and we can get water there no matter what hostiles are around. I had friends come with me from Fort Tullock to build the place. They were Danny Marks and Jack Peabody. They did most of the work on the place. They were carpenters before they joined up. I was a storekeeper. Ain't much good with my hands. How Laura loves it. We're going to stay there once my enlistment expires. Ten years with the army is enough for any man. It's a hard life. A hard life."

Slocum noted the rolls of fat around the quartermaster's waist. "For some it's hard."

The soldier reached for him. The motion surprised Slocum, who withdrew his hand. He let it return. The man's grip was wet and clammy with sweat. When he spoke, blood spattered his lips and Slocum felt the fine spume of the man's life on his face and neck. "I didn't mean it, with the blankets," he said. "It wasn't my idea. I was doin' what I had to do."

"You ever see someone die of smallpox?" Slocum asked.

The man let his hand drop limp. His eyes begged John Slocum. Slocum was irritated, and awfully damn bored. "It's always the same," he said, half to himself. "Man hurts you and if you hurt him back it's no different than if you let him ride away."

"Now, horse, you're speaking sense," Beckwith said. "Come on. It's been a hellacious day and I heard the sutler here sells uncut whiskey."

Slocum came out of his hunker easily as an oiled machine; the quartermaster's eyes followed him as he rose. "My wife," he said. "My daughter."

"Laura, you said she was called. And Opal. Now which one was which?"

Slocum would have stayed to hear the man's answer, but Beckwith was pulling him away toward the bank. Slocum shook Beckwith's hand off. "I don't suppose you'd like to cash in your checks," he snarled.

Beckwith looked at him sadly. "Son, I never thought you was that kind of fool."

"I don't take to bein' manhandled," Slocum said.

"And I don't much like to see a man doin' what's beneath him. You swim at a level below your own and you're gonna damn well get used to it. That's natural."

Slocum smiled easily. "Why, Jim," he said, "that's deep. I appreciate hearin' somethin' deep like that. Makes me realize what life's all about."

"The hell with you." But Beckwith's curse had more laughter in it than anger, and the two men moseyed toward the fort's sutler and the rumored whiskey.

2

The officers' wives had vanished from the parade ground and the landing. The smallest boys and all the girl children were inside too. Broken families had gathered to mourn as best they could and some houses already had wreaths hanging in the windows. The nurses had finished with the *Rosebud* and now the post chaplain and his assistant stepped carefully through the dead and dying.

Slocum and Beckwith found another sort of comfort inside the fort sutler's.

As always, the Fort Lincoln sutler was a civilian. He bought low, sold dear, and carried half the men in Fort Lincoln on his books. The sutler's store was a plank structure against the stockade. He could credit straight razors, Colt revolvers, officers' fancy epaulets, tobacco, and whiskey to any man on the rolls. All others paid cash.

The sutler's bar was a row of tall packing cases. Along the back wall he had three tables where a man could sit and talk to his whore or drink or play poker. The house rake-off was a dime and a half-breed dealt for the house and collected the rake-off.

The sutler stepped to the bar briskly—ex-military for sure—and said, "Your pleasure?"

They both ordered whiskey, which was two bits a glass or two dollars a bottle. The liquid they tossed back was pretty raw, but Slocum couldn't taste anything lethal and he dropped two cartwheels on the rough bar.

The sutler's hands were quick—slightly too quick; he was a very angry man. "You're new here," he said, flat.

"Just come upriver from the Platte," Beckwith explained.

"Nobody's come through those Indians since spring," the sutler said.

"Well," Beckwith said with a shrug, "we did."

"General Crook tried to come upriver by land but the Sioux turned him back."

"Maybe they thought we wasn't worth a bullet," Beckwith said calmly. "I didn't come all the way up this damn river to argue with you about whether I did it or not. I ain't particular quarrelsome, but if that's what you're looking for, let's have it now and get it over with so I can kill you and drink my whiskey in peace."

The man took a step back from the bar and raised his empty hands palm out. "No offense," he said, though it pained him saying it.

Beckwith grunted and the sutler moved down the bar where a couple of crippled soldiers were drinking. From time to time one of them—the younger—would burst into quiet tears.

"I hate a man like that," Beckwith commented.

For a change Slocum was the peacemaker. "He just lost a couple hundred customers today, and if I know pony soldiers, they probably were into him pretty deep."

" 'The Seizers.' " Beckwith took a drink of his whiskey. "The name suits them."

"Oh, hell."

Beckwith carefully looked at the back wall. "Sorry to hear about your wife. I hadn't heard the how of it."

Slocum didn't say anything. His grief was not for sharing. He drained his glass and made a face. He set the empty down on the counter. "I don't know what I want to do," he said. "But this ain't it."

Four more soldiers came in. Benteen's lieutenant was among them. When he stepped up to the bar, the sutler handed him a drink without his asking. The lieutenant had gotten used to being a messenger and figured to carry all the news. "I suppose you've heard that we're abandoning Fort Lincoln," he said.

"Oh, Christ!" the sutler said. "That's all I need."

"The War Department is sending two more sidewheelers upriver. Every man, woman, and child will be withdrawn to Fort Phil Kearny."

"What about Benteen and Reno?"

"We won't leave until they get here. We'll all go. It just isn't safe."

The sutler couldn't quite believe his ears. "My God," he said. "We'll leave the entire west to Sitting Bull."

"The westernmost post will be at Fort Bozeman," the lieutenant specified.

The sutler's wife, a huge woman, came out of the kitchen just long enough to chase the table occupants off. "You'll have to clear away in here," she said. "For supper we have buffalo steak or beef stew. Spuds and boiled tomatoes. Supper's two bits." She placed her hands on her hips. Two of the soldiers drifted to empty tables, but the lieutenant looked like a man with a bad thirst.

"How about it?" Beckwith asked. "You ready for grub?"

"No," Slocum said. Though he'd just poured himself another glass of whiskey, he left it there on the bar. He wheeled away. "I'll be seeing you later."

Outside, the afternoon sun cast long shadows across the parade ground. Somebody had thought to lower Old Glory with its thirty-six stars to half mast, but the Seventh Cavalry banner still flew at the top of the pole. The wind was gusting and the flags snapped and rattled their lashings. They'd come down when the fort was abandoned.

Slocum shivered. It was July, he reminded himself, so it wasn't the weather that was cold. It was his soul.

The post chaplain had finished his business and gone. When Slocum boarded the *Rosebud* again, he was the only whole man on the deck. The dead lay still. Twenty dying men were unattended. Several raved, several cursed. One sang. He sang "Tenting Tonight on the Old Campground" which never had been one of Slocum's favorite tunes. The singer's voice was high, off key, and cracked.

Once again he hunkered down beside the quartermaster and rolled a quirly. Without asking, he fired it up and passed it to the man. The soldier's eyes were wide open. The whites were muddy with poisons but now he was at peace. "You came back," he said, slightly surprised.

"Uh-huh."

"Why?"

"Can't really say. If you don't draw so hard on that smoke, you won't cough."

"Can't see how it makes much difference." He drew hard. His cheeks bulged with an effort that left him poorer, but he didn't cough. A pause. "I suppose you meant to kill me." Not a question, a statement.

"It crossed my mind," Slocum said. "It's better they did it for me."

"The Sioux? Hell, I never sold no blankets to the Sioux. They didn't have any grudge against me." His voice was petulant, like a disappointed child's.

"I wouldn't worry about your family," he said. "Benteen'll pick 'em up."

A bit of hope gleamed in the quartermaster's white face. "Do you think so? I told 'em they was to stay right there until I got word to 'em." He added, "We was going to open a roadhouse on the Powder River. Steamboat traffic. It's the coming thing." He smiled. The cigarette fell from his mouth and his eyes rolled back with a click. A few seconds later his guts churned convulsively and the fluids started running out of him.

Slocum said "Good-bye" in a perfectly flat voice. He returned to the sutler's. He wasn't sure why he'd wanted to be with the man while he died, and when Jim Beckwith asked him about it, he lied. "I wanted to be there to be sure the son of a bitch had his ticket to hell."

Beckwith cut himself another hunk of buffalo steak. It was tough. A man got used to the tender meat of the buffalo hump or the smooth muscle along the loin. When he got to civilization they fed him ham steaks cut off the oldest beast that grazed. Beckwith picked his steak up with his hands and stretched it until it tore. He dropped it across his metal platter. His wiped his hands on his trousers and stabbed at it with his bowie knife. "They could've skinned it before they cooked it," he grumbled.

More soldiers came in to swallow the bad news with the help of the sutler's whiskey. A couple of times the sutler's wife came out to announce supper but got no takers. She cleaned the platters off the tables as they emptied, and when a couple of soldiers brought out a battered, greasy deck of cards and started a little game of poker, she didn't object.

"I think that goddamn President Grant sent Custer up there to get him killed."

"Yeah. The colonel was going back to Washington to testify against Secretary of the Interior. Theft, corruption, bribery."

"Hell, Custer had done testified. He'd done the worst he could. He almost missed this particular fight."

"Better for him if he had."

A tall woman, veiled, dressed in black, came in and walked toward the rear of the room.

She wasn't usual and a silence preceded the woman as she made her way to Slocum's table. Slocum thought that, veil or not, he recognized the redheaded widow he'd seen earlier.

Her voice was quite husky. "Gentlemen, do you mind if I sit down?"

Beckwith hurried to his feet, upsetting his chair in the process. "Yes, ma'am," he said. "No, ma'am." Jim was every inch the gentleman.

Slocum waved at the third chair as if it didn't matter. "Suit yourself," he said. "If you eat here, you deserve what you get."

She settled herself gracefully, demurely. "I have a small appetite," she said.

"Yes, ma'am," Beckwith said again.

Slocum said, "Why don't you sit down, Jim? Unless you're tryin' out for the waiter's job."

"Oh, no. No, I ain't." Beckwith took off his hat and scratched his head. He beat the hat against his leg

and created a dust cloud. He blushed. "Nice meetin'
you, ma'am," he said. He went to the bar.

Slocum pushed his platter away. He had no more
room for the gristle. He sloshed the whiskey around his
glass. He'd always had a good head for liquor, but since
Bird-Calling died, it seemed he couldn't get drunk no
matter how hard he tried.

"You could offer me a drink, sir," the woman said.
Her voice was steady and iron-strong.

Slocum drained his own glass, refilled it, and set it
down before her. He leaned back and stretched.

Delicately she sampled the whiskey. The curve of her
chin behind the veil was very soft, very smooth. Slocum looked her over openly. She coughed gently
and found a handkerchief to pat her mouth dry.

Every damn eye in the place was on the two of them,
and one or two faces wore leers that Slocum objected
to. He got to his feet and said, "I ain't accustomed to
bein' regarded like I was a damn medicine show."

Heads turned. Conversation resumed, uncertainly at
first. There was a rustle and flap of someone dealing
cards. Slocum sat down.

"Aren't you going to say how sorry you are about
my husband, Edward, sir?" She had a very sweet voice.
It stirred him some.

"Never had the pleasure," Slocum said. "Never knew
you before either."

"But aren't you sorry Colonel Custer's brave command was slaughtered?" Her voice betrayed a bright
curiosity. Nothing more.

"Never met him either. We was on opposite sides
during the war. He fought in the Wilderness for Phil
Sheridan. I fought for General Lee. He was supposed to
be a good cavalryman. That's all I know about him."

"But haven't you heard how gallant he was? Our
brave Colonel Custer?"

"I've heard folks talk about him. I told you. I never
met the man."

"Surely, sir, you have some opinion of your own?"

"Uh-huh. I think the whiskey here is better than

some." His hand snaked out for the glass Beckwith had been using. He poured a couple of fingers and drained it in one swallow.

"My Edward. . . . Did you know what the Sioux women do to their husbands' kill?"

"Uh-huh. Do you really want to go into it?"

He thought he saw the faintest trace of her smile behind the veil. "Sir. . . ."

"My name is—"

She silenced him. "I do not wish to know your name, sir."

Slocum shrugged. He twisted his neck around on his shoulders. His neck was stiff. "I don't wish to know what the squaws did to your husband," he said carefully. "Ain't my affair."

Abruptly she nodded her head. "Good," she said. "Very good. Will you sleep with me?"

Oddly, his first impulse was to say, "But it ain't even five in the afternoon." He restrained the impulse. "I haven't slept with a white woman for two years. I haven't slept with any woman since January. My wife. She died."

"Yes," she said.

"What's your name?"

"Mrs. Edward Pollitz."

"Your first name."

"I don't wish you to have it. We are not friends, sir."

He nodded his head. He scooped the half-empty whiskey bottle and dropped it into the deep pocket of his duster. He set his hat firmly on his head. "Why me?" he asked.

"I don't know."

He shook his head affirmatively, as if she'd given him a good answer, and got to his feet, his arm held out to her. She took it and the two of them strolled out. Jim Beckwith's weren't the only eyes on the unlikely pair.

Outside, he felt that same chill as before. "Is it cold?" he asked.

"I don't believe it is."

Slocum wondered if it was his cold heart melting. "My wife was a Blackfoot woman," he volunteered.

Soldiers were unloading the dead off the *Rosebud*. They moved hurriedly, as if they feared an attack at any moment. Slocum tried to see if they'd removed the young quartermaster's corpse, but hell, he couldn't tell.

They strolled through the parade ground where, in happier times, the post band might have gathered for an afternoon concert.

"Did you have children?" the woman asked. Her touch on his arm was light as a feather.

"A girl. Just a baby."

"Her too?" Her voice was sympathetic.

"Yeah. They died together."

They walked in silence together for a bit. "Edward was planning to buy out his enlistment," she said quietly. "He had such plans."

"He wasn't a regular?"

"Until he met me, Edward Pollitz had no higher ambition than a bottle of rotgut whiskey and a whore on Saturday night." She was leading the way now and their stroll had some purpose to it.

"So. You changed him."

"Do you doubt me?" Her voice was harsh.

"I've never thought too much of people who take responsibility for other people. Seems to me that's falseness on both sides."

"Sir, I come from distinguished antecedents."

"Yeah," he said dryly, "I can see that. Let's walk to the river."

She protested, "Why?" but accompanied him with only that protest.

Slocum picked a point upstream from the *Rosebud*. He didn't particularly care to watch the blood run downstream. The river was muddy, as always. The color of yellow clay. It looked abrasive enough to wash his teeth in it. "Seventy-five years ago, Lewis and Clark came up this river," Slocum said. "There'd been a few white men in the Dakotas before them, French mostly, and a few trappers for the Hudson's Bay company. The

Indians didn't care. They thought there was land enough for everybody. Clark went right through this country all the way to the Pacific and never got in a fight."

She released his arm and hugged herself. "You're right," she said. "It is cold. I never cared for history."

"No?"

"I care for grace. I long for elegance."

Slocum looked at the muddy river and the barren plains on the far side of it. "You came to the wrong place."

"Edward was graceful." Her voice was detached and conversational. "For a plump man, he was very graceful, and on horseback, his posture was remarkable. It was his grace that first attracted me. I had come west with my brother-in-law, Captain Keogh, and met Edward at a post dance. When my parents learned that I was engaged to a sergeant, they were appalled."

"I'll bet."

"I'm quite a practical sort. I reminded my family that deficiencies in breeding can be cured by the judicious application of greenbacks. No wealthy man is refused admittance for long. I also noted that Edward, though no mental giant, would be, if not a family asset, at least not a liability like the wastrels my sisters married. They cut off his privates, sir."

Slocum winced.

"It was because his hair was thin on top and his scalp wasn't worth taking." She hugged herself hard and her voice came from deep in her throat. Her teeth created a barrier but the voice got by all right. "I presume they needed some form of souvenir."

"The army killed my wife," Slocum said quietly. "Come. Let's go back to the post."

"Why would they cut him like that?"

Slocum was wondering why the soldier who'd fed her the information hadn't lied. "Dead, I suppose it doesn't matter much," he said harshly.

She stepped back as if to measure him for a slap.

"I wouldn't," he said calmly.

She was so angry she swept the veil out of her face

and tugged her hat and veil off. The sun lit her red hair until it glowed like an ancient warrior's helmet. Her green eyes were tight and furious. "You bastard," she said.

"I hate to see anyone enjoying the tortures someone else has suffered," he said.

This time she did swing at him, but he caught her arm before the slap could land and held her arm until all the strength went out.

For the first time she dropped her proud head. Her voice got faint and very much softer.

"They buried them all, you know. In a common grave. I won't even be able to mourn his body. Sir, he was such a sweet man."

He took her arm again and turned back across the parade ground. He figured she'd gotten something out of her system and never considered that maybe he had too.

For the second time that day the bugles sounded at Fort Abraham Lincoln.

Major Reno and Captain Benteen were the highest-ranking officers to survive the Battle of the Little Big Horn, and they led their weary soldiers into the fort as though they were leading a column of the dead. The short column of soldiers—fewer than two hundred in all—were half collapsed on their horses and many of the horses were stumbling. Half of them were blown—ruined for serious riding ever again. Reno halted dead center of the parade ground and raised his hand. The riders behind bumped into each other.

Reno's commands were thin and scratchy, as if his voice had been ruined. "Dismount. Grain your horses. Troop sergeants dismiss the men." Without a backward glance Reno got down from his own horse and walked, not toward post headquarters, but toward Colonel Custer's house, where Libby Custer was waiting.

Some of Reno's troopers led their horses toward the stables. Many from the bedraggled column simply dropped their reins and headed for their barracks. They walked like zombies.

A couple passed near and Slocum called, "How close are the Sioux?"

"Mister, the damn Indians are *everywhere*. White man's got no more chance out there than bee honey in a bear cave. They chased us. My God, they ran us. . . ."

The woman's hand squeezed his arm. "Why do you care?" she asked. "If the army killed your wife and child, don't you wish them all dead?"

Slocum took her question to be an honest one. "I dunno. Sometimes I do. I wasn't awful sorry to see that quartermaster die."

She asked him, "What quartermaster?" and he told her about the Hudson's Bay blankets. She listened to his tale without a question, and when he finished, she didn't offer him a bit of pity. "So you tracked him here?"

"Seventh Cavalry. He had to be at Fort Lincoln. But when I found him, he was already too dead to fool with. Ain't that a joke?"

"I suppose it is." They'd passed through the remnants of Benteen's command. Uniforms were filthy and tattered. Most men showed wounds, some serious. The Sioux had taken the heart out of them. Their dearest wish was to travel downriver, the sooner the better.

The ranking officers at Fort Abraham Lincoln had dwellings to themselves. The NCO's and warrant officers rated only half a house, and the corporals and below were not allowed to have families on the post. The Pollitzes shared one of the larger houses with another sergeant. Two identical front doors side by side and two identical front yards. The warrant officer's side had a neat lawn and a neat black wreath on the door. Slocum wondered if army families learned to keep a wreath handy, just in case.

Pollitz's front yard was scruffy and uncared for, and no black wreath adorned the door.

Inside, the house was neat and small. Someone had managed to acquire a few nice pieces of furniture. The desk in the downstairs parlor was a hand-rubbed cherry.

A drop-leaf Queen Anne table was against the dining room wall.

Or so Mrs. Pollitz said—making conversation as the tea water boiled. Slocum set the whiskey bottle on the Queen Anne table. She eyed it with a grimace. "I do believe Edward has better whiskey than that," she said. "Though no longer a drinking man himself, he kept whiskey for entertaining officers. Under my tutelage he became quite popular with the officers."

"I'm sure Colonel Custer thought the world of him," Slocum said. "Break it out."

She smiled ever so sweetly and said, "You're a fine man, sir."

"And you're a fine woman," Slocum said easily. "Though you don't look your best in black."

Her hand went to her bright red hair.

"It doesn't go with your hair," he said.

"I suppose not." She set the bottle down on the table and he drank without waiting for the glass. It was straight unblended Kentucky sour mash. Good hooch. He said so.

"You're rather an animal, aren't you?" she said, her lips curling with distaste.

"Yes," he said. "It's getting late. I hate your black dress. Where's the bedroom?"

He had to give her credit for nerve. Without a protest she marched out of the room, every inch the trooper. Slocum followed. The hall was too narrow for more than one person at a time. The steep staircase took up most of it. Slocum followed her rump up the stairs and down the uncarpeted second-story hall into what had to be the master bedroom.

The bed was a genuine something like the furniture downstairs. It was old. Slocum had seen enough of spool beds in his own boyhood to know they weren't made anymore. The backs of her knees rumpled the bed cover. "I don't even like you," she said.

"No, ma'am. I don't think much of you either."

"Are you satisfied to be used?"

"I ain't usually satisfied," Slocum said, not knowing

if what he said was true. But she seemed to know what he meant better then he. Her brusque nod welcomed him. Her hands went to the neat pile of her hair and came away with a tortoise-shell comb as her hair tumbled free, framing her neck in red. Hair undone, she seemed about ten years younger and more vulnerable. Her businesslike fingers worked at the buttons of her bodice. She stepped out of her widow's weeds like a butterfly shedding its cocoon and stood before him, unbound and barefoot, in a modest white shift.

She sat on the bed. The springs squeaked. She patted the coverlet beside her. "Take off your boots— your shirt."

He stepped out of his boots and peeled his shirt off his wide shoulders. She eyed him with frank curiosity, willing and interested. "You have scars."

"I've been shot. Been stabbed too."

For the first time, she reached to touch him. Her fingers traced one of his knife cuts. Perhaps she was embarrassed by her show of tenderness because her fingers closed into a fist. It was like a clasp knife closing.

He sat and put his arm around her waist. The shift was silk and slipped slick over her warm body like a second skin. He felt the tremble underneath the shift.

"Your wife . . ." she started.

"Dead."

"Just like my Edward." Her words hung like hot-air balloons. "Oh, my God, what am I going to do without him?"

He bent to kiss her. Her lips were ravenous. The tears ran down her cheeks in a rush, flavoring her. Her hands scrabbled at his back as if she wasn't sure whether to rub him or claw him to ribbons.

Before his hands found the soft pillows of her breasts, her hands were at his belt buckle; unfamiliar with the buckle, they pulled and tugged this way and that.

"Take it easy."

"Oh, no. No."

So he unfastened his own pants and stepped out of them. Her eyes were on him, then, so hot that he wondered. . . .

She took his cock between her hands. "Edward had a nice cock too," she said. "Come closer."

He obeyed as she lowered her head and kissed the very tip of him, and his cock slipped into her mouth so smooth and warm. He wrapped his hands in her red hair.

She took his wrists and pulled them away. He put his hands on her shoulders. He slipped the straps off as she sucked, loving him. The shift slid down, baring her brown bosses, hard-nippled, with only a slight sag to show she was no longer a girl. When he rubbed her nipple she moaned.

She worked her tongue and cradled his balls. Abruptly, he jerked away. Her face was wet when she raised it and the tears were as bright as her question. "Why?" she asked.

"I want to be inside you," he said.

"Why?"

"I need it. You need it."

What he said was true. She simply lay back on the bed rucking her shift up to her waist as casual as that. Her hair was just as red and rather sparse. She raised her knees and he crawled between them. He waited then, poised until her hand found his wet cock and guided it to her. He pressed forward and popped into her. She gasped when they joined at the bone. Their pubic bones were like sharp beaks, rubbing together. She spread her legs wider apart and pulled him in.

He went to the back and stayed there. He didn't withdraw an inch. She was very tight and trembled around him like a glove. She'd never had a child, for sure.

She bucked. Her hands grabbed his hard buttocks and squeezed the flesh together. He came up on his toes to get further into her. She was saying something in his ear, a stream of obscenities. He didn't mind. He held himself there like a pouring lip ready to pour. She withdrew from him, and impaled herself again and grunted with the effort. Her eyes were blind and the moisture on her cheeks was sweat. He poured into her for a very long time as she bucked around him. He didn't hear her when she called out to Edward.

3

She was quick to roll out from under. They lay side by side in her marriage bed, catching their breath. Slocum jerked his shirt across his chest, his hand searching for tobacco. The rough flannel felt good on his drying skin.

"Edward never smoked in here," she said

"I ain't him." His fingers rolled the cylinder.

She let it go. In a dreamy voice she said, "I never met anyone quite like him. He had so much energy, Edward did. He used to say the sun never set on a busy man."

Slocum held his tongue.

"His energy and my direction. He was like a primeval force."

"Here?" Slocum swatted the rumpled coverlet between them.

She looked annoyed. "No. I don't know whether I should talk about *that*."

Slocum eyed her: legs apart, juices still slipping down the inside of her thigh. Her eyes locked on the ceiling overhead as if her body belonged to some other woman but her head was her own. "Suit yourself," he said.

She spoke his first obituary. "Edward was born in 1855 in Carrollton, Missouri. His father was a wheelwright and expected Edward to take up the trade. I never met his father."

"Dead?"

"I don't know, and I'm sure I don't care to. Edward spoke poorly of him. He was the reason for Edward's joining the army at such an early age."

Slocum drew on his cigarette. Mrs. Pollitz began detailing her husband's life, like someone repeating a litany as a memory aid. She feared to lose him, he understood that. The smoke curled up in a thin column and flourished when it touched the low ceiling. Someone had taken considerable trouble to stencil a decorative border below the ceiling, framing it with fleur-de-lis, and Slocum wondered which of them had done it. He didn't care enough to ask.

The blinds were drawn against the late sun to protect the carpet against fading, and the dim golden rectangles of the paper shades were like two shuttered eyes. From time to time voices passed by outside the windows. The voices were always hurrying.

She went on. Her husband had been mostly promise—what he could be one day—and Slocum thought that was sad and that it must have been a sad marriage too. Bird-Calling's face flashed in front of his mind and he shied away so fast his head spun.

"Let go of me," she said. "I was just repeating what Edward said to my mother." His hand was locked around her wrist. Impatiently she twisted in his grasp.

"Sorry," he said. "Any kind of ashtray in here?"

"You'll find a saucer in the kitchen. Edward always smoked in the kitchen when he couldn't control himself indoors."

"Fine."

She put her hand to her brow, still remembering. She wouldn't need him. Her pictures were unfolding in her mind, a square inch of canvas at a time, and she wouldn't welcome help deciphering it.

In the kitchen, he stubbed out his smoke on the linoleum-topped counter and pumped the hand pump. She called, "Bring me some cold water, please." So close to the river the well water looked awful damn muddy to him, but it tasted all right. He drank down a handful and found a small tin cup for her. He splashed some water on his face and wiped it with her clean dishtowel.

When he came back into the room, his cock was banging against his naked leg and she looked away. "Here."

She took one shallow sip before handing the cup

back to him. "Thank you. My Edward always brought me water when I needed it."

He sat beside her supine body and laid his hand on her belly, which was soft and round and warm. She covered his hand with her own. She wanted to speak more about Edward. Slocum rotated his hand so that his wiry wrist hairs rasped her skin ever so gently. She drew her knees up and put her other hand over his so he would be still. He withdrew his hand altogether.

Tears were brimming in her eyes. "Edward was such a gentleman. He never committed a single thoughtless act."

"More's the pity." Slocum covered her breast and felt her nipple awaken under his touch.

"What?"

"I don't carry any great love for gentlemen," Slocum said. "Good manners is like the fine-tasting frosting on top of bitter cake." He blushed. He hadn't meant to make a speech. His hand was fondling her now, with a will of its own. Her eyes flicked away and back to him, questioning. Her legs opened slowly like flower petals.

"Edward never—" she began.

He covered her mouth with his own. At first she was soft and passive. His hand slipped down to the core of her, and her lips grunted against him and her tongue came out to play.

This time, he mounted her with less urgency than before, just slipped on into her with the ease of a man pulling on a familiar pair of boots. Slowly he went in, slowly came out. He rotated his hips, exploring, seeking her out. She put one hand over her mouth when he leaned above her, and the eyes that looked at him were the eyes of a frightened girl. It reminded him of Bird-Calling.

"What's the matter?" she asked.

He was still, leaning on his hands. "Something I hoped to forget," he said. "Wait a minute." The sweat stood out on his forehead and the image of Bird-Calling's shy smile wouldn't leave his mind.

The woman threw her hips up against him and slipped her buttocks from side to side as if she were grinding flour. Slocum felt little of it. His hair hung down in front of his face and he tossed his head like a horse straightening its mane.

Her hand was on his back. She stopped twisting. "You don't have to if you don't want to," she said. For the first time, her voice was kind, and that unmanned him completely. He let himself fall to his side, and his half rigid cock slipped out of her and she winced. He laid his hands at his sides with his face pressed against her white cotton coverlet. His eyes were open but saw nothing but whiteness. Her hand on his back was hesitant. She was rubbing some of the same circles he'd implanted on her belly.

"Was your wife pretty?" she asked.

Slocum grunted. Damned if he couldn't feel the moisture at the corners of his eyes. Damned if he couldn't. He hadn't cried when he found Bird-Calling or when she died in his arms. He hadn't wept when he spoke to her brother Two-Medicine, one of the three survivors—the lucky immune—in a village of the dead. Neither he nor Two-Medicine had mourned her then. Two-Medicine had lost his own wife, his father, brother, and children. His sister was just another addition in a long list.

"My God, how I wanted to kill him," Slocum said into Mrs. Pollitz's white cotton coverlet. He wouldn't lift his head—not with that moisture in his eyes. "I never wanted to kill a man so bad before. Soon as Two-Medicine told me about the blankets I knew that's where the smallpox came from. Hadn't been any travelers at the camp and no white men either, and that smallpox, it had to come from the blankets. Still, I had to be sure. I rode into Fort Tullock the next week, to ask some questions, but the Seventh had been pulled out of there and none of the garrison knew anything. I found out the blankets had been guarded heavy, but most of the soldiers thought that was so people wouldn't steal 'em, not because of the pox. I found a medical man who'd talk, though I sure had to loosen his throat with booze."

"The army killed your wife? She was an Indian, you said."

Her voice rang louder in his ears than his own. He turned his face to ask, "What damn difference does that make?"

She was wearing a funny smile on her face. "Edward could tell you," she said.

"Well, goddamn," he said. That dried his eyes all right. Dried them fine. Roughly he pushed her legs apart. He thrust into her to the hilt with his eyes on her her eyes. They looked faintly amused until he bottomed, and then she gasped very slightly. They didn't kiss— wouldn't. Kissing was too kindly for what they had in mind. Slocum pushed deep as he could and returned until just the tip of his cock was inside her before slamming it home so hard she bounced and the bedsprings let out a scream of protest.

She smiled. "Indian lover," she said pleasantly.

He yelled his anger.

"Indian lover," she said. She wore her pleasantness like a steel mask.

His hips slapped against hers. His pubic hair patted her sopping wet hair. He put one hand on her breast and squeezed it, harder than he had to.

Her eyes narrowed at the pain. "Lover," she hissed between her teeth. She jumped under him like a shot animal. She opened her mouth wide and her eyes rolled back until he saw more white than pupil. She was panting like an engine.

He withdrew himself until he was barely contained within her lips.

"You son of a bitch," she hissed. Desperately she clung to his ass.

Somewhat wearily, he gave her what she wanted, slipped in deeper, and she twisted around him, held in place, affixed.

She went on deeper and harder, pushing against him,

and he rested, letting her do all the work, working herself out.

She stopped for a moment. "You finish," she said. Tired eyes. Heaving belly.

"I'm all right." But he thrust into her just the same and pushed into her delirium. Once again, like a horse flogged beyond its endurance, she shuddered around him, and when he thought she was done, he collapsed on her, not moving.

"You didn't. . . ." she said.

"Didn't feel like it."

"Edward . . . Edward used to say . . . a man had to finish."

"Edward sounds like a fool."

"Off me. Get off me."

"No."

So she wriggled out from under his weight. He heard the pat, pat, pat of her feet and the sound of hinges, and when he turned to look she was drawing on a robe. Her eyes were funny. They held something like sorrow and something like triumph all at once. "I suppose you'll be wanting something," she said. She found a brush on her dresser and brushed out her long red hair in quick strokes. When she turned back to him, she had the tortoise-shell hairpin in her mouth. "Hmmmmm?" she said.

Her arrogance got to him. "Don't know what," he drawled lazily. Making no attempt to cover his nakedness, he sat up and swung his feet over the edge of the bed. "I ate a buffalo steak only a couple hours ago and I fucked a hot woman just now. Isn't much more a man needs than that."

"Hot woman." She didn't care for that too much. "If you were a gentleman . . ." she began, but stopped when she ran into his lazy, smug grin. "I will make coffee," she said. "Come into the kitchen when"—she eyed him pointedly—"you're decent." And she whirled out of the room like a thief leaving the scene.

John Slocum took his time dressing. He tucked his pants into his boots and straightened some of the wrinkles out of his shirt. He used Edward's badger brush on his long raven-black hair. Edward had left some thinnings—blond—in the brush. Edward wouldn't be leaving any more. When he tossed the brush back onto the dressing table, it made a clatter. The woman in the kitchen stopped whatever she'd been doing. He could feel her listening. "I wouldn't mind taking a bath," he said. "I been on the trail for a week."

"I noticed," she said. He heard the clatter of the pump, the bang of the ash handle on her cast-iron cookstove. He could smell the odor of fresh coffee. Oh, well, he hadn't really had a hope of a bath. That was expecting too much.

All the same he eyed the hot-water tank. Her stove had a tin insert beside the baking oven with a spigot on the side. Handy. So long as you kept some kind of fire in the firebox, you had hot water at the turn of the tap. What wouldn't they think of?

He tapped the iron stove with the toe of his boot and said, "What won't they think of next."

"Yes," she said briefly. "It's quite ingenious. I'm sorry I can't offer you a chance to bathe."

"I didn't figure," he said. He drew back the kitchen chair and sat down, setting his elbows on the table like someone staking a claim. "I'll have some of that coffee, though."

Her hair was restored to its neat bun and she must have kept powder in the kitchen because her face was fashionably pale, not the flushed color of a woman fresh from bed. She set his coffee cup down with enough force to mean there wouldn't be quite enough time for a refill.

To annoy her he requested the cream he never used in coffee.

"We have some canned milk," she admitted reluctantly.

"Fine." He smiled innocently. "That'll be just fine." And when she punctured the can and set it at his elbow, he asked for a spoon and took his time about stirring. He eyed her over the cup. "None for you?" he asked.

"Not just now."

So he slurped deliberately. "Damn," he said. "This is hot."

"I'm sure you've had hot coffee before in your life."

"Ma'am," he said to annoy her further, "I never had nothin' so hot as you. My God. If you peddled that ass of yours, I'd bet you'd make a fortune."

Her smile dripped with sweetness. "And I suppose you'd be just the man to, uh, help me. . . ."

"Why, ma'am. Are you callin' me a pimp?"

"No more than you're calling me a whore," she snapped right back.

He nodded. He looked up at her set face and her hands tapping nervously on the counter top. He let out a roar of quick hearty laughter.

"I don't see anything funny in this," she said.

"No. I don't suppose you do." Her coffee was just as good as he expected. "What'll you do now?"

She went to the high kitchen window. "I'll return to St. Louis," she said. "My family is there."

"Think you'll marry again?"

She wheeled. "Think *you'll* marry again? Will you take another wife?"

He looked at her and then answered seriously. "I figure one wife and family is enough for any man's lifetime. Maybe I'll feel different in five, ten years, but I don't think so. Man with a family can get hurt to death. Anything I ever had was taken away from me— my homeplace back in Georgia was stolen by carpet-baggers; my country—the Confederacy—it went down in defeat. My pa and ma died of the cholera, and my only brother was killed on Cemetery Ridge. I was there that day too. On Little Roundtop. I watched Pickett's charge coming out of the peach orchard toward that goddamn stone wall. The wall was blue with Yanks. I fired my rifle until it was too damn hot to hold and the other sharpshooters did the same, but I fear we weren't much use. The charge faltered right at the stone wall. I saw George Pickett go down. They shot him to rags. You could always tell the officers because they were with the flags. I knew my brother was with Pickett's bunch, but I didn't see him die. I found out that night when we were all out scouring the battle-ground for our wounded. He made that wall but no further. I never wanted to have too much after that because I'm a grasping sort of man. What I have I hold to me fast, and when it's taken, it likes to tear me all to pieces. Now I ain't got nothin', and I expect I'm better off."

For a moment, her face was softened. Then it hardened up. "My," she said. "Such eloquence."

He didn't heed the sarcasm. "It's like that quarter-master. Duffy. Hell, he may have been a murdering son of a bitch, but I wouldn't want to die like he did. When it comes my turn, I'll go, and gladly enough. If you die and all you got is your guns and your horse, somebody's bound to steal your horse and somebody else'll steal your guns, so you don't have anything to worry about. Man like that quartermaster dies worryin'. I wouldn't wish that on any man."

"Duffy. I know him. Benteen's quartermaster. War-rent officer. His home is just two houses down. He had some family, but they were never on the post."

"His mistake," Slocum shrugged. "Duffy's wife and daughter are in God's hands now. Somehow I don't think God's gonna have the time to fool with them."

"I met her once. At Fort Tullock. Pretty little thing. A little flightly, I thought. He had a daughter too. Let me see. . . ." She put her finger to her lips. "I remem-ber. She was one of those blond-haired skinny girls. Always looking down at her feet. Big eyes. She looked like a woods colt, so she did."

"Uh-huh." Slocum finished his coffee. Without a thought, she filled his cup up again. This time, Slocum didn't bother with the canned milk. Made the damn coffee too sweet.

"He had them settled on the Powder River some-where."

"Mizpah Creek."

"That's right. That's right. Edward mentioned it. Duffy wanted Edward to throw in with him. Set up a wood yard on the river and a roadhouse. I opposed the plan, of course."

"Of course?"

"The day of the river steamboat is done. As soon as the Northern Pacific completes its northern branch, these river towns will shrivel and die on the vine. Can't you see that?"

"And what about the Indians?"

She waved her hand airily. "The handwriting is on the wall," she said.

"I ain't sure it reads so good," Slocum said. He was sorry he spoke, because she'd been dreaming about the future and his words took her back to the past and her face closed up as if she'd closed a shutter.

Her lips made an ugly grimace. "Yes. I suppose I was getting overexcited," she said. She looked out the window again. He sensed her shriveling up and for an instant he saw her as she'd be when she was bent and very, very old. He wanted to put his arm around her but hadn't the right. Noisily he set his coffee cup down and pushed his chair back. "I suppose I'll be goin'," he said.

She turned with a puzzled expression. "You don't suppose Duffy's wife and daughter are still out there?" Her gesture included most of western America and Canada.

"He said they were."

She blurted, "But they'll be killed!"

He nodded. "If they're lucky they will be."

"But that's terrible." Her hand went to her mouth.

"Yes, ma'am." He set his hat straight.

Once again she withdrew to her private world. "I wouldn't mind dying so much. But the terror. And that little girl. What was her name?"

"I don't recall."

She snapped her fingers. "I do. Her name is Opal."

"I expect you got it right."

Suddenly she smiled at him, a warm smile, one she had (he suspected) reserved especially for Edward. "And you're going to get them, aren't you?"

He returned a grin. "Now, why would I do a damn fool thing like that?" he asked.

Her response probably surprised her as much as him. "Because it isn't finished between you and Duffy," she said. "If you don't go, your revenge will eat you up inside and make you small."

Slocum headed for the door. "You sure got a way with words," he said.

But she intercepted him. "You are going, aren't you?"

He sighed. "I guess I will. I guess it's the only way I'll be quit of it."

"What's your name?" she asked.

"John."

"I'm Caroline."

"Nice to make your acquaintance, Caroline," he said. He took off his hat.

Affectionately, she rumpled his hair. Then she took his face between her two hands. "I'm sorry about your wife," she said softly but deliberately.

"Yes." He nodded. "I'm sorry about your husband."

Slocum got his bath behind the barracks, where Benteen's men had heated huge kettles of water. Most were in their cots but there were plenty of bathers. The hot water was beside the riverbank and once a man had scrubbed himself, he could rinse in the muddy river and replace the dirt he'd lost. Slocum borrowed a good long-handled, stiff-bristled brush to clean his back.

He didn't talk to the soldiers and they didn't talk to him. They were half scrambled from their fight and the retreat, and John Slocum didn't care to press for details.

Not so Jim Beckwith. As he often said, Beckwith "never could know too much about the redskin." He asked everybody every question he could think of: weapons, chiefs, even the type of Indian pony. The troopers all knew the old scout as a fixture in the west. He found Slocum at the river's edge.

Slocum indicated the hard bristle brush. "You can use this once I'm done," he said.

"I had my bath this year," the mountain man said complacently. "First warm day in spring, same as always."

Beckwith squatted down. "You should have seen these boys six months ago," he said. "They was full of piss and vinegar."

Slocum shrugged and waded out into the river covered with suds. "Ain't a man alive can't be beaten," he said before he launched himself into the water.

Even this late in the year, much of the Missouri water came from snow melt in the Rockies and it was cold, very cold. Slocum's head ached from the sudden shock. He kicked himself in a quick circle, churning and thrashing like a sidewheeler.

On shore he danced up and down. He didn't own a towel and hadn't thought to bring his horse blanket.

"You got bumps all over you, boy," Beckwith observed.

"At least I don't stink like a carcass in the sun," Slocum said without his teeth chattering—not once.

"Lord, listen to him." Beckwith was undisturbed. The soldiers deserted the riverbank as silently as they'd come, and now Slocum and Beckwith shared the beach with the piles of abandoned clothing the troopers had left where they'd stepped out of them.

Beckwith had a gleam in his eye. "Pity those clothes are so ragged," he said.

Slocum got into his pants and hung his shirt over his frame. "You just help yourself there, Jim. Blue uniform's just the thing to wear when the Sioux find you."

Beckwith laughed. "Well, I expect they're a little ragged even for an old carcass like mine. But this pilgrim ain't meetin' no Sioux no way. When those soldier boys go downriver, I aim to be sittin' on deck. There's a time to stand and a time to bolt, and I make this out a time to bolt. The Sioux—once they start killin', they can't help themselves, they can't stop. They'll cut down any white man west of the Missouri for completeness if nothin' else."

"Uh-huh." Slocum looked up at the sky. Two and a half hours of light left. "You figure they're watchin' the fort?"

Beckwith spat. "Hell, yes. Of course they're watchin' the fort. If we're real lucky, Old Sitting Bull will let us get on those sidewheelers before him and his bucks come in here and have themselves a good time burnin' and lootin' the stores. If we ain't lucky. . . ." Beckwith shrugged.

Slocum was a little bit tired of Jim Beckwith's wisdom but didn't feel like telling him so. "I think I'll go see to my horse," he said.

"Mind if I mosey along?"

"Yep."

The main corral was full of weary horses, many of them still saddled with high-cantled McClellan saddles, canteens, and Sharps carbines. Two horses lay on their sides and didn't even switch their tails. Two hostlers—one on crutches—had more than enough to do. The army couldn't take these animals on the boats tomorrow, and Slocum didn't think they'd leave them for the Sioux. He grained his own mare and curried her down—though he'd done that this morning once already. He eyed her hard. She'd been used hard but right now was probably the fastest horse on the post.

The sun dropped into the crazy red sky and the half-moon came up. John Slocum had cornered a big stall for his horse and it had plenty of room for him too. Slocum guessed that the empty stall had been meant for some officer but didn't know who. He settled into the deep straw, listening to the quiet chewing of his horse, the farting and bellyaching, the occasional thump of a hoof.

John Slocum rarely dreamed and never had what the Indians know as a medicine dream.

Bird-Calling was sitting outside their lodge with the baby in her lap. Bird-Calling was lacing up the sole of a moccasin, pausing every now and then to show the work to the baby, who gurgled and groped for it.

In the dream, John Slocum stood before them. He spoke to them too, but neither his wife nor his child heard. The sun was very bright and gleamed on Bird-Calling's braids, just as dark and shiny as his own. The baby cooed. He called to her but she did not hear. His feet were set in mortar and he couldn't move to her. A cloud fell across the sun and she decided to move back inside. She stood up, brushing at her long deerskin dress—the one she'd worn on her burial litter. The baby was asleep with her head on Bird-Calling's shoulder. Bird-Calling looked at him then. That was all.

And in her mute appeal, his heart skipped a beat, and another. For the sake of his dead family he had to save the quartermaster's wife and child. That was Bird-Calling's message.

He sat bolt upright, covered with sweat and staring. The straw was pricking his skin. The stable smelled bad. Restless, he went outside and rolled a smoke. He watched the wild stars wheel overhead until first light. When the low morning star was the only survivor, he saddled his horse, the Appaloosa with the oddly shaped brown and white patches. One day of rest was all the Appaloosa needed. That and a little grain. The horse nickered softly and suffered herself to be bridled and led out into the morning. Beckwith's horse, the big part-Morgan, stayed half asleep when Slocum tied him to the pommel of his horse's saddle. The two horses moved so quietly through the corral that most of the broken horses of Benteen's command didn't even waken. Many of the houses on officers' row had lights in their windows. Slocum would have bet money most of those lanterns had burned all night.

When he reached the sutler's, he led both horses around the side to the loading platform and climbed up to hammer at the door. He didn't expect any quick response and he didn't get one. He banged away patiently until a window slid up somewhere over his head and an angry voice shouted, "If you don't get away from there, you damn drunk, you'll find out what's resting at the bottom of my damn chamberpot!"

Slocum stepped back to eye the sutler, dressed in a flannel nightshirt. The sutler's wife's frightened face appeared briefly but withdrew.

"Got business with you," Slocum called.

"I'm closed," the sutler hollered. "Come back in a couple hours."

"I'll want supplies," Slocum called back as if he hadn't heard. "And it'll be worth your while. Hell," he added reasonably, "you're awake anyway. Why not show a profit for it?"

Apparently the sutler found that argument convincing, because a few minutes after the upstairs window slammed down, Slocum heard someone fumbling with the heavy bar on the inside of the storeroom door.

The sutler wore a robe over his flannel nightshirt and black dress shoes on his stockingless feet. "Get in here, dammit, man," he said. He closed the storeroom door behind him but didn't bother to bar it. The sutler showed Slocum a suspicious face. "Now, what might you be wanting that I might have?" he demanded.

"Ammunition. Forty-four caliber—Remington Centerfire. And I want some of the new wax-covered bullets too. Nothing older than six months. I'll want forty-four forty caliber bullets for my carbine. Winchester'll be all right. Two hundred for the pistol and five hundred for the carbine. I'll want a good bowie knife. Something to hold a decent edge. I'll want a rattail file, a flat file, number sixty grit. . . ."

"Wait a minute, friend." The sutler held up one weary hand. "Ain't you heard?"

Slocum waited for him. Might as well get it over with.

"By noon today, the sidewheelers will be loading. And my goods will be burning to keep them out of the hands of the damn redskins. We are all gonna hightail it downriver like the Devil was behind us. There'll be room for every man, woman, and child in Fort Lincoln, but we'll bury the dead right here and shoot the horses and my damn trade goods will go up in smoke."

"Then you'll give me a good price," Slocum said. "Some light gun oil, needles, and carpet thread. . . ."

"Pilgrim, you didn't hear what I said."

"I heard you. They're gonna burn your goods. Fine. I'll buy some instead. I'll want twenty pounds of cleaned oats—and they better not have any rocks or hulls. A couple spare cinch buckles. Ten pounds of wheat flour. Wrap that in oilskin. My slicker ain't no account, so I'll take a new one. A couple good pounds of plug tobacco. I'll want coffee, tomatoes, and beans."

Shaking his head, the sutler retired into the depths of the storeroom to prepare Slocum's order. No business of his if this man wanted to buy goods he could have free that evening.

"I said new bullets," Slocum said.

"I always sell the old stock first," the sutler said. He had pride in his trade.

Slocum sighed. "You silly son of a bitch. Bring the fresh ammunition."

And the man did.

"One set of number three horseshoes and a small paring knife, and, uh, two dozen horseshoe nails."

His hands full of bundles, the sutler clattered them down on the counter. "What d'ya need all this stuff for?" he asked. "They ain't gonna let you take it on board."

Outside the steam whistle started hooting again. It sent a short shiver down Slocum's spine. The *Rosebud* was greeting her sister ships, and soon three whistles were hooting at each other and doors all over the post were opening and slamming. "That's them now," the sutler said, stupidly.

"If you got a salt-cured ham under twenty pounds, I'll take it. Bag it up good so it can breathe. Twenty tins tomatoes, let's see, dried beans, and a tin of molasses."

The sutler called upstairs to his wife. "Get our valises down to the landing. If we get loaded, maybe they won't have the heart to unload the luggage." To Slocum: "Hurry up, man, time's a-wasting."

Horses were rushing by outside. Running feet too.

"Wax-tipped lucifers. Five boxes of a hundred. Flint and steel. New punk for it." Slocum pulled off his plainsman's boots and inspected the sole carefully. "Damn," he said finally. "I hate to break in boots. I'll just make these do. Do you have a good pair of officer's glasses?"

"Captain's glass or binoculars?"

"I'll want them weatherproof."

"Then you'll want the captain's glass." The spyglass he produced would have done credit to a naval officer.

"I can't see a damn thing through this," Slocum objected.

"Take it outside where you got some space."

Slocum watched the running figures around the hastily tied-up sidewheelers. The wives had precious household goods ready to be loaded, but the soldiers weren't letting those treasures aboard. There was room for the humans only. No property except for a single small handbag and a change of clothes. The angry faces jumped right out at Slocum.

"It's the strongest glass I ever carried," the sutler said proudly. " 'Course, you got to have steady hands to use it."

Slocum carefully stowed his new gear inside waterproofed leather pannikins that'd ride both sides of his packhorse. He took his time about it too, though the sutler was anxious to be away and kept wringing his hands.

He was almost finished when Jim Beckwith climbed up on the loading platform. "You intending to steal my horse?" he asked pleasantly.

"Yep." Slocum didn't bother to explain.

"Well, I suppose I won't have any use for him." The older man removed his hat and scratched where it itched. "You're a damn fool. You know that."

"Never doubted it for a minute."

"Your hair's gonna hang from some Sioux lodge-pole."

"Likely as not," Slocum agreed. He cinched the pannikins closed. "Here, you can help me lash these to your horse."

The mountain man tied his thongs with great attention to details. "He ain't fast, but he's got plenty of bottom," Beckwith said. "If they start to ride you down, you can yank this cinch loose and lose all your baggage. You'll be able to swap riding horses then."

Slocum checked the older man's neat rigging. His eyes traced each knot and the single dangling cord that'd turn his packhorse into a spare saddle horse. He nodded. "That's a hell of a good idea," he said. "I thank you for it."

"What do I owe you?" Slocum asked the sutler.

The sutler wore a strange expression on his face. "You're riding west then?" he asked.

Slocum didn't answer.

"He's pretty heavy laden for a trip downriver, you fool," Beckwith snapped.

"Well, I'll be damned," the sutler said, shaking his head. "I'll be double damned." In honor of the occasion, he only overcharged John Slocum twenty dollars for the entire load.

4

"The wicked flee when no man pursueth" was the disconnected thought running through John Slocum's mind as he stood on top of Red Butte watching the flight of the white man.

The trail to the top of the Butte was gradual but winding, tracing its thin way on the north and western side of the Butte. Slocum half expected to meet Sioux scouts as he made his climb, but didn't.

On top, he found the charred remnants of a campfire; the underside of the wood was still warm, so he figured he hadn't missed them by more than five or six hours. They'd been up there this morning when the two additional sidewheelers made their way upstream toward the fort that was now just a column of smoke in the north. Red Butte was a thousand feet higher than the sagebrush plain and the air was clear, and Slocum could almost make out individual buildings at the base of the smoke, but not quite. The army had decided to fire the fort after all.

Three hours ago the soldiers had started killing their mounts. It was an ugly business. Nobody likes to slaughter an animal that has meant the difference between life and death. It's hard to gun something that every instinct insists you should spare and even cherish. But the army wasn't going to leave any horseflesh for the Sioux: the heavy chargers that brought Benteen from the Little Big Horn to safety; the delicate thoroughbred Major Reno called Daisy; the matched black hacks that pulled Libby Custer's gig on Sunday drives; the red pony Tom Custer, Jr., called Carrot. They were all herded into the post corral, and troopers with Springfields surrounded them and began shooting.

Slocum hadn't stayed around for it. His own two horses became focal points for the resentment many troopers felt at killing their own animals, and more than one man called, "Hey, where you goin' with those damn animals?" as if the escape of any horse cast doubt on what they were doing. The young soldiers at the gate meant to stop Slocum. One unlimbered his carbine as the other approached the lean rider. The gate guard wore his campaign hat low over his eyes and his boots were polished to a high shine, and Slocum thought he'd been left behind at the fort when Custer and Benteen and Reno rode out. He had the harshness of untested youth. "Get down from that animal, mister," the boy soldier commanded. Looking down, Slocum couldn't see anything but the boy soldier's hat. He wondered what the boy would do if he spat a stream of tobacco juice all over the hat's pearly crown. Probably die for his hat. That's what he'd do. "I'm comfortable right here, son," he said easily. His right hand was on the reins in plain sight, his left hand on the Colt in his saddle holster. Already the thong was off the hammer and the pistol was half clear of leather.

"Goddamn you." The soldier's voice cracked and his hat jerked back and his young eyes were small and furious. "I gave you an order!"

"I ain't in the army, son," Slocum said, still easily. "You got any orders to give me, it's you givin' them, not the U.S. Army." Without being in any way threatening, Slocum took the Colt out and laid it across his lap. Slocum never had been an ambidextrous shooter. He favored his right hand. But at this distance, even left-handed, he couldn't hope to miss. The other soldier threw his carbine to his shoulder. Slocum spared him a glance. The bore of that damn carbine looked big enough to walk into with his arms stretched out. "I'll be ridin' out now," Slocum said, forestalling trouble. "I don't expect you'll be botherin' with me again." The crash of shots from the fort corral swelled, and though the boy soldier opened his mouth and said something, Slocum couldn't hear what. He nodded as though the soldier had given him permission to pass and holstered his Colt and leaned forward in the saddle, and the horse ambled out the front gate of Fort Abraham Lincoln into Indian country.

He cut south right away. Red Butte was a perfect watchtower just an hour south. From its broad top he could get a look-see at some of the country he meant to travel. He'd been down in the Powder River country a couple of times, trapping Crazy Woman Creek. The Yellowstone described a semicircle to the north, and the fastest route for a horseman would be west and slightly south for Mizpah Creek. He hadn't explored Mizpah Creek ever before, but he knew the broad shallow bar where it entered the Powder River.

It would be two hundred miles as the crow flies, maybe more, if the Duffy woman's cabin was very far up the Creek. Slocum figured it would take him a week.

Below the lip of Red Butte, the wide muddy Missouri flowed, indifferent to the currents of men's lives that depended on it for transportation, communication, and, on this day, escape.

The first army sidewheeler churned by. Slocum could look down directly on its deck. The army had loaded most of the able-bodied soldiers on the first and fastest vessel. A crew stood at the swivel gun on the prow and they were ready for anything. The low railings were lined with soldiers with carbines at their shoulders. The soldiers were very alert, and mule deer would have picked the wrong moment to take a drink just then because the Seizers were very angry and ready to kill most anything.

The second vessel was the familiar *Rosebud,* loaded this time with officers' wives, children, and some of the slightly wounded soldiers—those still able to bear arms. Someone had affixed an awning over the back of the deck, and Slocum supposed that was where the women and youngest children would find protection from the sun's glare off the water. That awning provided a fine target for any Indian eager to loose an arrow at the fleeing Seizers and partake in Sitting Bull's triumph.

The soldiers lay along the deck or sat if they couldn't lie down, and their carbines were just as ready as the carbines in the first vessel. They were ready for a sustained attack. Slocum doubted they'd face it. They'd have an uncomfortable all-night journey downstream, but by noon tomorrow, they'd tie up at Fort Pierre.

The third and last sidewheeler was past him now, downstream, its decks cluttered with the same wounded who'd been unloaded yesterday. All three vessels were pouring on the fire and all three hoped to make miles before dusk fell. The column of smoke bent. The last vessel rounded the bend and was lost to sight. In its wake a couple of abandoned boxes and trunks bobbed like buoys. One sidewheeler blew its whistle, a faint toot, the last salute of the cavalry to Fort Abraham Lincoln. A little wind dusted the top of Red Butte and blew some grit into Slocum's face.

It made him smile. A couple of thousand miles of wild country and he had it to himself. Except for five thousand Sioux, the land was his. No man to tell him "No trespassing," none to say "Don't spit here." The hoot of the steam whistle passing downriver could have been lonely as hell, but to John Slocum it sounded like a hoot of joy. He slipped up again on his Appaloosa and clucked softly, and his two horses started down the side of the Butte, turning their backs on the Missouri, turning away from the white man's river.

Slocum's Appaloosa found the level going at the bottom of the Butte more to her liking and stepped out briskly. Slocum reined in slightly. No sense hurrying into anything. He had all the time in the world and wasn't in the mood for startling anyone.

He kept heading south of the sun. The great Buttes looked like iron-clad Merrimacs steaming across the plains. The wind pushed the clouds around over his head, but didn't fool around much at ground level. To the casual eye, these plains would have seemed barren, but Slocum's eye knew better. Here was a high rocky ridge where even sagebrush couldn't grow, and under that slab of rock, probably rattlesnakes. It was too ideal a home for them. Slocum's packhorse pricked up his ears and snorted as he circled the spot, and obligingly one rattlesnake returned the horse's remark with a hiss of its own. "Easy," Slocum advised. At the sound of his voice, the horse straightened out.

A sage thrasher ran ahead of them, beating its white barred wings. Twice, in the eye of the sky, a mote turned into a hawk. He scared up a half-dozen prairie chickens just before dusk.

As he rode, he felt the eyes on him. Some of the eyes belonged to birds and ground squirrels and prairie dogs, but he felt the heavier pressure of other eyes too. Except for the high buttes, the plains were flat, but there were plenty of coulees where a hundred men could hide if they didn't move much. Slocum had seen two dozen Sioux hiding on an absolutely barren plain that wouldn't conceal a canary bird.

He made no concessions to those eyes. He noted their weight and kept a sharp lookout, but rode straight on ahead at his own leisurely pace.

His father had meant for him and his brother to inherit and work Slocum's Stand, the four-hundred-acre farm that crossed the Georgia mountain valley. His father had shown his sons everything he could about farming. They grew wheat, barley, corn, and oats. They raised cattle, sheep, a few horses, and hogs. John Slocum always preferred the livestock over the grain farming. His brother, Glavis, was the opposite way.

They had figured to farm the place together, to bring wives home and raise the farmer's best crop—a good bunch of children. The war changed all that. It killed Glavis outright and his pa indirectly.

Still, he'd tried to make a go of it. A battered, bitter John Slocum rode home in August 1865 on a fifty-dollar horse with a Colt and a shotgun tied to his saddle. His family was gone, but the homeplace was still there, and he knew his pa'd kept up the taxes though the fields were empty—as he'd expected—and thieves had pretty well cleaned the machinery out of the barn. He set to work and was beginning to see results for the labors that went on into the night and by lantern light, when someone else eyed Slocum's Stand. The man thought Slocum's farm would make a fine place to breed thoroughbreds and showed up one day with a hired gun to back his legal play.

John Slocum killed them both, and killed his own chances at the same moment. He'd shot a judge.

He'd ridden alone since that time, through the Nations, and north into the Dakotas. He'd crossed Texas and across the border into Sonora. He'd got used to the idea of loneliness and begun to value it, taking pride in his solitude. That was before he rode into Two-Medicine's camp looking for horses and saw the doe-eyed slender girl whom he later came to know as Bird-Calling.

That was John Slocum's second try at settling down, but he had no luck at it. Other men had wives and children, and passed their lives at the warmth of the hearth and in the warmth of their family. John Slocum rode by their homes late at night and only the barking farm dog marked his passing, and only the moon overhead gave him light. He was happier. He risked less —just a lonely death with no one to tend him or say good-bye.

Slocum shifted in his saddle. It wouldn't be too awful long until the sun turned the sunset colors and disappeared. There was moon enough to keep on going, but he meant to spare his horses. Thirty miles a day across rough country isn't impossible for a strong horse, but it takes the fat off, and Slocum saw no sense in pushing the matter. If the woman and child were dead when he reached Mizpah Creek, there wasn't any help for it. In some matters, John Slocum was a fatalist. Now he was looking for a campsite. It was more than ordinarily important, because the Indians' eyes on him would note his camp too and add its character to what they already knew about the strange white man.

The sky got gaudy, bands of red-purple and black against a sky translucent blue as Chinese porcelain. Shadows got funny on the ground—eighteen-inch sagebrushes throwing tree-size shadows. John Slocum found what suited him: a clump of alders at the base of a low rocky mound, some harder place that had been imperfectly flattened when the glaciers gouged this country millennia ago. The hummock—for that's all it was—was sixty feet above a fine spring.

A white man would camp beside the spring, grazing his horses in the alders and cooking his dinner on a bonfire that would blind him to the night. Slocum dismounted and loosed his horses' cinches and waited patiently while they drank from the sweet water. He hung the dripping canteens and let the horses graze their fill as the sky squeezed the sunset into the west. Then he led them up the bare ridge to a spot just below the summit where they wouldn't be silhouetted. He unsaddled, but didn't break his saddles open. In a few seconds, he could throw his gear on the animals and ride. He sat down on his saddle and dug some beef jerky from his saddlebags. From the low hummock, Slocum could see three hundred sixty degrees around him, and from time to time, his eyes sought the white and black prairie, but he wasn't working hard at it. If the Sioux wanted to come up on him tonight, they were welcome to.

The signals had gone out. The runners had been dispatched. The Indians had plenty of time to understand who he was before they killed him. There was no honor to be won by murder in the night of an unknown enemy.

It had been the reason the Indian lost so often. A foolish abundance of honor. To touch an enemy with a counting stick and leave him alive was more dangerous, and thus more valued, than taking his life. And when the bravest of the Indians were trying to get in close enough to demonstrate their bravery, white soldiers picked them off from cover. Slocum had seen it happen. And done it a time or two.

He got another hunk of beef jerky. He heard the

ching, ching of his grazing horses' bridles, and the tiny sound as hooves dislodged a pebble. The saddle squeaked when he shifted his weight. He'd use the saddle blanket for warmth and the saddle for his pillow.

The moon popped up, half full and very bright. A few airy clouds slipped across the night and the moon shone right through them. The stars were big and close, and the Milky Way splashed across the southern sky like spilled paint. Guarded only by his ground-reined horses, Slocum slept, dreamless as a child.

Before dawn he came awake. His right side was stiff where he'd pressed it into the rough shale slope, and his arm was stiff. When he sat up, he rubbed life back, flopping his wrist until it was flexible. He kept the blanket wrapped around him while he loosened up, because it was chilly and damp. Below, a fog had collected in the alder grove where the springs touched the colder morning air, and it looked ghostlike, and Slocum wondered if the Sioux were in the grove this morning. Wouldn't hurt to find out. He scrambled to his feet, stretched and yawned, worked a few of the kinks out. He unpacked a collapsible bucket and filled it with oats, one quart per horse. They'd be working today. He pulled on his boots, wincing when the sharp shale stabbed his feet. Here and there on the plains the fog hung low, as if the clouds that would form later in the day were born here in the before-dawn chill. Slocum's boots and hat were slick with dew.

When the horses had finished the oats, he saddled them carefully, pushing the air out of their bellies with his boot. He settled his cross-draw rig on his left hip and buckled the Winchester's scabbard to its rings before he led his horses downslope into the fog. It retreated before him, but at the bottom, deep in the grass, he couldn't see the ridgetop anymore. The horses were more interested in the grass than speculation, and he ground-reined them where they'd have some to eat. Then, walking soft and empty-handed, he scouted the grove. The Sioux hadn't decided to make this the place and this the time. He collected some low dead branches from the alders and snapped them smaller over his knee. Tiny pops wouldn't travel ten feet through this mist. He found a bare spot, which he ringed close with stones, forming a circle not much wider than six inches but deep. His wood formed a neat pyramid. He shoved strips of bark underneath for tinder. He immersed his coffeepot into one sandy-bottomed spring. A couple of handfuls of coffee. Dead alder burned hot—but you'd better have everything ready because it didn't burn long. He used flint and steel to set the bark alight, blowing carefully at the glowing ember until he coaxed flame from it. He'd save his matches long as he could. He washed his hands and face in the spring water and rubbed his chin which already showed rough black bristles. He sat down with a tin cup full of cold water, soap, and a straight edge to shave himself. He wouldn't get scraggly-looking. This country killed the scraggly and the failures without mercy.

When the razor lost its edge, he stropped it on the inside of his soft pistol belt until it was as sharp as he liked. When he was finished, his face felt scraped and raw, but it was okay when he washed the soap away.

His coffee had boiled and the fire was out by the time he poured coffee into the rinsed cup that had just served as his shaving mug. The coffee was bitter, oily, and excellent. Its aroma was the grandest odor in the world.

He would not build a fire at night because it would be a beacon for miles in directions he couldn't control. But he would build a good hot smokeless fire in the mornings because he would ride out soon. He wasn't afraid of leaving sign. They'd picked him up already.

He fried up some ham with his coffee and finished one can of tomatoes, juice and all, before he passed the bad news to his horses. "Look, fellas. I know you wouldn't mind grazing here all day and all week, but we got to put some miles behind us today."

He'd already pulled the caps and recharged each of his pistols: the one that rode on his hip and the brace that hung beside his saddle. The three pistols were identical Colts because Slocum didn't want to have to confuse his hands if things suddenly got loud.

His saddle was cinched. Tight enough for an all-day easy pace, but loose enough to permit a laboring horse's chest to expand during a chase. Two separate lines attached his packhorse to rings at the back of his saddle, and if he lost one line, the other was strong enough. A doubletree hitch held the cinch of the pack saddle. Brush or branches couldn't loosen it, but one tug on the right line and the pack saddle would hit the dust, and John Slocum would have two horses for his escape.

His Winchester held five in the tube—he never kept one under the hammer. His Colts held five each; ditto the hammer. He could kill twenty times if he had to.

Thus armed and prepared, John Slocum rode out of the mist on the second day of his journey. Almost immediately, he crossed a broad track where a Sioux scouting party had passed. They'd meant him to see it. Their trace was perpendicular to his own, and his quick glance counted twenty horses, maybe fifteen riders. A couple of the horses dragged travois—their sharp points cut the ground, and that was surely unusual for a war party. But the tracks were from well-cared-for young horses, and the Sioux had meant for him to see them. Indians left marks or not as they desired, and no village on the move likes to advertise itself and no hunting band has so many fine young ponies.

Why had they let him see the tracks? They were curious, Slocum knew. If he had ridden right over the tracks without stopping to examine them, an arrow would have killed him directly. He'd be revealed as the most ignorant of white men—one who doesn't see the world he travels through—and thus deserving nothing better than death. On the other hand, if he'd read the truth in the tracks and turned tail, they'd probably run him down. Once again, their curiosity about him and his place would be satisfied. But a white

man who examined the tracks of their band of mounted
Sioux and then simply continued in the same direction
as he'd been going, and at the same pace—Aiiiii, that
was a curious matter. Curious Indians don't kill. It
is a difference from the whites who often satisfy curiosity with a bullet.

The country was sagebrush plains, interrupted by
the towering indifferent buttes: Heart Butte, Camel
Butte, White Butte, Coffin Butte—buttes as serene as
the British imperial fleet. The sky was clear and hot,
and he sweated through the neckerchief that protected
the back of his neck. He found no water that day, and
the sagebrush quit in favor of greasewood and tumble-
weed that liked more alkaline soil. Water here wouldn't
be drinkable anyway. He consoled himself with that
thought.

At noon, he walked his horses for two hours and
chewed on more beef jerky. At night, he watered his
horses with a canteen poured into the leather feed
bucket. He drank a pint from the other canteen. The
next morning he made a fire of buffalo chips and cut
a slice of ham and opened another tin of tomatoes.
He drank the juice gratefully, every drop. No coffee.
The cigarette tasted harsh and rasped his throat.

The sun glowered on the morning horizon. "We'll
go a ways," he said as he swung aboard his Appaloosa.
The horse looked at him worried, a little thirsty. "We'll
find water today," Slocum assured her. The sun got
hotter, and his two horses threw up little dust streamers
behind their hooves. He couldn't see similar streamers
from the Indians' horses but knew they were out there
just the same. Riding parallel, like as not.

Sometime in the afternoon he came on a dry streambed, wide where flash floods had slashed away the
banks, and cobblestoned on the bottom. He rode beside its banks until he spotted a couple of bushes and
four thin cottonwoods. He dug near the cottonwood
roots until he found damp ground, and waited an hour.
The pool filled with murky water, and he let his horses

drink. He wasn't too worried about himself. A man didn't need as much water as a horse.

His face was scaling where the sun burned it, and his cheeks were sore. He walked his horses half the thirty miles they traveled that day, and that night they made another dry camp. He didn't have much appetite in the morning, and the prospect of more dry meat was distinctly unpleasant. But he built a fire and sat in front of it, trying to melt irreducible beef jerky in a mouth without saliva. He sat beside his buffalo-chip fire as long as he usually did and shaved with a cup of his remaining water. He emptied his canteen into the leather bucket for the horses.

The plains climbed like a monstrous slab set on edge, interrupted by narrow deep slashes negotiated at the cost of pain and time. He traveled until noon, covering less than five miles, but in the afternoon the interruptions were fewer and he made better time. He saw no sign of the Indian scouts but knew they were still watching. He guessed they had water too. This was their country, not his. Of course they had water. He put a stone under his tongue. It helped some.

He and the horses smelled the stream at the same time. He stood in the stirrups. His Appaloosa raised her head too, hoping to confirm what her nose had already announced. The horses picked up the pace.

The water was protected by a screen of deep brush where earlier in the year a second current had run.

Once he broke through the brush, there was a stretch of dead flat land and then the glistening shallow river. It sounded nice to him, like a melody.

He reined up. The Indians had been here first and had created for him a piece of magic—a test.

The ground was covered with white stones, larger than his fists and smooth from the water that had rushed over them for eons. Above, a line of something faced him. He rode forward. Buffalo skulls—twenty of them, painted red, facing due east. His horses smelled Indians. The Appaloosa cocked her ears and snorted. Slocum drew up. The horses could see and smell the

water, and it had been three days since they'd had
their fill. John Slocum had trained the Appaloosa himself, but he was surprised she suffered herself to be
ground-reined when he dismounted. Slocum's nostrils
were wide with water smell, but he could not broach
the magic line carelessly. He felt the weight of Indian
eyes. Black eyes, hidden back in that brush. They had
left no tracks on the smooth white stones, just the
line of ochered skulls. The paint job had been quick
and rough. Red was someone's magic color: red over
bone. He'd file that fact away.

With their empty eye sockets, the skulls faced the
way that the white man came. Faced the dirt farmer,
the railroad man, the miner, the telegrapher, the herd
slaughterer, the Seizer. Slocum waited. He stood there
in that water-starved world waiting to understand.

After fifteen minutes, he stooped, picked up the
center skull, and moved it. The first instant was the
danger time when the arrows might find him, and he
knew that but did not hesitate. Though it was nothing
but bone, the skull was surprisingly heavy. The ants,
worms, and sun had long ago bleached all the nourishment out of it. He set it down where he wanted and
picked up another skull. Smoothly and carefully he
shifted the skulls, leaving none of the original line in-
tact. The last skull—which must have belonged to some
huge bull buffalo—he placed in the exact center of the
circle he had created. The circle was open to the east
to admit the rising sun. Each buffalo skull was turned
toward the center where the bull buffalo skull stared
sightlessly into the void. The circle Slocum had created
was the medicine circle, the exact shape of every
Cheyenne or Sioux village. The central skull occupied
the precise place of the medicine lodge. After he placed
the last skull, he walked around the circle once to the
east, once to the west. He returned to his horses.

He led both animals to the shallow river running
so clear and brisk over the stones, and they drank
heavily. He paid no attention to the brush at his back.
The watching eyes couldn't see what he had done and

would be consumed with curiosity. He grinned. Let them earn their look-see, same as he had. His cracked-lipped laugh would have gotten him killed if any Indian had seen it. "Easy, girl, that's enough now." He heaved the Appaloosa's head up and hauled both the animals back from water's edge. Cold water after a long, hot ride. There was no surer way of foundering a horse, and he didn't intend to get killed for a fool's mistake. After a ten-minute rest, he let the horses drink more and then knelt and moistened his own lips. The water was sweet and cold, and it hurt the space right behind his eyes. Another two hours of daylight before the long dusk. Camping here appealed to him but would be pressing his luck.

The plain climbed again on the west bank of the river. Behind him, the country spread out like a map. A half-hour out, he pulled up and stood his stirrups. He uncased the sutler's telescope and put it to his eye. Through the powerful magnification, his medicine circle was plain. And the Indians crowding around for a closer look were visible too. He clicked the glass closed and cased it. He thought, "He will prepare a table for me in the presence of mine enemies." He didn't know why he was remembering Bible verses, but they were surely crowding his mind these days. The ground was more hospitable and the soil changed color from the sickly alkali whites and yellows to black and white speckles of granite sand. Tufts of sweetgrass appeared among the sagebrush. Now, when he dismounted, he let the horses at the sweetgrass and they went at it with a will. The low peaks of the Powder River range were like a mirage ahead. Though they looked no more than an hour away, that was the fine clear air. He'd be lucky if he reached the mountains tomorrow evening.

That night he camped beside Big Box Elder Creek, a narrow, mad creek that hurtled out of the mountains to connect with the Little Missouri. The water was pure and good. The grass was lush, and he must have been climbing because he had to put another shirt on

over the one he was wearing. John Slocum fired a
small campfire though its solitary glow could be seen
for miles. He figured he'd earned it. The aroma of
cooking ham and brewing coffee traveled a distance
through that chilly night and may have made a Sioux
warrior's nose itch.

His horses cropped peacefully at the creekside all
night and didn't wake John Slocum when they smelled
strange smells that sometimes came to them. Smells
of other men and other horses.

In the morning, Slocum peeled off his clothes and
dived cleanly into the icy water. The water tumbled
him and scraped him along the bottom, but it felt
marvelous. He got some of the trail dust washed off him
before he shaved, squatting naked beside the water
next to his guns.

It was perhaps his public nakedness, so innocent and
so threatening, that forced the Indian shaman's hand.
The original buffalo line had been the shaman's work,
and Slocum's conversion of his magic had upset him and
made him lose face in the band. His next ploy was
perhaps more hurried and thoughtless than it should
have been.

Slocum was crossing the sunrise pass through the
Powder River range, some nine thousand feet above
sea level and four thousand above the long flat plain
behind him. The pass here was as high as the mountain
tops, huge hogbacks, scoured clean of vegetation except
in the lee of boulders where the brilliant alpine flowers
bloomed. The trail was wider than a game trail, and
the People had been using sunrise pass as long as there
were people.

Slocum's horse snorted and spooked. The sunlight
caught the magic and glistened. Slocum rode closer,
sawing the reins from side to side to control the Appaloosa. Her hooves clacked. Up here the sounds
carried cold echoes.

A shout would ring and bounce through those hard
peaks like a whisper of paradise among old men.

Slocum had seen ant heaps like this magic heap, but

ant heaps didn't glitter so. The glittering was sharp
and dangerous, and when Slocum got close enough
to see how the Indian shaman had constructed his
magic, he credited him. The shaman had captured
"threat" pretty well.

Where the Yellowstone River first dives into its
high-walled gorge, there, near Hell Roaring Creek,
are the black glass cliffs, the obsidian cliffs the Indians
used to make their finest arrowheads. These cliffs are
sheer, lifting two hundred feet out of the deer meadows.
To gather the stuff, a man has to climb, placing one
foot above another on the sharp hand and foot holds.
Of course a man might gather his arrow material from
the slabs and chunks that lay fallen in the meadow
below, but such points would turn aside under the
deerskin. Such points would never penetrate the buffalo hide. Such points would leave a man at the mercy
of his enemies. So the wise gatherer climbed high above
the meadow, clinging to the sharp rock with his hands
and leaving some of his blood behind for the arrowhead
stuff he took.

So obtained, a piece of obsidian could make a year's
arrowheads for a careful hunter: arrowheads so sharp
that each head was wrapped in split moose hide cover
in the quiver. A five-pound piece of the black glass
from Hell Roaring Creek was as valuable as a young
horse, even before it was turned into arrowheads.

A heap of broken obsidian glittered in the hard
noonday sun. The blackness of the obsidian was a
glitter of power. On the top of the conical pile something glowed more softly, winking at Slocum like the
friendly eye. Slocum leaned back in his saddle, considering. When he tipped his hat back against the
eyes, the glitter diminished, but he still couldn't make
out what the softer object was, though he knew what
the obsidian was. His heels nudged the Appaloosa
forward. The horse's belly grumbled.

"Well, goddamn." A brass cartridge case capped
the top of the shattered obsidian. It was very shiny
and not tarnished at all—part of the Indian's medicine.

The bullet from that case had brought down a particularly large animal or brave enemy. The obsidian the shaman had smashed into chips to block Slocum's trail was more valuable than the magic he'd created from it. This pathetic heap of glittering black glass and the single cartridge case were mighty weak. Slocum's horse rumbled again and spread her hind legs, and the tail arched up in a high bow. Slocum made his decision as the grin crossed his face. He dug his heels in again and the Appaloosa stepped wide around the cone, and Slocum backed the horse so she was standing in front of the shaman's magic when the first plop splashed down. The horse had been going since dawn with no chance to rest and really void her bowels. The cone vanished. The Indians were ahead of him, but where was hard to guess. He wasn't altogether sure they wouldn't kill him for what his horse had done, but the joke had been too damn good to resist. The brass cartridge stuck out of the steaming mound.

The downslope was easier. He tapped his Appaloosa into a canter. He was feeling fine. He was a full mile below the peaks in the long shadow of the afternoon, below the echoes. He loosed his laugh, laughing until he cried, laughing until it hurt. He would have given a horse to see that shaman's face when he saw what Slocum had left him. "And that damn brass cartridge, like a shiny top hat." He laughed again.

Not more than a mile further, the trail passed into jackpines, stunted by the northern winds. There hadn't been one evergreen on the eastern side of the range and he wondered why that was. Maybe the snow banked up more on this side.

Old growth forest now. Blue spruce, and big fir trees. Few branches at the base, but towering clumps a hundred feet over Slocum's head where they crowded each other for light. The trail diminished and faded among the lichened boulders. Slocum stopped his horses at a small spring that burst from a slab of granite and trickled into a pool. The pool overflow went just five or six feet before disappearing underground again. The bottom of the pool was plain white sand, and the hole looked finger deep, but it covered Slocum's canteens completely. It was quieter in the forest than it had been on the ridgetop, and hotter too. A couple of camp robbers flashed white through the timber. A moment later came their harsh caw. Squirrels chattered away angrily, reminding Slocum he'd disturbed their domain. "You watch yourselves," he said. "I have eaten a few squirrels." The squirrels fell silent when he mounted up. He spotted elk tracks—mulies—twice the heavy splay-footed mark of buffalo, one a cow and the other a small bull. And rarest of all was the mark of the curly horn, the mountain sheep. Usually they grazed in the high glacial moraine where a man would swear there wasn't sustenance for a mouse. Slocum got down to check for the little tip at the front of the hoof which gave the mountain sheep away as surely as the dewclaw identifies the dog. Yep. Slocum remounted happily. He took the hoof mark to be a sign of good fortune.

The forest quit and Slocum came out on a shelf above the Powder River valley. The buffalo grass waved, and he watched the ripples of the wind in the grass as each blade deferred to its passage. A small band of buffalo grazed beside the cottonwoods and aspen that lined the riverbank. One old cow, doing sentry duty on the outskirts, had her head raised, and Slocum swore she knew, though the buffalo's eyesight was notoriously poor. Anyway, she didn't lower her head, and after a minute she snorted, and the band of animals moseyed on downstream, cocking their heads back from time to time to make sure nothing followed.

Mizpah Creek was upriver. One very annoyed Indian shaman was planning Slocum's death, and there was no sense getting Mrs. Duffy and her kid involved in that dispute. Slocum figured they probably had enough trouble without him carrying more to their heads. He wondered if Mrs. Duffy was pretty. His horse began picking his way down toward the river. Slocum didn't think it was likely Mrs. Duffy was pretty. A picture began to form in his mind, a portrait of a chubby little woman with a face as round as a pie plate.

Near the bank a broad empty space of a streambed identified the place where the bank was too low to hold the raging water in the spring. The campsite was open and vulnerable from three sides. The trees on the far bank provided concealment from the west. John Slocum used his packhorse to skid dry cottonwood, aspen, and alder to his campsite, where he stacked it high. He shoveled a trench around his fire site because a grass-fire ruined everything in its path. His Indian companions would kill him for sure if he set the earth on fire. They didn't care for that kind of waste.

The Powder River was milky blue. It must have rained upstream, though Slocum hadn't seen a single cloud. It cleared up in his coffeepot once he let the water stand, and the horses drank readily enough.

Slocum started his baked beans early in the evening, burying the bean pot under the place where he'd make his bonfire. Beans, molasses, a little mustard, and a couple of ham scraps.

He'd had a fine day, and he hunkered down on his heels and smoked a couple of quirlies, watching the bands of purple and orange and red and blue swirling on the horizon. He didn't think much about anything.

There was some light in the western sky when he fired his bonfire. The bonfire snatched all the light, making everything darker. It was an enormous fire. The aspen caught and fueled the punkier cottonwoods and the willow chunks he'd broken off a big downed tree at water's edge. The flames rolled around the base of the pyre and clambered over each other in their hurry to reach the top. Like rivers of fire running uphill, it looked like, and the fire could have been seen from the peaks of the Powder River range upstream and down for fifteen miles. The tallest flames crashed twenty feet over Slocum's head and he stood back from the heat of it, and still his whole front was cooked and his back was ice-cold unless he revolved like an ox on a damn spit. He smiled, wondering what the Indians were thinking. They might think he'd totally lost his mind. He hoped they'd come to some such opinion because Indians generally let crazy men go their own way.

The fire was vivid and he couldn't see the stars. It got so hot, the grass on the far side of Slocum's fireline smoldered and blackened, and he had to stamp out one small fire with his boot.

When the fire burned down, the cold rushed in with a fury and dropped the temperature so quickly that, though he wrapped himself in his horse blanket, he couldn't get warm. He hunched himself forward like the rawest tenderfoot until he was sitting almost on top of the coals and embers.

By now the Indians would have crept in close. Perhaps they'd be wondering whether this was the night to kill him. This immensely wasteful, futile fire should keep them guessing until they understood it as the gesture of contempt it was. Slocum was spraying contempt all around with the enthusiasm of a skunk in a contest.

The morning dawned cool and dry and the sun's warmth chased the light across the plains. Slocum scraped the ashes of his bonfire aside. The fire had burned so hot that there wasn't much left except a fine gray ash that rustled and wafted like butterfly wings. The earth underneath was baked dry, and Slocum used his knife to penetrate ground he'd dug with his hands the night before. The bean pot was sizzling hot, and he used his shirt to hold it. When he pried up the small circular lid, it smelled fine. He scooped a couple of spoonfuls into his tin cup, blowing on them. It was good. He refilled his cup, ate again, and that was okay too. He rolled a quirly and smoked it and washed his cup out with sand and packed his bean pot with the same care he would have used if this wasn't probably his morning to die.

It was a beautiful morning. The wild clover and mustard were blooming, big red flowers and smaller yellow ones. The aroma was heady, and as soon as the dew was off, regiments of bees set to work, drunk on the scent. John Slocum rode real slow, enjoying his life. He was one of the luckiest men on this earth.

He rode well away from the trees along the river and steadily south along the broad shallow river. In a bit, the sun was directly before him, shining into his eyes, turning his horse's ears into black silhouettes. It would be soon, very soon.

His hat brim shaded his eyes and he could see pretty well, half so well as, say, the average hawk, and he picked out the creature.

Might be a man, though it was too motionless to be alive. Steadily he rode on and no motion of his alarmed his horse, though his pulse rate picked up and he felt a slight tingling along his arms. Now he could see the Indians. All in a row. Fifty yards past the creation—a scarecrow? He started to count the Indians, but quit after ten. Probably fifteen with two men out front who'd be the leaders of this particular bunch. And out in front of them, their scarecrow. There was something mannish about its shape. Slocum wished he didn't have the damn sun in his eyes. The Appaloosa's bridle glared brightly when she threw her head back, all bug-eyed, alerted finally to the other horses. She swished her tail. No more than seventy yards separated the lone rider from the Indians. He closed steadily.

The creation was a scarecrow all right. But the Sioux weren't farmers and it was no surprise they'd got it wrong. A crucifix of wood for a frame, lashed together. Something perched on top for a head. Something draped from each limb and tapering to the ground. The material was just as dark as the silhouette, either brown or black or blue, Slocum couldn't tell.

He spoke softly to his horse. "Now, don't you get all nervy now, old girl, because we may need your services in a sudden, and I'd like for you to have your wits about you."

Blue. The fabric hanging from the scarecrow was blue. Looked like a pair of trousers hanging from the cross arms, and a chill went down Slocum's back until he was damn sure there wasn't part of a dead man hanging there too. Just his trousers. And his cap.

Twenty yards away, Slocum reined up. The horse got a whiff of something and jerked her feet, suddenly all dancy.

"Easy now. Easy."

Slocum waited, both hands in plain sight, eying the scarecrow and the Indians beyond who were eying him right back.

John Slocum was beginning to understand. He might have ridden closer to be sure, but it would have been a clumsy move, and anyway, the meaning of the magic would sink in if he gave it and himself a chance.

Sure enough, it came to him. The pants would have a yellow stripe along the seam. He was sure of that. And the cap on the slender pole had once rested on the back of a cavalryman's head. Still he waited, his horse's nostrils flaring at the unpleasant odors, and maybe John Slocum's nose was wrinkling too.

The stain was darker than the cloth, but might have passed for a shadow at this distance. And since the stain was dry, there would have been no odor. The trousers were draped with the legs bent over the cross-members and the braces hung almost to the ground. The stain at the crotch was no more than six inches across and might have been urine except it glistened with a hard crusty brightness. Slocum swallowed. It would be a bad way to go, with a Sioux knife at your cock.

So.

He pressed his heels into his horse's flanks because he didn't want to change his mind. He kept his eyes on the Sioux. The uniformed scarecrow couldn't hurt him more than it had.

The morning was warm and his jacket was tied behind the saddle. His hands went to his green checked flannel shirt. He undid the hooks and eyes and quickly stripped the garment off his arms as he rode forward.

The sweat was cold on his forehead. Details were very sharp, very clear. His muscles rolled under his skin, awakening to the challenge.

He was riding directly into the sun, but he thought he could make out who was who. One man was probably the war chief. The second Indian was very short and very stocky and young enough to be the shaman Slocum had been testing his wits against.

Slocum came off his horse when he was at the scarecrow, fluid, graceful—he didn't even rein up, just came down on his horse's right side, sliding his Winchester from its scabbard as he did. Snapping the reins a second before he turned loose of them, he let them fall as his feet touched the ground. The horse was ground-reined, stopped as effectively as if she'd been nailed to the spot. Slocum thought he heard a murmur of appreciation from the line of tribesmen. Might have been. They were men who valued horsemanship above most skills.

He loped toward them casual and loose-gaited as a coyote. Slocum saw the headbands and paint of the Lakota Sioux, which didn't surprise him. They were young and well armed for Indians. The possession of a repeating rifle was very great wealth to a tribesman, and Slocum saw four of them. The presence of some deerskin-clad Cheyenne, with their elaborate beadwork stomachers, did surprise him, because the Sioux and Cheyenne lost no love for each other.

The chief was Sioux. The shaman looked to be Cheyenne. Slocum paid no attention to the scarecrow until he was abreast of it, and then he bowed to it as if it were the personal idol on his home altar. It deserved a little recognition. The trousers would have fit a fairly large man, he could see that, and he wondered if maybe they'd belonged to Mrs. Pollitz's husband. No telling now. It wasn't blood glistening on the front of the trousers. It was a cloud of blue-belly and green-belly flies, clustered so thick on the blood they made another layer.

"Hyuh!" Slocum shouted and, two-handed, lifted his Winchester over his head. With the rifle outstretched, he marched around the scarecrow chanting. He chanted, "Oh, I wish I was in the land of cotton, old times there are not forgotten, ahy-yea-uhuh-yea Dixieland," in a steady, monotonous kind of way. He circled to each of the four directions and made his obeisance at each corner. He did this Blackfoot style. He wished he knew a little Sioux magic, but probably he was better off ignorant. Part knowledge of another man's magic is one of the quickest ways to die.

When he faced the motionless tribesmen again, he set his rifle down against the main brace like an offering. This was the dangerous moment. He had established himself as a brave man, and now the worthiest of the Sioux and Cheyenne would feel justified counting coup. So he turned his back to them. They were less than forty feet behind him and he faced the back side of their magic scarecrow, his own bare back twitching, the muscles bunching.

Though the Sioux and Cheyenne were both plains Indians, hunter-horsemen and warriors, and though they occupied the same range and one summer the Sioux would roam where the Cheyenne had roamed the summer before, the two peoples were not identical. The Sioux had knowledge of the upside-down men. The Cheyenne did not. Once a year, in the spring, when the first green showed in the land, the upside-down men had their day. The Sioux were organized into warrior societies, the Dog Soldiers, the Loon Society, and so forth, but the upside-down men came from every society. On their day, it was the duty of the upside-down men to do everything backward: to run when they should walk, go uphill when they were meant to go down, stand on their heads, dress like foolish animals.

And wear their clothes upside-down. John Slocum unwrapped the trouser legs from the scarecrow. They were bound to the cross-members with vines that parted easily in Slocum's hands. For a second, the Indian line started and several exclaimed as the crazy white man flipped the trousers into the air like a great sail and settled on his back.

John Slocum tied the trouser legs around his neck. The blood patch faced the Indians. The trousers were very warm against his bare skin. Almost hot.

The line of Indians stirred again, restlessly, as the white man wearing the trousers where his shirt should be backed toward them. No warrior can count coup on a brave man's back though some fingered their foot-long stone-tipped coup sticks nervously and a couple of horses pranced, tingling from the bursts of nervous energy that passed through their master's thighs.

The white man stretched one leg backward, and when it seemed he could stretch no further, he dug in his toes and hauled his body back to the stretch of his leg. Then the white man waited. Always he faced away from the sun. Always he faced the magic animal the Cheyenne shaman had constructed.

The Cheyenne shaman was muttering now, and some of his brothers heard him but could not call out because the Cheyenne were only five among the dozen Sioux, and the Sioux were stronger in guns too. The rifles they had taken from Seizers. The shaman and his small band joined the Sioux two days after the battle of the Greasy Grass and had taken no rifles or horses, though Lame Bear had taken clothing from the dead Seizers for his magic. He had not earned the clothing but he had taken it, and that lack was in the forefront of his Cheyenne brothers' minds as the white man backed toward the combined band.

It is fair to say the Sioux cared less about where the Cheyenne's medicine had come from than whether it worked.

The buffalo skulls in a line—now that had been very strong medicine, everybody could feel that. The buffalo had been invoked to turn the white man back. If the buffalo and the red man cannot turn the white man back, then they shall perish together. And once this white man turned, they would count their coup and kill him and travel on toward the Pumpkin Creek where Crazy Horse was waiting. But the white man rearranged the magic. Created a medicine circle of his own that shamed the Cheyenne shaman. The Sioux had said nothing because they were bound by Sitting Bull and his dream, but they noted that Cheyenne magic was not so strong as the white man's.

The cone of broken arrowheads was a different matter. The Sioux had heard the shaman's chants and seen his medicine smoke and watched him sing around the cone as he shattered the rare black obsidian, but the act made many of them sad, because it was many fine arrowheads destroyed wastefully.

The Sioux never held with sacrifice. Death could be fine and was inevitable, but life was hard enough without wasting the precious.

But they kept still while he reduced a hundred fine arrowheads into splinters. When he crowned the heap with his own brass cartridge case, the Sioux were more hopeful.

The Sioux chief led the way to the obsidian cone once Slocum left. The chief was a man of very great dignity and self-restraint named War Bonnet. When he saw the horse flop on top of the cone, he laughed so hard he almost fell off his horse. One Sioux did fall off his horse and rolled around on the ground hollering something about "Horseshit magic. Medicine. Great Cheyenne medicine!"

The Cheyenne shaman would have killed the disrespectful Sioux on the spot, alliance be damned, but he would have died in the next moment, and he wasn't ready to take the trip across the shadowland. The color mounted to his ears but he stayed quiet.

Once the subject had been breached, the Sioux showed little restraint and practically no mercy. At the campfire that night, the Sioux called out as if they were addressing the creatures of the night. "Hey, Coyote, you noiseless one, have you heard about the new magic? You can smell it further than you can see it." "White Owl, tell us about the great Cheyenne medicine heap. There are many such medicine heaps here on the plains and they are all Cheyenne."

The white man, shirted with his dead brother's clothing, marched toward them walking just like an upside-down man, and the Indian horses were nervous because of the strange jerky way he moved, and a few Sioux braves were speaking openly now, telling their horses not to be afraid of this white man who had more magic than the Cheyenne shaman. Each jerky backward step brought him closer to the Indian line, and the hair on the back of John Slocum's neck was standing up and swaying, but there wasn't a breeze. Each jerky step was hard on his back, and the flies, dislodged when he swung the bloody pants over his head, were back now with a vengeance. They liked Slocum's fresh blood as well as the dead soldier's dried stuff.

He hadn't wanted to stumble into the close-drawn ranks of Indian ponies, and before he set out he'd eye-balled the distance, but estimating how much ground a man is covering backward is hard. It was the wood-smoke smell and the sulfur they used in their warpaint that brought Slocum to a halt. He couldn't feel the horse's exhalations on his skin, but almost felt like he could.

Forty feet in front of him, the scarecrow remained, forlorn without its blue cloth covering. The forage cap leaned on the edge of the stick, as if held aloft by some celebrator, and the Winchester held the upright like two sticks leaning together. Slocum took a deep breath. A horse nickered softly, and he would have sworn the animal wasn't more than three inches from his ear. The damn Sioux were so close he could feel their body heat, and his torso was shiny with sweat. He relaxed. As much as he could.

Some of the Sioux wanted to draw back from the crazy white man, but their own courage wouldn't let them. The Cheyenne shaman was five feet from John Slocum's skull, which was protected by the soft cloth of his Stetson. Lame Bear longed to drive his war club into that hat, but knew he could not, because the men would never let him forget as long as he lived that he'd killed this enemy from behind. The shaman's eyes were fixed on the white man, and his hand was flexing and unflexing.

The white man's hand jumped. Noise. Roar. Jumping

horses. It was the white man's small gun flaming, more continuous than thunder over Grizzly Peak.

With Slocum's first shot, the forage hat dropped six inches because the heavy bullet severed the stick holding it, as a headman severs a neck.

The second slug tore the leather brim right off the cap and sent it spinning high in the air. To the Indians it looked as though a hand appeared and flung it, spinning, toward the sky.

The third bullet took the air out of it. The fourth tore cloth next to the earlier bullet and made a hole big enough to let daylight through.

The top of the cap billowed and the air streamed through the bullet holes and it settled toward the ground.

It landed with a soft plop.

"Ahh." That's what the Indians said.

John Slocum holstered his Colt and turned to face the Indians. Nobody said anything for the longest time. They were studying each other. John Slocum read the shaman's fury in the set of his mouth, the narrowing of his eyes, his busy Adam's apple.

Slocum's eyes had a faint smile. Win or lose, it had been a hell of a run.

"It is easy to fight hats." The shaman spoke in Sioux. His hands made the universal motions of the sign language that is understood among all the plains tribes.

"It is ghosts I fight," John Slocum spoke in the language. "Not hats."

The shaman had powerful short arms. His wrists were as big as many men's thighs and he was a famous wrestler among his own people. When he drew the short buffalo horn bow from under his knee, he was able to do what few men can do—he strung it on horseback.

The horn bow, curved at both ends, is the strongest bow the Cheyenne make and is only used by a strong man in his prime. Many a fine warrior cannot pull a horn bow, and few can string it. The sweat stood on Lame Bear's brow as he slid the rawhide to the notches that would hold it firm. His muscles stood out like cordage. For a second, the rawhide slipped back and it seemed as if Lame Bear's very great strength wouldn't be enough for the job, but he found the extra somewhere and the rawhide caught. It was a beautiful bow—jet black and shining as if polished. The shaman set an arrow into the string and cocked it. The bow threw short arrows and they were very strong. John Slocum found himself looking at an obsidian arrowhead which was the close relative of the pile his horse had shat on yesterday. From this distance the arrow would probably go right through Slocum's skull.

"It is easy to kill men," John Slocum said. And yawned. Elaborately, he patted his mouth.

The bow trembled in the shaman's grip. The muscles on his arm stood out like cable.

"It is hard to count coup on a brave man," the shaman admitted.

Slocum eyed him. He rested his hand on the butt of his Colt to remind them all what he had done and could do again if he chose.

"But a fine way to die." Slocum's smile spread across his face. The sun went behind a cloud. It came out again. The shaman's arms began to tremble, just a shiver at the arrow point. Slocum's Appaloosa nickered to the Indian ponies in a friendly fashion, and the Sioux war chief's pony nickered back.

War Bonnet put his hand out on the shaman's arm. He didn't say anything. He didn't need to. His grip was very strong, nearly as strong as the Cheyenne's, and his power was very much greater. The shaman slackened his bow. He put his arrow back into his quiver, though his hands were shaking very badly. He looked at the strung bow in his hands. He had tears in his eyes. Somewhat clumsily he swung his leg down and came off his horse. He put his foot through the bow to unstring it because he had used all his strength in the contest with John Slocum's eyes.

The Sioux chief said, "Who are you?"

Slocum answered in Blackfoot, but made the gestures for his name too. "I am called the Owl Child," he said.

"War Bonnet." The chief pointed at his chest. He added that he was a very great warrior and had fought at the battle of Greasy Grass and counted coup five times and took scalps from four men.

"You are a great warrior," Slocum conceded. "But what of this . . . Cheyenne?"

A murmur from the Sioux. The Cheyenne shaman looked at the dirt. "And what of this one?" Slocum gestured. "How is he called? Bad Arrowheads?"

The Sioux chief stared, disbelieving. Then he laughed. He laughed until the tears ran down his cheeks. The other Sioux laughed too. The Cheyenne edged together until they were a solid block. But none of them got close to their shaman. Slocum stood empty-handed, still smiling.

"Are you a friend of the Seizers?" the young war chief asked.

"No," Slocum said. And he told the truth too.

The flies were biting his chest, gorging themselves and falling off to the dirt. He didn't feel a thing.

"Are you a friend of the Sioux?" the war chief asked.

"I am no enemy of the Sioux," he said, and that was true enough too. "I am called Owl Child," he repeated, because he didn't want to say he was no man's friend because the Indians would have killed him where he stood. The Sioux always killed rogues.

5

The young war chief's black eyes sparkled. Evasion, like stealing horses, was a much appreciated skill among the Sioux.

The tension went out of the band of warriors and they came in closer, forming their circle around John Slocum. Many dismounted, and Slocum had to stand still as hands pinched him and prodded him. The dignity of the body was no particular big deal to the Sioux, and though they were masters of the mortal insult, they wouldn't have understood a man who refused to be touched. Their touches were not particularly rude, but they gave Slocum the creeps. Unlike most white men, he didn't quail at their touch, but he would have liked it better if they were Blackfeet instead of these damn Sioux. Blackfeet . . . well, they were the People, and that was all there was to that

When one young Cheyenne touched the thong of his pistol holster, Slocum covered his fingers and squeezed. He caught the other's knuckles just right and, without loosing his smile, he poured his strength into his hand and the brave howled and dropped to his knees. Slocum said, "My weapon is mine until I die."

A sharp command was barked in Sioux and the tribesmen stood back, forming up close to their leaders. They were two bands now and one outcast: the Sioux, the Cheyenne, and the shaman. Divide and conquer; that was how the white men always beat them. Not that the Indians didn't make it easy for them. It was perhaps Sitting Bull's greatest achievement to get the tribes to ride together.

Slocum turned his back and went back to his horse, peeling the stinking pair of trousers off his shoulders.

He tossed the trousers in a heap over the cap, and for a split second, the tiny heap looked more human than you could imagine, and it gave Slocum the chills, as if that dead horse-soldier had ridden his shoulders to make the magic.

He fastened his shirt neatly, though his fingers were trembling. He would have liked to reload his Colt, but didn't, because weaponry is too easy to misinterpret, and he didn't dare chance anything just now. In a minute and a half, he'd used a year's luck. When he swung aboard his Appaloosa, he took the time to study the Sioux leader, War Bonnet, and the Sioux returned the compliment.

The Sioux had plenty of laugh lines running from the corners of his eyes, but that might mean one thing or it might mean another. Torture could be funny to a Sioux. Certain kinds of dying were plain hysterical. Those laugh lines didn't necessarily indicate a man who told many jokes.

The chief's legs were awful damn skinny. His leggings were long and soft and baggy, but Slocum saw his ankles above his mocassins and they were as thin as a boy's. The man's shoulders seemed overdeveloped— maybe to compensate for his legs—and his neck was bull-thick. His black hair was drawn back in two short, fat braids. He wore two white and one red line slashed across his forehead, meaning the man who has recently killed. His cheeks bore his own magic sign and that of his society.

"Dog Soldier?" Slocum guessed.

"Aye." Carelessly his hand flopped behind him. "We Sioux are all Dog Soldiers."

"And the Cheyenne?"

Carelessly and falsely, because he knew the Cheyenne's societies and rank to a fine point, War Bonnet said, "They are what they are. Where do you travel?"

Slocum bent to gather his Winchester. He slid it back into the scabbard. "I go to the mouth of Mizpah Creek. How many days?"

The Sioux lifted his shoulder, meaning not of any consequence, not so very far.

"Is there game on Mizpah Creek?" the Sioux asked.

"Maybe yes and maybe no."

"Are there enemies on Mizpah Creek?" That prospect made him smile. "Perhaps we could meet them together." His long war lance was tucked into its boot below his knee. The lance was decorated with four fresh scalps. Two brown, one black, and one blond. When he got back to his own lodge, he'd drape them over a rack before the fire and smoke them until they were cured, but now pieces of flesh still clung to a couple of them, and on the blond one, fat cells had burst under the skin and turned the whole skin a yellowish red. Noticing Slocum's interest, he turned so Slocum could better admire his trophies. "My enemies," he said proudly. "Enemies of the Sioux."

"Uh-huh. Very nice."

"You are Blackfoot?" War Bonnet was too polite to mention the fact of Slocum's white skin and his white man's dress. It would be a matter to consider later, how a white man could be a Blackfoot too. He cocked his head up at the sky. "Come," he said and wheeled his horse and gave it a hell of a kick and raced back toward his band with his fat braids straight out behind him.

Slocum put his heels to his Appaloosa, and the horse, who'd been treated so gently all morning, jumped about five feet and almost pulled the packhorse off his feet before the two animals swung into a gallop.

"Yi-yi-yi-yi-yi-yi," the Indian yelled.

Slocum yelled back, barked the scream called the rebel yell. And if Slocum had heard the Indian's cry before, no less certainly had these warriors heard the rebel yell, and it made 'em uneasy.

The chief galloped right through and Slocum behind him and the others kicked their horses, and the whole band was strung out behind them going like hell.

Maybe Slocum could have caught the chief, maybe he wanted to be politic, maybe he wanted to spare the

Appaloosa, but he dropped back noticeably and pretty soon he was right in the middle of the pack with the chief and two others a good distance in front of them. They galloped along the Powder River, on the bank when it was broad enough and through the river meadows. They galloped for half an hour, blowing off steam. The shaman rode with them, but in the drag where dirt clods thrown by the other's hooves dirtied him and his horse both.

His horse puffing and blowing, War Bonnet pulled up where the river meadow was wide and the river near. With so many warriors, he didn't need to select a more cautious campsite, and there was plenty grass here for the horses. Quickly, he slid off his animal's back and landed on his stick legs.

"Rickets," Slocum thought, because the legs seemed almost to bend when the chief put his weight on them.

"We will ride with you," War Bonnet said, grinning with the happiness of the ride.

"So long as we're goin' in the same direction," Slocum said.

One of the Cheyenne had killed a pronghorn the day previous, and now he pulled the haunch off his horse's rump and dropped it in the dirt. Gruffly, he commanded others to build the fire and cook the meat. He was the hunter—others could do the women's work. Well, this stirred up a quarrel.

Slocum sat beside the young chief on the riverbank. The man had his moccasins off and dangled his feet in the milky water. "You are a fine joker," the Indian said. "Like Coyote, the prankster. You are my friend."

The Indian jabbed his finger toward his chest, and Slocum felt pretty good because the Indian's generosity practically guaranteed his life. His new friend would think nothing of going into battle for him, and if he should die there, well, that happened too sometimes. Among the Blackfeet, if a man gave another a horse, he'd arrive, riding his gift. Since camps were often three days' horseback journey, the gift-giver faced a formidable walk home, but that's what a gift meant, and what value was a gift not valued by the giver?

Slocum made the sign accepting the friendship, and offering his own in return. The tie always bound two ways.

The resentful Cheyennes threw the joint of antelope meat on the fire as soon as the flames got hot enough. It landed on a couple of thicker sticks, which were the only grate it was ever to have. Another stick served to poke it around so it burned evenly. The braves watched the meat roasting until one became impatient and pushed the meat out of the flames. When he raised his hunting knife to attack it, the chief snapped a single word of command, and with great solemnity, he cut himself a much larger piece than he'd ever eat. John Slocum, as War Bonnet's new friend, came next and followed his example. They ate the rich meat, though it was burned on the outside and cool in the center.

They ate like there was no tomorrow. Men on a constant protein diet eat differently than men who dine on more varied fare. They eat all the animal, except its hide. The jelly in the hooves and the bone marrow are considered special delicacies, and like other predators, they prefer raw liver to anything.

Slocum was awful damn hungry—tension release—and when he finished his chunk of antelope meat he returned to the ham and whacked off some raw meat from the knob of the hip joint. Slocum was none too quick. Even as he returned to his place beside War Bonnet, a brave picked up the ham and cracked the bone with his war club, and others gathered for the marrow.

The Cheyennes did not eat particularly well and their young shaman ate the worst of all. If Slocum had had a nervous stomach, it would have bothered him—the way that boy sat on the outskirts, glowering at him. Slocum had eaten under worse circumstances and was real hungry besides.

When he was done, War Bonnet wiped his hands on the grass and on his trouser legs. He mounted his horse swiftly, and Slocum followed his example. War Bonnet's snapped command brought the band to their feet and, done dining or not, the Indians mounted their ponies.

The ponies were as tough as their owners. Most of them were Appaloosas, but Slocum noted a few cavalry remounts among them, and two of the Cheyennes rode animals that had pulled a plow before.

The finest light cavalry in the world—that's what General Crook called them, and likely he was right. The Indians rode like extensions of their animals, so simply and gracefully it looked like the easiest thing in the world, and only a very fine rider could recognize how especially fine they were.

Without command, outriders took their place, two hundred feet on either side of the main column. One Indian hung back and the Cheyenne shaman rode with him.

It had been months since he last rode with a war party on the plains, and Slocum slipped back into the old habits with a little start of recognition. His eyes moved constantly, never still, searching always for the tiniest suspicious sign. A man sees better when he is unfocused, and Slocum's eyes rarely stopped searching the near distance. He didn't speak. Riding through enemy country was not time for gossip, and though this country belonged to the Indians now if it belonged to anyone, that was no reason to throw caution away.

They rode from point of concealment to point of concealment, and each time, the angle where an enemy could spot them was different. They presented views of themselves as reluctantly as the gray wolf and never the same angle for very long. If an enemy on the far side of the river could see them, then an enemy in the meadow could not. If an enemy in the foothills could have seen them disappearing into a coulee, he wouldn't have been able to see where they rode out. That was the secret of travel with a war party. Move fast and don't spare the time to be invisible and still cover forty miles a day.

As quick as they came, they surprised three mule deer drinking at the river; twice, flocks of wood ducks sailing serenely downstream; and once a bunch of prairie chickens lifted off at their passage like a sudden cloud. One of the Sioux exclaimed and lifted his bow, and the *thum* of the bowstring was chased by the *thwock* of the arrow and the bird's hopeless gasp.

It was a remarkable shot, and the rider who broke from the column scooped the dead bird from the ground at a full gallop and earned a murmur of appreciation from the warriors.

They drove south through the afternoon. Twice, they dismounted to spare their horses. When they walked, covered ground, it was with the long stride of the plainsman. Slocum settled right into the rhythm. While they moved, his eyes continued their automatic search of the country around him, and not much moved that he didn't see. It was oddly comfortable, riding with these men. Sometimes, John Slocum thought he understood the Indians better than the white men. They were more all-of-a-piece. Probably he had some wild blood in him. His hair and high cheekbones might have come from the Cherokee buck who'd split the blanket with his great-great-grandmother. It was an easy life and a good life. What wounded you generally killed you, and that was all right too. The men he was riding with had killed men—his new friend the war chief might have done for fifteen of his fellows. Slocum was comfortable with that too—the warrior's ease—the warrior's bitter jokes—the realization that always, the stay-at-homes took the finest things in life but lost life itself.

They splashed through the Powder River at a gravel-bottomed ford. The outriders didn't expose themselves until the leader signaled them, and they didn't spend much time in the open when they did cross.

The country changed as they moved south. The buffalo grass got sparse and the alders came in closer to the riverside. The band of green on both sides of the Powder River narrowed as the ground began the odd ripples that'd convulse into the spires and crevasses of the badlands, just twenty miles south. Though it was certainly no hotter here, it felt hotter, and though the sun was, if anything, lower, Slocum's neck started to burn. It was the way the earth held the heat and the way it bounced it right back at you.

Now the ground between the alder and quaking aspen was sandy and the front of the column couldn't see the rear. They closed up. Slocum's face was gritty. He'd been eating dirt so long he could polish his teeth by rubbing them together.

A couple of miles north of Mizpah Creek they came out into the last lush meadow this side of the badlands. Every raiding party traveling through this country used this meadow, like the oasis it was, and the signs of old campfires were numerous.

And there was another band of Indians in the meadow, though at first John Slocum overestimated their number and War Bonnet did too because he ordered his band forward as soon as he saw the first few horses coming into the meadow from the other side. The alders must have been thick over there because War Bonnet just had enough time to shout his shout before all the joy fell from his face.

He'd hoped for Crows or Kootenai or even Sheep Eaters—just a small hunting party his band could chew up and spit out.

Ten mounted Sioux rode into the meadow, and one of them shouted something back to the advancing band, who rode harder for the chance to show horsemanship.

War Bonnet's band pulled up before the smaller band, and men shouted their exuberance and their need for news of those they loved.

When War Bonnet rode forward to parley with the leader of the other band, naturally Slocum rode along too. War Bonnet answered looks with the following brief introduction: "Owl Child. Blackfoot. My friend." And that was all that need be said on the matter; War Bonnet's comments erased the color of Slocum's skin as quickly as paint.

They were a war party of Sioux—the Loon Society. Normally they would have ridden under the leadership of a wise man and once-famous raider named Snow Fox. Today, the leader of the band was his son, Squirrel, who was one of the tallest Indians John Slocum had ever seen and one of the skinniest. His bare amuleted arms were awful damn thin, and he rode his black and white pony like a circuit preacher. Wildflowers were tied to his horse's mane—blue flowers that Slocum didn't recognize. None of the other Indians had flowered horses, and War Bonnet asked about it right away. "Do you seek a woman, Squirrel?" he asked.

"I seek a woman." Squirrel's voice was surprisingly deep for such a beanpole, gravelly as an old man's whiskey voice.

"It is time you got a wife," War Bonnet noted. "Your famous cousin's example must be constantly before you."

Squirrel's color mounted into his face, which wasn't unusual, but the color moved into his wrists too. His hands twitched but lay still. "I am not my cousin," he said in that frog's voice. "I uphold the honor of my brothers and the warriors who killed the Seizers."

Slocum noticed that the young man's lance, unlike War Bonnet's, was undecorated, and before he could make his observation, War Bonnet made it for him. "Killed Seizers? Tell me, Squirrel, of the Seizers you have killed."

Maybe that would have been too rough an insult for Squirrel to swallow, but War Bonnet didn't give him a chance, one way or another. With a laugh, he raised his hand for his band to follow and they broke off, questions half answered, news half exchanged. They'd found out one important thing: The main camp was just twenty miles west, just a half day's ride. Well, now, that raised the ante. Five thousand of Sitting Bull's warriors just half a day from here. Slocum made no particular sign that he had heard this piece of news, but the Cheyenne shaman wasn't so poker-faced about it. He was positively grinning with delight. When War Bonnet and his Sioux passed through Squirrel's larger band, the Cheyenne pulled up. It puzzled War Bonnet, who'd expected the Cheyennes' commitment to remain, but not Slocum. Why suck hind tit when you don't have to?

War Bonnet rode to where Slocum waited by himself. His new friend was angry. "If I ride with you, that . . ."—he paused seeking the precise description —"that dogmeat will take his Cheyenne and attach to Squirrel and the Loon Society."

Slocum didn't really want to ride into Duffy's roadhouse with War Bonnet's Sioux backing his play, but didn't want to offend his new friend either and so said nothing. Squirrel was aloof. The Cheyenne shaman looked very pleased at his new ally's side. War Bonnet was mad as hell but resigned himself to this tactical defeat. War Bonnet said, "The upside-down man will understand." He cocked his head for Slocum's response.

"Sure. You go on ahead. I reckon I won't be too hard to find again."

The Indian grabbed Slocum's upper arm and Slocum returned the favor. The flesh they gripped would be bruised in the morning. The Sioux thrust his arm in the air, hollered his yelp, and the whole amalgamated bunch galloped west, hoping to reach the main camp while there was light enough to ride.

Slocum watched them to their disappearance. He rolled himself a quirly. Their path across the meadow had beat the grass flat for fifty feet on either side, and soon the smell of crushed grass mingled with the aroma of Slocum's tobacco. Surveying the mark they'd left, Slocum thought, "They ain't so much easier on the land than whites. There's just fewer of them."

He stayed pretty close to the Powder River. He wouldn't miss the place now.

The grass got sparse and the alders fewer and patches of white alkaline earth came right down to the riverbank, and Slocum could see where it picked up the milky color it carried downstream.

Mizpah Creek was a bustling little thing, chortling over a sand and gravel bottom, blue as the sky. Slocum could see one reason why the Duffys had chosen to build here.

He never did see another one.

The roadhouse was just above the place where the creek entered the river—barely high enough above the spring flood line. The tufts of grass were sweetgrass and cropped close to the roots. Slocum crosssed a heavy Indian track at the gate to the place.

The corral was very large. Ten freighters or twice that many buckboards could have put up there. A short run of creek was enclosed and watering stock would be automatic and effortless. The front gate swung open easily on greased hinges.

In the corral were two saddle horses, a small donkey, a milk cow, and two goats, who ran bleating for the front door at Slocum's approach. As he rode up, with goats bleating and his horse nickering hello, the door opened six inches or so. The door shut before he was close enough to penetrate the darkness. He tied up at the hitch rail in front of the low-slung house.

Duffy's was a well-built place, and maybe the claim of Duffy's carpenters to excellence in civilian life was justified. The front roof rested on square posts, eight by eights, mortised and tenoned into the rafter plate. The roof was split cedar shakes, uniformly gray from the weather. Cedar shakes always looked real casual, but they'd take more weather than most, year after year, and that justified the extra work it took to set them in place.

The walls were board and batten and the line of the wall was straight. Though the low single-story building didn't look too elegant, the nearer a man got to it, the better it appeared. It made John Slocum sigh.

There were three windows on the front of the house. Each of them was shuttered closed with oak shutters meant to turn away a bullet and loopholes just above the sill where a man could return fire in relative comfort. Slocum knew that eyes watched him from those loopholes and maybe a gun or two as well. So under the overhung front porch he stopped to shout his greeting. "Hello! Hello! I'm a stranger, come peaceable and meanin' no harm to any herein."

He waited, and heard some kind of scuffle inside before the door swung open.

The woman wore a gray dress with a white bodice of some other material. Her hair was drawn up in a neat bun. Her eyes were pale blue, and full of anxiety. "Welcome, stranger," she said, with forced heartiness. She bowed in a parody of an inkeeper's bow. "Welcome to Duffy's Roadhouse." She looked right past him, as if she were reading a newspaper just above his left shoulder. "My husband, who will return shortly, always says Duffy's has the finest eatin' and the softest beds between Fort Lincoln and the Bozeman Trail."

"Well, then," Slocum said. She'd spoken all of her invitations but seemed to be stuck right in the middle of the doorway, and a man'd have to be awful damn rude to come in. "John Slocum, ma'am. Pleased to make your acquaintance."

The repetition of the old formula had the hoped-for effect and Mrs. Duffy said she was Laura Duffy and wouldn't he come in? It was too early for dinner, but perhaps a cup of tea. She added, "My husband is out chasing horses. Perhaps he'll be back before the tea gets cold."

The inside of the roadhouse was dim, though light outlined the shutters. The guest parlor was set up with four long board tables and pine benches along the walls. They could have seated a company of men here, and Slocum found himself wondering how much it had cost them to get set up in such fashion. There were vases on each table—two of them made for the purpose, two of them that had started out as jam pots. There were flowers in each jar, blue ones.

She rubbed her hands together. "Do sit down, Mr. Slocum. I'll put water on for tea."

"I'll take a whiskey if you got it," Slocum said.

"Oh. Oh. You don't drink tea. Well, many men don't. Of course, my husband is a tea-drinking man himself, but he is exceptional, I suppose. . . ."

"Rye whiskey if you got it." Slocum sat down on a bench and rested his Winchester against the wall. Now that he was here, he wasn't sure what to do. Without another word, she hurried out of the room. Slocum tried to remember if her husband had been short too and decided he probably had been, though Slocum never saw him on his feet.

She brought the whiskey in a tall fluted milk glass, about half a pint of it, and said something more about her husband's liking for tea. John Slocum took a sip of the whiskey and it went down like it was burning a new route to his stomach, splashing warmly around when it got there. "Yes, ma'am," he said. "Sit for a minute. I got news."

She said, "Well, I certainly don't know what news might concern us. I mean we are rather, uh, remote, out here, don't you know, and the big world goes on its ways without trifling with us. . . ." But she was sitting down on the bench as she spoke and the color was draining out of her face like somebody'd pulled the plug.

Slocum took another stiff belt of whiskey. "Your husband's dead," he said. "Warrant Officer Duffy was killed by hostile Indians at the battle of Greasy Grass. Almost all the Seventh Cavalry was killed and elements of the Fifth Cavalry as well." He waited for her to faint if she was going to. Her lip trembled.

"Now, maybe you're thinkin' I'm not tellin' you the truth," he went on, "but I was with him when he died." Because this woman had never done anything to him or his, he added, "His last thoughts were for you and your daughter, Opal. He told me to tell you how much he loved you both and he'd see you again on the other side."

He pushed the whiskey at her. In a soft voice, just a hair louder than a whisper, she said, "No, thank you,

sir. I do not drink strong spirits. My husband . . ."
Her face broke up but she brought it back together.
"I forget my duties, sir. Do you require some light
refreshment? My husband . . ." She couldn't get far
without running into him, and she was much too proud
a woman to do her weeping on a stranger's shoulder.
"If there's anything you require, sir, my daughter will
fetch for you. I beg you not to pass this weary news to
her ears. . . ."

"Whatever you say." Stiff-backed but tottering, she
made her way out of the room. Slocum twiddled his hat
in his hands. He sipped the whiskey, which tasted
pretty damn tasteless if you want to know the truth.
He walked around the room, noting the freshly filled
flower glasses and the shutters drawn against attack.
He leaned down to look through one loophole and,
sure enough, it commanded the whole corral. The shutter was made from pin oak, which would stop most
bullets smaller than a Sharps .69 and every arrow. The
loophole was wide enough for a rifle or shotgun, your
choice, and the shooter could rest on the window sill
for better aim.

Built too well and built in the wrong place. Unless
someone came here special, there was no reason to
journey to the mouth of Mizpah Creek. It wasn't really
between anywhere. The shortest distance between Bozeman and Fort Lincoln was the Missouri, and such land
travelers as there were weren't likely to skirt the badlands. Duffy's would get the trade of a few hunters
and as many outlaws as poked their heads out of the
badlands, but nobody was going to get rich on that
custom. Slocum examined Warrant Officer Duffy's
snug dream and thought, "So this was why Bird-Calling
died."

"Hi," she said.

The girl was standing twined around the lintel post
in the doorway like a Virginia creeper. Slocum nodded.

"Hi. I'm Opal. Do you like our house? My father

built this house for my mother and me. I'll like it better when we get busier."

"Slocum's my name."

She curtised, smooth as a dancer, and Slocum wondered where she'd learned that eastern grace out here. "Pleasure, Mr. Slocum. I'm Opal Duffy. My father is an officer in the cavalry and General Custer's personal friend, so you had probably consider very carefully what you say to me."

"Huh?"

"Yes. Well, it might do very well for you to express your surprise because you aren't expected to know everything. Have you been to France?"

"Nope."

"Well, neither have I!" She put her hands on her hips and sailed right into the room. It was a little hard to guess Opal's age. She was slight enough for a child but moved like she was in her early teens. Her hair was blond and fine as spun gold and the blue ribbon flattered its grandeur. Unlike either her mother or father she had a fine-featured face, that aristocratic sort of face General Custer had and every damn card sharp in Boston. Her nose was too narrow. She was dressed like a child, but two soft mounds in her bodice suggested the mature figure that lay underneath. "But I will," she said.

"Will what?"

"Go to France." Hands on hips again. She thought he was stupid. "When I'm a few years older, I've promised myself I'll go to Paris, France, and I never break a promise I make to myself."

Slocum had seen a few trappers like this girl. They spent so much time alone, they'd gotten used to talking to themselves, and when they did run across another human being they were terrible conversationalists. Since nothing was required of John Slocum, he said nothing. He took another pull on his whiskey and was surprised to finish the drink. He hadn't thought he'd taken so much.

"First Paris and then London and then France,"

the girl prattled on. As she talked she whirled through the tables, pirouetting. "I'll see the London Tower and the Castles and the Rhine and the Seine too." She pronounced *Seine* to rhyme with *tiny*.

Slocum stood up. The girl followed him without showing interest. "And you know what then?" she asked.

"Nope." Slocum put his glass down beside the sink. Though the stream wasn't far away, even that distance was too great for the fine folks of Duffy's Roadhouse. A new shiny pump perched to the right of the sink. John Slocum wet his handerkerchief and washed his face and hands. The child babbled on about her travel plans, but he didn't pay her more mind than the gurgle of the creek water just audible outside.

He unfastened the shutters. The kitchen faced due west and light flooded inside, all pink and red and violet.

"My mother says we have to close the shutters," Opal protested.

"Damn place feels like a prison," Slocum grumbled. "I'm a guest, ain't I?"

He had changed categories. "Yes, sir!" she said, with the enthusiasm of the recently converted. "Might I get you some tea?"

Slocum worked the pump handle a couple of times. It squeaked. The leather cups needed greasing. The water that spouted out of the pump ran over his wrists and into his glass. The water stank real bad. It was alkali water, okay for washing but you wouldn't drink it for fun and you could never cook the foul taste out of it. He made a face.

"Our water's all right. You get used to it." The girl was defiant. She pushed her kettle onto the hot stove-plate of the stove. "I make a fine pot of tea," she added.

"Uh-huh. Where does your mother keep the whiskey?"

The girl pointed at a high cupboard. When Slocum swung the door open, his jaw dropped. Whiskey.

Bourbon. Rye whiskey. Some rum. Even a couple of bottles of that Scotch whiskey you could get at Brown's Hotel in Denver. Slocum read the label pasted across the bottle of rye: "U.S. Army Officer's Stores."

It was a fine supply of booze. "Where's your storeroom?" Slocum asked.

"Why?"

"Where's your storeroom?"

The girl led him to a room beside the kitchen where it'd stay cool in the summer and warm in the winter. The storeroom was perhaps twenty feet long and six feet wide, and it was full of U.S. government stores. The walls were lined with casks of flour and molasses and salt and corned beef and mutton in brine. Row upon row of U.S. Army–stamped hams hung from the rafters. Stacked cases advertised their contents: applesauce, tomatoes, beans, pork loins, and peas. Slocum recognized an issue rifle case behind the salt beef.

"They're father's," the girl said. The edge in her voice revealed her suspicion.

"I can see that," Slocum said. He closed the thick door behind him with his heel. He felt like a grave robber and an outraged citizen both.

He poured another whiskey. The woman called from the other part of the house.

"In here, Mama," Opal called. "Mr. Slocum and me have been looking at the storeroom."

The woman's face was quite composed, though her eyes were ruined beyond repair. "The stores, Mr. Slocum? Are you from the army, then?"

"No. I don't care what your husband stole."

Her eyebrows climbed. "Stole, Mr. Slocum? Stole? How can you speak of theft?"

"Ain't hard."

"Perhaps you don't care to take supper with us, then. Since we are the wife and daughter of a man you choose to brand a thief."

Slocum looked out the windows where the last glow of the sun wasn't more than inches above the horizon. "Ma'am," he said tiredly. "I am not indifferent to where

I sleep or what I eat, but I will not pay a very great price for either."

The innkeeper again: "Sir, I doubt you will find more reasonable accommodations nearby. The meal is twenty-five cents and the bed is the same. Since we are at present unoccupied, you may have the finest room in the house."

"Sure," Slocum said. "And, ma'am, there's no reason to fasten all these shutters. If the Sioux wanted to walk in here, they'd damn well do so."

"I presume you're keeping count of the whiskey, sir? Unless you'd rather buy the bottle at two dollars."

"I expect that'd be all right," Slocum said. It was better whiskey than he'd find anywhere north of the officers' mess at Fort Phil Kearny. "The pony soldiers have pulled out," he said bluntly. "They packed up their gear and vacated Fort Abraham Lincoln, kit and caboodle."

"After they buried their dead."

"Sure," Slocum said.

"What dead?" Opal asked.

"Never mind. It isn't important."

Slocum gave Laura Duffy a look. He also offered her a drink, which she didn't take. She said she had a roomful of whiskey if she wanted any. She also said she would get dinner together, if nobody minded.

Nobody did. She meant for Slocum and Opal to go elsewhere, leaving her alone in her neat, well-ordered kitchen, but Slocum didn't see any sense in going in the other room and sitting in the dark, and said so. He turned up the wick on the lamp and fired a lucifer on his thumbnail. The lamp glow was unexpectedly bright and he blinked. Mrs. Duffy's kitchen was whitewashed and neat, and she had heavy-gauge pots and pans to feed an army. Which was as it should be since they were issue. A mental picture came to Slocum: the late Mr. Duffy smuggling war goods out of Fort Tullock's stores, a wagonload at a time, scared to death some unbribed sentry might happen across him. Men drew twenty years in Leavenworth for smaller thefts than Slocum saw all around him.

Despite her elaborate collection of pots, Laura's dinner that night was a large can of bully beef and another smaller can of tomatoes, which she poured right in the pot with the beef before she slid it over the fire. "You can get some more firewood, dear," she said to Opal. Opal dragged her heels some but started bringing in the night's kindling, a stick at a time. She left the door open as she went in and out, and her mother didn't remark on it though the stove was heating the great outdoors and it was a chilly evening.

"Did you plant a garden?" Slocum asked.

She motioned toward the closed storeroom door. "With that many provisions, wouldn't a garden be superfluous?" she asked.

"Uh."

If Mrs. Duffy had meant to say anything to John Slocum away from the girl's hearing, she didn't get a chance. The girl knew something was going on she should know. Her time outside was short. Presently she had the stove filled and roaring. She rubbed her hands over the stove and shot a sideways glance at Slocum. She stuck her hands into her armpits and said, sulkily, "I can't take care of my nails."

"That's a shame," Slocum said. To her mother, "The child, was she born on an army post?"

"I ain't no child." Opal's face got very red.

"Opal has always lived under better circumstances than these," Laura Duffy said. She gave the bully beef a brisk stir and said, "There," with some satisfaction. She put a heavy lid on the pot and kept the fire very hot. "Opal was a 'love child.'" Laura Duffy's face was smug. She expected Slocum to be appalled at her frankness, or maybe she was just pleased at herself for so precisely naming her daughter. "Her father was a prominent officer in the army whose name you would know if I were to divulge it."

"Mama . . . please!"

Mama didn't heed. "I was more child than woman

at the time and he betrayed me, oh, yes, he did, but I shall never betray him, and the secret of his identity shall go with me to the grave. My husband understands."

Slocum noted her present tense. "You understand, then, too," he said.

"Why, of course."

Opal tightened her hands into fists and smacked them together smartly. "Well, I don't understand. Not at all. I don't understand anything."

This provoked a seraphic smile from her mother. "Yes, dear, I know."

Steam was leaking from the pot.

Slocum sipped at his whiskey and thought that it was good to be warm here with fine whiskey.

Laura to Opal: "Why don't you take the soap and wash?"

"Do I have to?" High-pitched whine, the first childishness from the girl.

On second thought, John Slocum would rather have been out on the prairie with coyotes for company.

The girl dipped water into a shallow tin basin. She took basin, soap, and towel to the washstand at the far end of the room. She was all ears.

"When will they return to Fort Lincoln?" Laura asked, adult to adult.

"Hard to guesss. I expect they'll want to bring more troops up from the Mexican border. If I was plannin' it, I'd try to have the fort manned by first snow, but I never been any great shakes predicting the military mind."

She held up fingers, calculating. "Last year, first snow was October eighteenth at—"

Slocum interrupted. "And this year it might be end of August. . . ."

"July, August, September. A hundred twenty days until the soldiers return."

"Hell, lady, there's no tellin' when the soldiers will—"

"I suppose the sutler is closed at Fort Lincoln?"

"Burned all his goods and got on the sidewheeler same as everyone else."

That stopped her momentarily. "Burned *all* his goods? Oh, my!"

"Will Daddy be traveling with the other soldiers?" Opal asked.

"Nobody could ever get me to burn our goods," her mother said stoutly.

The lid of the kettle was bouncing on the pot.

"I'm sure."

"Mama, where's Daddy?"

Laura Duffy put her hands to her face and pushed as if she were trying to squeeze dough. "Will you please be quiet, Opal? It isn't mannerly to interrupt your elders." To Slocum: "Sometimes I don't understand how the Mister adopted this brat, but he did, all legal when he married me, and treated her just like she was his own. I can't understand it."

Slocum poured himself another glass of whiskey and drained it.

"Well, his misfortune is our good fortune, I suppose. There's no wind so it doesn't blow good."

"Who?"

"The sutler. He was our nearest competitor to the east. Now that he's gone, all the travelers will have to stop by here, and business will be so much better."

"Travelers, ma'am?"

"Oh, yes. Between Fort Phil Kearny and Bozeman, if a man wants a safe place to rest and a good meal, he'll have to stop here."

"What travelers, ma'am?"

"The traders. The drummers. The gold seekers and immigrants. Oh, I tell you, Mr. Slocum, this country is going to bloom someday, and only those on the spot will catch the blossoms as they fall."

"I see," Slocum said gently. "Your husband tell you all that?"

"That's one of Mister's favorite expressions," Laura

said. Her smile was ghastly. "He's very foresighted. He's a man of the future."

"Mama? What about Daddy?"

"Didn't I tell you to keep still!"

"Do you think . . ." Slocum began.

"I think Mr. Duffy's vision will be vindicated, that's what I think. He's no fly-by-night."

Slocum said, "If you're done stewin' that beef, we could probably eat some of it."

Bully beef was canned beef in gelatin. The process that canned it destroyed all toxic bacteria and disintegrated the beef into long ropes that jelled at the slightest provocation.

She pulled the pot off the stove, with her apron, and spooned three portions into metal bowls. The tomatoes made it look like a red stew of some sort. It didn't smell very good, and Slocum knew it would taste that way.

Slocum sat down heavily. "You eat this good every night?" he asked.

"Oh, yes. We have plenty of provisions."

"Mama, I'm not hungry."

"Sit down and eat your supper."

Opal sat, unhappily, but made no move to pick up her fork. Slocum shoveled the food into his mouth. It was hot. That was most of the good that could be said about it.

Still, Slocum wasn't awful damn proud. He just shoveled it in and the woman did too. She may have had manners once in some other place.

"This is swill," Opal remarked.

Laura turned and pointed to her daughter. "That'll be the last we hear from you," she yelled. "Tell me, Mr. Slocum, how did Colonel Custer die?"

Slocum choked. "Pardon me, ma'am. Something must have got down the wrong tube." He coughed into his handkerchief.

"It must have been dreadful for the ladies at the fort. We knew so many of them."

"Woman named Pollitz?" he gasped. "Sergeant Pollitz?"

"Oh, no! We only associated with the officers' wives."

"Yes, ma'am."

To her daughter: "And of course you remember gallant Colonel Custer, dear. Remember what a fine rider he was?"

"The colonel is dead!" The girl spoke with real outrage in her voice, as if she'd been personally betrayed by her mother, and maybe she had.

"Yes, dear. With all the men in his command." Cheerful as a bird she was.

With a scraping noise, Slocum pushed his plate back. Without asking for a by-your-leave he rolled a cigarette and fired it up. When he had it going good, he looked into Laura Duffy's eyes. They were very strange eyes.

The girl's eyes were flooded with tears and her lower lip was fluttering like a piece of loose canvas in a Nebraska wind. When in Bedlam, do as the Bedlamites do.

"You get many travelers, ma'am?" Slocum asked.

"You didn't finish your dinner, Mr. Slocum. I'm afraid we can't give a refund for that. We can't be responsible for an appetite that's less than the guest expected. You do see, don't you?" She leaned toward Slocum and he nodded stupidly.

When he took hold of his wits again, he said, "Many travelers, ma'am? Am I the first?"

She clapped her hands together like a child while her daughter wept. "In a manner of speaking, sir, you are. I wonder if I should keep your money as a good luck token? Tell me, sir, how did my husband die?"

Slocum was getting used to it and didn't bat an eye at her change in direction. Opal wasn't hearing anything she hadn't guessed, but she let out a sob.

"He died at Fort Abraham Lincoln," Slocum said. "He had been shot in the chest and was brought downriver with Benteen and Reno's wounded."

"Did he suffer so much, then, at the end?"

"No, ma'am. He wasn't feelin' much of anything."

"That's good. And you said his last thoughts were of us?"

"That's right. He asked me to come by here and bring you out. I expect you'll find assistance at Fort Kearny."

Her eyes grew puzzled. "Leave here? Leave Duffy's Roadhouse? Surely you must be mad."

The daughter stumbled out of the room. Her mother pulled her plate to her and began to finish her untasted dinner.

Slocum eyed the whiskey bottle. He'd need more than this one. He sighed. "Ma'am," he said quietly, "you and me and your daughter are the only white faces for two hundred miles to the east and twice that to the north and south. We're the only live whites between River Platte and Bozeman. Now, there are five thousand Sioux camped just a half-day's ride from here. They just killed a good piece of the United States Army and run off the rest of it. Now, tomorrow morning, we're gonna pack what we can pack on your miserable horses and we're gonna hightail out of here, and by God, we won't sleep until you been delivered to the fort."

She looked up from her dinner, a piece of beef at the corner of her mouth. "Mr. Slocum. This roadhouse is everything my husband and I ever worked for. Do you know how long Opal and I have been here alone? Since March, Mr. Slocum. A total of one hundred and eighteen days today. I am quite beyond fear, Mr. Slocum." She scraped her spoon along the bottom of the metal bowl.

"The Indians won't let us leave."

Slocum remembered the wildflowers on each of the otherwise bare plank tables.

"Oh, Jesus," he said.

She got angry. "I do not allow profanity in my house, Mr. Slocum. I might make an exception for travelers in the common room, but my own kitchen is sacrosanct."

"Squirrel," he guessed.

"Who?"

"Tall fella. Big Adam's apple. Short-haired for a Sioux. He's some relation to old Crazy Horse himself, though I didn't catch what. He's the one, ain't he?"

"He was here, today," the woman said vaguely. "I never allow him beyond the public rooms."

"He rides right in here with fifty warriors?"

"Oh, no. I never allow them beyond the corral. Just him."

"Squirrel."

"I suppose that's the name he goes by. His English is very poor. If the Mister were here, I wouldn't allow him in the house at all, but since I am defenseless, I have had no choice."

"Uh-huh. You don't think he'll let you leave?"

"Oh, no. He has said as much." She lowered her head demurely. "He has marriage on his mind."

What Slocum wanted to say wouldn't be welcome in this woman's kitchen.

"He isn't a bad-looking man—for a redskin. And he, by their standards, is very wealthy."

Slocum was sick of this woman and it showed. "Well, hell. Maybe you ought to just get hitched. You got a considerable dowry."

She pointed at her chest and her mouth fell open. "Me?"

"Well, who the hell else?"

She laughed, a silvery pearl of laughter. "Oh, my, Mr. Slocum. You must think me quite the merry widow. Oh, no, Mr. Slocum. I am wed to Mr. Duffy in this life and in the next. He will be waiting for us in paradise and watching too, I wouldn't be surprised. Squirrel isn't a bit interested in me. He wants Opal."

6

"The black spotted horse and the burro," the old man added reluctantly. "That makes a total . . ."

"Five horses and one burro. I can count," John Slocum said. His face was quite impassive. Squirrels' father's face didn't show much either. Four men faced each other across the fire in Snow Fox's lodge. Behind them Squirrel's older wives bustled and chirped, pounding out cornmeal cakes and grinding the herb tea they'd use for the nuptial celebration when this business was finished.

War Bonnet, Slocum's adviser, was slightly behind the white man but close enough to lean forward to whisper in his new friend's ear, "You aren't going to do better than that. Squirrel isn't a rich man and neither is his father. Crazy Horse has plenty of ponies, but Squirrel is just a second cousin. Squirrel claims the relationship, but it doesn't work the other way. The stream of kinship flows from the heights to the lowlands."

"Sure."

The old man spoke for his son. "The burro is a fine burro. It was trained by whites so it will speak Owl Child's second tongue." The "second tongue" was a nice touch. Since Slocum rode into the camp that morning, polite fiction had it that he was a full-blooded Blackfoot, Owl Child. If he'd been a white man, they would have killed him.

He'd set out in the morning from the roadhouse figuring it would take him a while to find the Sioux main camp because he only knew the general direction. He hadn't reckoned the size of the camp. The hunter's trails approaching it were worn deep as mine roads, great roads across the trackless prairie. When he was three miles out, he could see the campfire smoke, like a haze over the valley. They'd pitched their lodges on the bank of Pumpkin Creek, which was clearer and deeper than Mizpah Creek, but three thousand warriors, their families and horses leave a hell of a mark on empty wilderness. The great pony herd was ringed with boy guards, and grazing a good mile out from the camp because they'd browsed it bare nearer. When he came into sight, the pony guards started up and the nearest rode away to join his brothers. These boys carried only short bows, useful for ground squirrels or rabbits, but they were Sioux and recognized him as a white man. He hadn't dressed especially for this particular meeting, though he did tie a white duck feather to the muzzle of his Winchester, which he held upright like a lance. The white feather was the sign for peace and a parlay, and if the Sioux didn't kill him too quick, maybe they'd honor his request.

Horses. So damn many horses. Old ones, young foals, burros, donkeys, cavalry horses, teamsters' horses, and a few horses that had once carried riders for the Pony Express. Many of the horses were magnificent and all of them spooked when he passed near, offended by his "white man's stink."

Some of the boy watchers galloped into the encampment to warn the warriors; others collected and herded the horses that separated at Slocum's approach. Four of the bravest booted their horses into a run and, yelling war cries, bore down on him. They seemed like flat brown patches on the backs of their horses, galloping full tilt, straight in his face. They might have used their rabbit bows but chose not to, and Slocum swore under his breath when he figured their intentions. No doubt these boys—a Sioux was a man at twelve—meant to count coup on the strange white men. When they got near enough, they would strike him and gallop away, greatly honored. He couldn't let that happen because a man so shamed couldn't hardly talk to a Sioux warrior, and one of the lesser ones would take his scalp, just for the hell of it. No. If the boys whacked him with their coup sticks, he'd have to gun them all. Foolishness. Pure foolishness. A hundred yards, fifty. He held the rifle over his head, its white feather dangling plain enough for a blind man to see it. One of the boys dropped out at thirty yards, but the other three had their coup sticks ready and only veered off at the last instant, shouting their disappointment.

Slocum said, "Goddamn," meaning no blasphemy.

The four did take one honor for themselves, the honor of escorting John Slocum into the main camp, two on either side. He was met by the bucks who had lodges nearest the village entrance (and were selected for that post because of exceptional strength or skill), and twenty Dog Soldiers who were just going out to hunt. Slocum reined up and held his empty hand up. In his other hand he held his feathered carbine like his banner.

They could have killed him right then and there. But the curious outnumbered the warlike, at least in that band, and nobody killed him before he told his name and tribe and the most important fact of all, that he was War Bonnet's brother and wanted to speak with him.

He had a piece of luck. In an ordinary village of ten to a hundred souls, everybody knew everybody, but in this capital city of villages, the biggest assemblage of Indians in the history of the west, he was lucky that Dog Soldiers were at the gate because War Bonnet's name meant nothing at all to the gatekeepers.

And it was a good thing War Bonnet was at home instead of off on a hunting or scouting trip. Sitting Bull and Crazy Horse fully expected another attack by Custer's fellow Seizers because in identical circumstances, that's what they would have done.

The camp was spooky. Many of the braves wore portions of cavalry uniforms, and the braves who guarded the medicine tent in the center of the tribal circle wore complete uniforms, though the shirts and pants hadn't always come from the same corpse. Some of these uniforms were ragged, some powder-stained or stained black with dried blood. They all carried the history of wounds. Many braves had fresh scalps on their lances or drying on racks beside their fire, and a few of them looked at John Slocum like he was fresh meat.

War Bonnet didn't seem surprised to see him and spoke his hello with some real enthusiasm. Slocum felt his tight muscles loosen. They'd been tight since he left Mizpah Creek. His scalp muscles had been particularly knotted.

War Bonnet snapped out a command and one of his small sons took Slocum's bridle while a torrent of rapid Sioux advised Slocum's escort that Owl Child was indeed his brother, a great shaman, and a great warrior whose next boasts would be earned by slaying each and every one of those present unless they skedaddled. Which they did.

Slocum returned War Bonnet's embrace enthusiastically. He really was glad to see the man. "Inside, my Blackfoot friend," War Bonnet advised. "Some of these stupid Dog Soldiers can't tell an Indian from a white."

Inside, War Bonnet offered the honor seat to Slocum: far side of the fire, facing the tunnel-like opening. Light streamed in overhead. War Bonnet's life and autobiography were painted on the skins that formed the conical lodge, and the latest of them showed, with figures, the battle of Greasy Grass. Politely, Slocum leaned over to examine the man's story. Here War Bonnet was counting coup on a mounted Seizer. Here he was, braining that same Seizer. Here he lanced another. Here he killed a dismounted Seizer though the bluecoat already had the drop on him. Slocum murmured polite approval, wondering if any of the men his friend had killed had been a fat sergeant with a red-haired wife.

War Bonnet's first wife was a plump thing whose smile was good despite the teeth blackened and shortened from chewing hides. Hospitably, she set a bowl of steaming something before John Slocum. It was white and lumpy but it smelled a hell of a lot better than last night's dinner, which had kept his stomach grumbling until well past midnight. He waited until it cooled enough for him to dip his fingers in the pot. The meat was some kind of rodent: ground squirrel, prairie dog, chipmunk, or woodchuck. The grain was pounded manioc and oats, seasoned with sage. He didn't have to feign his enthusiasm. When she returned, she had a bowl of warm water for him to wash his hands. When his hands were clean and his belly full, his friend offered the pipe. The pipe was a long-stemmed stone-bowled affair, wrapped in beads and feathers. It was very light and the tobacco, kinnikinnick, was aromatic. Formally War Bonnet offered the pipe to the four winds before he took a puff himself, and Slocum repeated the offering before he took his turn.

Behind them, the women and children went about their business. Some sewed; the youngest played with stones and dolls. A grandmother dozed on a pile of furs, her arthritic fingers clenching and unclenching as she faced her nightmares.

War Bonnet lowered the pipe. Politely, Slocum asked about the game, number, and strength of buffalo herds, the location of the pronghorns and the mulies you could find in the dense alder groves. Politely, War Bonnet replied to his questions, considering each singly.

Next, Slocum complimented War Bonnet on his lodge and the epic that ran around its inside walls and the number and comeliness of his wives.

War Bonnet admitted that he had the best lodge in the village and that his wives were the youngest, most beautiful, and the hardest workers. That caused a slight stir and a couple of giggles, which the men didn't deign to notice.

"How can I help you, my friend?" War Bonnet asked.

"Squirrel pays court to the younger woman at the lodge on Mizpah Creek. She is named Opal, after the stone of great radiance, but is not much to look upon. Squirrel would marry her."

War Bonnet cocked his head, puzzled, waiting for the rest of Slocum's story. When it didn't come, he signed, "So what?"

"She doesn't want him."

Still puzzled: "But why not? Squirrel is a man of some substance, cousin to Crazy Horse himself—though a distant cousin from a most conservative part of the family. He is a young man but owns a few horses of his own and his father owns more. Why does she not wish the match?"

Slocum said, "Because her father was killed by the Sioux and she has sworn enmity to all Sioux and Cheyenne."

War Bonnet's brow furrowed. He looked about him for something and Slocum tossed him the Bull Durham pouch, which War Bonnet poured directly into the stone bowl of the pipe, neglecting the ritual. "White men make good guns and good tobacco," he said. "But their whiskey is awful and their horses unthrifty. Their women, like this Opal, are weak and cannot do much work. I do not understand why Squirrel wants this girl, but I will ask him his reasons." He smoked the pipe for several minutes before he rose, saying, "If the white's whiskey was as good as his tobacco, he would be a good friend to the Sioux."

Slocum thought his doubt but didn't speak it.

While Papa was gone, Slocum was the object of the children's curiosity. Solemnly and carefully he was examined by four boys and as many girls, who wouldn't desist no matter what their mothers said.

Abruptly the lodge flap whipped open and a breathless War Bonnet took his old seat. He hadn't been gone fifteen minutes. His children rediscovered their company manners and retired to the outskirts of the light. "It is no use," War Bonnet said. "You can demand more horses than the woman is worth, but Squirrel will have her or kill them both, and his father, Snow Fox, backs him up on the matter."

Slocum fired up the pipe. The remnants of kinnikin-nick mixed with the tobacco smoke tasted like the underside of a leaky sewer pipe. He coughed and waved the smoke away from him.

War Bonnet took the pipe and inhaled greedily.

"She will not," Slocum said. "She is not a woman yet."

"She has no breasts? Her mound is not mossed?"

Slocum shook his head. "I am not her father," he said.

"But you act for him, do you not?"

And John Slocum faced up to the unpleasant fact that either he acted for Warrant Officer Duffy's interests or nobody would. It galled him when he said, "I suppose so.'"

War Bonnet shook his head. Anything could be solved if reasonable men talked long enough about it. "Let me tell you of Sitting Bull's dream," he said. "Three weeks before the Seizers came to Greasy Grass, Sitting Bull had a medicine dream. He had fasted and cleaned himself for three days and three nights, and when he slept he dreamed of Seizers falling out of the sky. The next morning, when he sent the boys through the villages with his songs, the people knew that he had dreamed a very great dream and all gathered that night in the council to hear it. When he told his dream we all understood that a very great many Seizers would come to our home and we would kill them all. Runners went out to the other bands, the Lakota, the Shoshone, the Gros Ventres, and all came back with 'Yes, we will come; yes, we will come.' Sitting Bull would make the magic, but Crazy Horse would be the war leader. Sitting Bull has no father or mother or sisters, only his wives and his brother, Strong Bull. Everybody else is dead. But Crazy Horse comes from the Loon family, a very strong, very powerful family. In the old days they were as strong as the Dog Soldiers, but that is not true today. They are very concerned with old values, they are 'guardians of the old ways.' Thus, their honor is very high and very tender.

"Crazy Horse had a wife. A beautiful wife of sixteen summers. While he was away speaking to the tribes, she crept into the tepee of another one night and again the night after. Crazy Horse's other wives tried to hold her, but she was too clever for them and slipped out every night to this young buck who must have been a magician lover."

War Bonnet's plump wife put a few more sticks on the fire and set a pot of water in the embers to heat.

"Soon enough, everyone was talking about it," War Bonnet continued. "She was the wife of the war chief of all the Sioux and Cheyenne and she was quite open about what she did. When Crazy Horse rode back with his honor guard, we knew that soon she and her lover or Crazy Horse would sing the death song. All the laws of the people make that clear. A husband should cut the ears of an erring woman or cut off her nose so she is not tempted anymore, and then he must kill her lover or drive him into the wilderness. Her lover was an unproven warrior, and a coward. When Crazy Horse came back into the village, the lover hid with the woman at the river, washing clothes. Oh, how they jibed at him. The half men—those men who look like women—they jibed at him too. They were all waiting for Crazy Horse to come to the river and kill his wife's lover. He did not. He went to her and brought her back to his lodge. He did not disfigure her. He did not mark her in any way. He ignored the younger brave completely. He made it like nothing had happened—nothing at all. The Loon people were outraged. Here was their war chief swallowing a great slur on his honor. Crazy Horse would not talk of it. He would not defend himself even when they talked about it. He said only that he meant to kill Seizers and not his brothers. After the battle of Greasy Grass the shame disappeared from most men's minds and perhaps nobody remembered Crazy Horse's dishonor except for the Loon people. Snow Fox said since Crazy Horse had given his wife away to slaughter whites, the whites owed the Loon family a wife. Squirrel was chosen. Now Squirrel will court Opal at Mizpah

Creek or he will kill her, but he cannot commit a second slight on the Loon people's honor. His life would be ruined if he did and likely it'd stir up that old business about Crazy Horse too, and maybe some harm might come to him. Squirrel is like a man on a crusade. Will you act for Opal's father?"

John Slocum found himself saying "Sure," though it was the last word he wanted to say.

War Bonnet wanted to get right to negotiating, but John Slocum said they might as well wait until morning. He'd never seen an encampment like this and owed it to his grandchildren to take it in.

Crazy Horse and Sitting Bull were up in the Medicine Lodge with an envoy from Chief Joseph of the Nez Percé, so Slocum didn't get to see the most famous shaman of all. He caught a glimpse of Rain-in-the-Face's gaunt, scarred figure limping into his lodge, and Red Cloud of the Cheyenne rode past a scouting party. Red Cloud had discovered a small wagon train of immigrants who, with his assistance, had immigrated permanently. Red Cloud was in a fine mood, boasting and waving scalps. The long-haired scalps were women's. The smallest were children's. At first, War Bonnet had to explain Slocum's presence every few yards, but after a while news of War Bonnet's Blackfoot friend got ahead of them and nobody else bothered them anymore.

Sitting Bull's band moved frequently, as quickly as the game and graze disappeared. They described a great slow circle, like a rabbit turning back to its origins, this slow moving of peoples. Sitting Bull held them together with reminders of their great victory, though many of his allies would have been very much happier in smaller bands.

As usual, the warriors were underarmed, but thanks to their recent success, there were a few more Spencer carbines than usual. Except for the weapons they'd taken from Custer's command, the Indians had no new arms at all. On the south side of the camp, where the sun was hottest and the wind kept the flies off, women gathered at the stretching racks to peel the hides off the animals and scrape the scraps of flesh off the skins with flint knives. The wives from the wealthiest families had trade knives and iron scrapers for their work. The hides staked out to dry covered a hundred yards, side by side. Slocum had never seen anything like it. War Bonnet didn't comment on the hides, though he did comment on the young women doing the work. Proudly, he pointed out a particularly pretty black-eyed girl, who ducked behind her mother. The mother's glance wasn't all that friendly. War Bonnet explained airily, "The negotiations have not started. Her father is as great a warrior as I am and has only one other daughter. Many fine warriors wish a connection to his house and she will be worth many ponies. I have sixteen ponies, four for war, two hunting horses, three with foals, three too young to break, and one colt whose mother died foaling. One of my war horses belonged to a Seizer, the officer Tom Custer. Rain-in-the-Face wanted his heart but I got his horse. Hah! The heart rotted days ago, but my war horse will carry me against the Crows, before the snow flies!"

This was no war camp, though all the warriors were here. This was a camp of the whole Sioux. Plenty of little kids running around, busy with their games. Tiny bows, tiny arrows—many boy children picked Slocum as a good target for aim, though none loosed his arrow, not one. To shoot a guest of the People even in play— what a horror! In the evening, the smoke from the lodge fires made the sky black, and the smell of meat cooking was very strong. Two of War Bonnet's wives had spent the day gathering blackberries high up on Pumpkin Creek. The children's hands were black with the juice, and their mothers scolded them and ordered a wash before they were allowed to eat. Children and wives ate together while the two men sat at the fire. Slocum was pretty hungry. One of the younger wives served them, getting up from her own circle whenever she saw they were lacking something. She brought the iron bowl filled with lukewarm water for Slocum's hands and the piece of fur, the fox skin, to dry them.

Belly full, War Bonnet became philosophical. He spoke of the shadow land and how it must take us all. He spoke of how it had been in this country before the Seizers.

"How was it in this country before the Sioux?" Slocum asked. "When the Crow and Sheep Eaters and Assiniboine had it? And the Ree, you pushed them out, didn't you?"

"We did." War Bonnet grinned. "And a fine fight it was, too. The Crows are very brave."

"And the whites will push you out."

War Bonnet's smile stayed just as wide but became wintry. Maybe it was the way he was showing his teeth. "There will be mourning in many a white man's lodges before that day."

Slocum shook his head. "I reckon that's true."

"Have you many horses?" War Bonnet asked Slocum.

"In my home I have many horses," John Slocum lied because only a rogue owned just two horses. "I have fifteen horses," he added. "Three of them are war horses and as many for hunting. Many of my horses are the spotted ponies of the Nez Percé—Appaloosas—because of their footing and fine nerve."

"The Seizers' horses have great speed."

"But not so much nerve. How long can they travel on an empty belly?"

"That is true. And I have never seen a Seizer's pony who could follow a mustang where water is scarce. They are too big and too heavy and need to eat too much."

"But they are fast."

"Yes. They are very fast."

And that's how the two of them spent the evening, talking horses and weapons and warfare. Slocum showed War Bonnet the new Winchester, which the brave had heard of but not seen. He put it to his shoulder happily and squinted down the barrel. He shuddered. "Oh, it is a wolf's weapon, it is," he said.

And they talked about battles. Since the Blackfee,

and Sioux had a common enemy in the Crows, they told
stories of famous fights with Crow raiders. "The Seizers
use Crow scouts against us both," the Indian said.
Which was true enough. Only the Crows hated the
other tribes enough to scout for the army, though
occasionally you would find a Ree or an Assiniboine
brave who was willing to do it.

"Many of Custer's scouts are white," Slocum said.

"They scout the shadow land." War Bonnet laughed.

Slocum didn't laugh, though he understood the joke.
"I used to know a white man who scouted with Yellow
Hair," Slocum said. "Man by the name of Hickok. Wild
Bill is his summer name."

War Bonnet's hands described Hickok's broad shoulders and long hair. "Yes. That is the man."

War Bonnet shuddered. He said that he had seen
Hickok in action once, at the battle on the Marias
River, and Hickok's guns saddened many lodges that
night.

"Uh-huh. He's quick all right." John Slocum took
a stick and traced in the dirt next to the fire. Outside,
the murmur of voices was surprisingly loud. In the heart
of this village you couldn't even hear the damn birds
sing. John Slocum traced his own initials in the dirt
and then rubbed them out with his boot heel.

They talked long into the night—about war and
horses and country where the grizzly and the shaggy
beard (mountain goat) could be found. When they
were both rolled up in their furs and asleep, Orion rose
in the east.

Breakfast was some sort of overcooked cereal sweet-
ened with honey and some of Slocum's molasses, which
War Bonnet's wives reluctantly accepted from him. One
of them giggled while licking her sticky fingers and the
spot of molasses on the tip of her nose.

War Bonnet went outside after breakfast, and when
he returned he announced the time of their meet with
Squirrel's representative. With the help of his first wife
he began the elaborate toilette that was required of
him. Since he was the go-between, his dress had to

be elaborate enough to indicate his own high status without outshining the status of the participants. He wore two single strands of his grandfather's wampum and offered John Slocum three strands to wear, but Slocum had a clean green flannel shirt in his pack and thought that would do to honor the occasion.

"Snow Fox will expect you to look right." Meaning that he would expect Slocum to wear wealth across his about the courage and hospitality of the Loon people and Squirrel will wear riches too."

"Yeah. Well, we Blackfeet don't go in for decoration like you Sioux," Slocum said, accepting a couple of strands of jet trade beads as his only concession.

Since the Blackfeet were widely known among the most elaborately dressed and beaded Indians, this statement earned Slocum a disapproving look from his Sioux friend.

The two men stood outside Snow Fox's lodge and hollered until one of the junior relations popped through the lodge flap and motioned them inside. War Bonnet had barely enough time to finish an oration about the courage and hospitality of the Loon people before he found himself enjoying the latter.

The fire was neatly arranged, each stick precisely balanced on its fellows so that as one burned through, another would topple into the fire cone to take its place. The sand around the fire was raked clean and spread with the Loon family's lushest robes. Snow Fox remained seated when the two visitors entered, but both his attendants got to their feet. The two were Squirrel and Slocum's old friend, the Cheyenne. Squirrel wrinkled his forehead in a gesture of formal welcome, but the Cheyenne's face was black and ugly, and Snow Fox's face hardly moved at all. He raised one hand in greeting and lowered it before the two men in the doorway had time to reply. Wordlessly the two sat on the robes provided for them. John Slocum facing Snow Fox directly. The old man's face was crinkled with the lines of many winters and his hair was dead white, but Slocum figured he was still a fine warrior and hunter in his own right. It would be years before Squirrel took over the leadership of the Loon family.

Snow Fox began abruptly, "You are the girl's father."

Slocum and War Bonnet exchanged surprised looks. "I speak for her," Slocum said. "Among the Blackfeet it is customary to call the blessings of the mother earth upon a gathering with a pipe of tobacco. Do not the Sioux follow this custom?"

Snow Fox opened his mouth to say "We do, with friends," or words to that effect, but John Slocum and he were locked, eye to eye, and whatever the chief saw in Slocum's eyes backed him down. He grunted. He said, "It is our custom too," and signaled for the pipe. The Cheyenne hissed something in Snow Fox's ear, but Snow Fox chopped him short.

The ceremony of passing the pipe was brief, satisfying the letter but not the spirit.

"Her father is a white Seizer," Snow Fox said, as soon as he had the pipe put away.

"Her father died at Greasy Grass. Perhaps one of your braves killed him," Slocum said. Slocum smiled a bland, knowing smile. Snow Fox's eyes narrowed a notch or two. "How many horses does this Squirrel have?" Slocum asked.

Now it was War Bonnet's turn to hiss, as the three Loons exchanged glances. "Don't be so rushed. You insult them!"

Slocum ignored the advice. "I have heard the Loon people have many fine horses." He spoke those words as if they were too worn to have any significance at all. "If rumors are thought to be true."

"Our famous cousin, Crazy Horse, has many horses," Snow Fox corrected Slocum.

Slocum let his eyebrows show mock surprise. "Crazy Horse is your cousin? We Blackfeet had not heard of this. Surely he is not your close cousin."

Snow Fox's "That is true" was more a growl than a reply.

Slocum was relentless. "And this Squirrel—is he such a famous warrior that none in the Blackfoot nation has heard of him? Is he so fierce that the name Squirrel is unknown among us?"

Squirrel couldn't stand much of that and jumped to his feet and shouted something at Slocum, and Snow Fox snapped something at him, and unhappily he sat back down.

"Squirrel has killed a Crow and a Ree and taken the Ree's scalp," Snow Fox replied.

"Oh. He has killed two enemies! How could such a famous and fierce warrior as Squirrel not be known to us? I will sing the praises of the warrior who has killed twice. How many times has he counted coup?"

"He has not counted coup."

"How many horses has he stolen?"

Slocum was merciless, and once again War Bonnet tugged at his sleeve. He whispered, "Do you shame them? You will make enemies for life. Careful!"

"The woman is weak!" Snow Fox shot right back. He might not have mentioned the white girl's second, most obvious defect, but considering the line Slocum took, he didn't mind.

Slocum smiled. He was thinking of Opal Duffy as he'd last seen her the morning he left the roadhouse on Mizpah Creek. As soon as he got matters straight with the Indians he intended to take them back to the fort. Mrs. Duffy said she wasn't going anywhere—that she meant to stay where her husband, the warrant officer, had put her. Slocum felt obliged to reply that with Squirrel intending to marry her daughter, it wouldn't be awful safe here. The woman put enough pause in her voice before she resumed objections to let Slocum know she didn't give a tinker's damn whether Squirrel married her daughter or not. At this, Opal squealed in outrage and attacked her mother, beating on her breasts with clenched fists and clawing at her face. It took more strength than Slocum would have guessed to pull her off.

"She is not weak," he told Snow Fox. "She is very strong. Stronger than her mother and father probably. Squirrel has made a fine choice." He grinned thinking what demure little Opal would do to Squirrel's face if the two of them ever split a blanket. It tempted him for a minute, to tell the truth.

Then the two men got down to serious business, counting the horses. Snow Fox was reluctant to offer very much for the girl. He didn't think she would be much of an asset to his other wives or the Loon people, but his son, Squirrel, wanted her very much and she would solve the problem of Crazy Horse's shame that had descended on their family. At that moment, Snow Fox didn't know whom he liked less: Crazy Horse for making it necessary for the family to spread itself so thin and accept a new (expensive) wife, or this white Blackfoot who kept refusing the terms that he offered. The woman was worth three ponies, no more, by any reasonable man's calculations, and John Slocum was pricing her at five ponies and one burro and no end in sight.

"A burro?" Slocum asked indignantly. "What use have I for a burro? Can a warrior ride to war on a burro? Can he chase buffalo? Is that why the Loon people are such fierce warriors and do not count coup, because they ride burros to war?"

Once again Squirrel jumped to his feet and once more his father bade him sit down. The Cheyenne glowered at Slocum openly and fingered his medicine bag. Slocum smiled right into his face as though his curses were the greatest joke in the world.

"How many horses do the Loon people have?" he asked brightly, ignoring War Bonnet's restraining hand.

"Many horses," Snow Fox spoke from between his teeth.

"Look," Slocum began, quite reasonably. "Let us speak like equals and men of the world. Let us look at this as warriors." His glance included the old man but not Squirrel or the Cheyenne. "The girl is young and strong and has fine teeth. She is obedient to her mother and has strong thighs that will carry many sons."

"She does no work," Snow Fox interjected, still trying to strike a bargain.

"How many horses do the Loon people have?" Slocum bored on. "Do they have forty horses?"

The Loon people had eighteen horses total, barely two for each one of its nine warrior members. Of course, Crazy Horse had very many horses, but he never really counted himself a member of the family.

"We have very many horses," Snow Fox said. Both Squirrel and the Cheyenne were standing and Snow Fox did nothing to restrain them.

War Bonnet's grip on Slocum's arm was like iron, but Slocum paid no attention to it at all. "If Crazy Horse wanted the girl," he said in his mild voice, "I would use my authority to give her to him. Three horses would be the price. Because Crazy Horse is a warrior. To the Loon people, the price is forty horses, no less."

7

War Bonnet won the location but lost the choice of weapons. He would have preferred it the other way around but wasn't the man doing the deciding! Crazy Horse was. War Bonnet was just Dog Soldier's representative and John Slocum's second.

The Loon people considered it an honor for Crazy Horse to be the arbiter of the combat to come. For years, Snow Fox had been trying to involve his famous kinsman in family matters. Since Crazy Horse was as interested in his poor relations as the Loon people were interested in their poor relations, Snow Fox's efforts had not been crowned with success until John Slocum insulted the entire Loon family, sneering at their courage and wealth. Fifteen minutes after Slocum and War Bonnet left Snow Fox's lodge, a picked young warrior was on his way to Crazy Horse's much larger lodge to let him know of Owl Child's gross misconduct.

Sitting Bull joked sometimes, but he rarely smiled. When the messenger came to the lodge where the Sioux leaders were planning their strategy, Sitting Bull smiled. "Let the Nez Percé wait for you, my brother Sioux," he said, dismissing the Nez Percé representative as if he'd suddenly lost his right to sit by the fire. "Take care of your family's business."

For the last four weeks, Sitting Bull and Crazy Horse had been doing nothing but negotiating. Crazy Horse was a great boaster, but even he tired of boasting of his achievements at Greasy Grass. Sitting Bull was working to bring more tribes into his alliance: The Nez Percé were wavering and the Shoshone were almost certain to join. Meanwhile, the Cheyenne in the big camp were restless and some had already started off to the more familiar hunting grounds farther south. Sitting Bull and Crazy Horse had forged this sword and wanted to use it more than once. But without the danger of immediate attack by the Seizers, their weapon was getting awful damn unwieldy. Crazy Horse walked back to his own lodge. He'd been at it since dawn, trying to convince the stubborn Nez Percé that the white man was their enemy too. The Nez Percé had helped many of the early white settlers, and even kept a few immigrant families from starving. The Nez Percé land included some of the richest valleys in the western Rockies, and Crazy Horse had been unable to convince them that the white men were unlike the Indians. The Indian never forgot an injury and never forgot a friend. The white man never forgot an injury. That was the gist of Crazy Horse's argument, and it was still going through his tired mind as he tossed aside the flap of his lodge and stopped to face Snow Fox's messenger.

"Where is Snow Fox?"

The messenger said, "He will be honored to know he is invited to your council," and got away before Crazy Horse could correct the impression.

Crazy Horse was a very big man, well over six feet and over two hundred twenty pounds. His face was slab-sided like an ax and his eyes were slanted thin. His hair started far back on his high forehead, making it seem higher. He wore no ornament or beads, but his breechcloth and leggings were of the finest calf elkskin exquisitely tanned and his moccasins were lined with the white winter fur of the mink.

War Bonnet waited silently while Crazy Horse sized him up. War Bonnet was one of the first among the Dog Soldiers. He and Crazy Horse had fought together and couseled together and even danced the sun dance together.

Snow Fox arrived and greeted his kinsman with the outraged dignity of a broody hen.

War Bonnet spoke. Snow Fox spoke too. War Bonnet referred to John Slocum as "Owl Child, our

Blackfoot ally," and Snow Fox called him "the white Blackfoot who calls himself Owl Child"—a distinction not lost on Crazy Horse.

Crazy Horse was a very great warrior and had killed more men than his friend Sitting Bull, but he didn't share Snow Fox's attitude toward whites. Whites, Crows, Blackfeet—to Crazy Horse they were all the same: opportunities for a warrior to test his mettle, his lance, and his skills. Sitting Bull didn't trust the whites, and his plans all demonstrated that fact. Crazy Horse didn't care much whom he fought. He didn't think he'd ever run out of enemies.

Usually, any chief called in to arbitrate a dispute between two warriors was inclined to make peace between two offended and deeply touched men. Many of the Sioux chiefs preferred peace within the tribe. Ways could be found, compromises discovered.

Crazy Horse wanted to know what Owl Child would fight with.

"He would fight with the long gun," War Bonnet suggested. "Such a course is fair since Squirrel has a fine Hudson's Bay musket and has fought with it many times.

Crazy Horse barely restrained a snort. "Many times he has fought with it and yet he has killed no man with his fine musket!"

Snow Fox put it more kindly. "Though Squirrel has shown his bravery on many occasions with his musket, he wishes to meet this white Blackfoot more closely. Face to face."

"Yes," Crazy Horse said. "I understand."

So did War Bonnet. Squirrel had one rare proficiency among Indian braves. From childhood he had learned to handle knives—first the flint knives that children play with and, when he became a man, he wore, always, two steel knives. It was said among the Sioux that no hunter could skin an elk faster than Squirrel with his two flashing steel knives. War Bonnet said, "Hand to hand, man to man. Wrestling to the death. That most honorable form of combat."

Snow Fox sneered. "Squirrel does not wish to touch this enemy with his hands."

"Owl Child is no fighter with knives."

"The white Blackfoot insulted us gravely. Insulted all our family."

Crazy Horse wasn't going to give the Loon people all the edge. He figured maybe he'd give them this much and they'd quit pestering him, so he put on a solemn expression and said, "That is justice. That the insulted party choose the weapons."

War Bonnet was doing some very fast thinking behind his mask. Choice of weapon was strong medicine. But the killing ground, that could make a difference too. He figured Squirrel had a couple of inches reach on John Slocum, but wouldn't have the stamina. "We will fight by the Stinking Springs," he said.

Snow Fox didn't want that spot. Crazy Horse didn't think it made any difference. With a curt movement of his hand, he finished all discussion. "It is my decision that this Owl Child and Squirrel settle their differences with knives at the Stinking Springs. They will fight the fight of many cuts."

The refinement Crazy Horse added to the fight between the two men was simple but pretty well canceled the advantage War Bonnet had won with his choice of ground. The two men would fight with a length of bridle rein between their teeth. The first man to loose his end of the rein would forfeit his life to his enemies' kinsmen standing on the sidelines with notched arrows.

Crazy Horse made his favorite clear when he said, "Tell me, Snow Fox, will Squirrel fight like a man?"

"He will fight." Snow Fox's face swelled with pride. The old man had waited a long time for this sort of intimate chat with his greatest relative. "He will strive to be worthy of you, Crazy Horse."

Crazy Horse's reply was genuine. "But how can he be worthy of me?" he asked. "How many braves has he killed? How many times has he counted coup?"

When Squirrel's miserable tally was related, Crazy Horse got annoyed. He'd been bothered for a trifle. It would not have been a trifle, of course, if two great warriors were to fight, but between Squirrel and some half-breed trader the fight wouldn't be worth watching. Two men killed. No coups counted. Indeed. Crazy Horse showed his relative out, making vague promises to honor the boy after he won the fight. He turned to War Bonnet and said, "And is this Owl Child a great warrior?"

War Bonnet smiled. "Did you know the Loon people have a Cheyenne shaman advising them?" he asked.

"Should I care?"

War Bonnet shrugged. "They are your family."

Crazy Horse wriggled his great hawk nose. He looked like a hawk imitating a rabbit.

"Owl Child is the greatest of the Blackfoot warriors!"

Now, that interested Crazy Horse. The boast was too large to lack every element of truth. "Bring this Owl Child to me. I would speak with the greatest warrior among the Blackfeet."

Despite himself, Slocum was curious. He hurried to meet the man known to have killed over fifty men. Inside the lodge he inclined his head with a slight nod. He signed his name and his band.

"But that band has been murdered by Seizers," Crazy Horse said.

"Yes."

"How then are you from Two-Medicine's band?" Crazy Horse asked.

Slocum shook his head. "How many bands does a man belong to?" he asked. "They are all dead, and now I fight all their quarrels. My wife and daughter were killed by Seizers."

A tiny spark of sympathy appeared in Crazy Horse's odd flickering eyes. "Why do you fight Squirrel?"

Slocum raised his head and locked eyes. "His challenge. He did not offer enough for the woman I speak for."

"Woman?" Though the Loon people had planned the marriage to Opal Duffy to avenge the slight they thought Crazy Horse had put on their honor, he hadn't heard a word about any of their actions or the reasons for them. Slocum told him the whole thing.

Crazy Horse frowned through most of the recital but didn't ask any questions until Slocum got to the point where Snow Fox offered five horses and a burro for the girl, "to redeem the honor you took from the Loon people."

Crazy Horse interrupted with a laugh. He laughed until the tears ran down his face, and he hiccupped with the effort to stop. When he found his tongue again he said, "All this is meant to redeem my honor?" He wiped his eyes with the back of his hands. "Oh, my."

"I didn't ask for this fight," Slocum went on.

"You turned down that many horses for a white girl who isn't a proven worker? What makes you say you didn't ask for this fight? Will you kill Squirrel?"

Slocum shrugged. "Depends."

"The weapons are knives. You'll fight where the ground is very slick and muddy. Neither of you will be able to get away from each other because you will have a length of leather between your teeth."

Slocum thought about knife fights. There was that Comanchero trail driver down in Arizona territory and, of course, he'd used the bayonet a couple times during the war. The war had been twelve years ago. "Is he good with a knife?" he asked.

It was Crazy Horse's turn to shrug. "So they say," he said. He stood up to signify the interview was over. Standing, he towered over John Slocum. His smile was fairly fierce. "I will come to watch you fight tomorrow when the sun is low in the sky. If you die, I will watch you die." He meant this as a very great compliment.

"Yeah," John Slocum said sourly. "I hope you get your damn eyes full."

War Bonnet was very interested in Slocum's report of Crazy Horse's doings but sighed when Slocum's account was done. "He did not grant us anything. I hoped he would change his mind. Wrestling—that would be fair. You could have strangled each other," he concluded on a cheerful note.

John Slocum sat cross-legged in front of War Bonnet's fire and inspected his bowie knife bought new and untested from the sutler at Fort Lincoln. Yeah," he said. "Wrestling would have been better." He turned the knife in his hand. The original knife had been designed by Colonel Bowie as a pure fighting knife. Until the bowie came along, every knife on the frontier had to serve a variety of uses, from skinning a deer to cutting a man's throat.

The bowie was a slightly shorter version of the old Roman sword with the addition of a gutting tip that made the point look like a dead pike. In a pinch, the thick brass guard separating the haft from the blade might protect the hand by turning an opponent's blade. No matter what the handle was made of, the bowie's balance was forward. The bowie Slocum was turning in his hands had a ten-and-a-half-inch blade. The blade was marked "Unwin and Rodgers, Sheffield" and bore the legend "Rio Grande Camp Knife." The blade was stout enough to split a hambone and it did take an edge. As a butcher knife it was entirely satisfactory. As a fighting knife—well, it'd have to do. He found his hone, oiled it, and began the long process of making the blade razor-sharp. It wouldn't hold the edge, of course, once Squirrel's steel began scraping against it, but even a dull knife can kill a man.

War Bonnet watched and listened to the soft burring sound of scrape and whisk. After a bit, War Bonnet withdrew his own knife from its neck sheath and tossed it at John Slocum's feet. His toss was good and it landed flat. Slocum picked up the blade with two hands, holding the edge free. War Bonnet's knife was a Green River knife, and on the widest part of the blade it had the maker's name and home state: Massachusetts. The blade was shaped like a modified bowie. The tip was a dagger point. But it had the bowie's blood groove and the heavy tang to disengage an opponent's knife. The Green River knives had been famous for twenty years since the first mountain men began to favor them. The steel was excellent. It wasn't easy getting an edge on them, but once it was there the knives would cut anything. "Squirrel fights with two knives. You should carry two knives."

Slocum nodded thanks and went back to work on his bowie. At times like these it was good to have something to do with the hands.

The fight would be at sunset at the Stinking Springs, and Slocum ate an early lunch though he didn't feel like it. He wouldn't want to have much in his stomach in case he got cut.

Once he had his bowie sharp as he wanted it, Slocum wanted to sleep for an hour or so, but War Bonnet wasn't having any.

As the fight got near, warriors gathered outside War Bonnet's tent, arguing and betting on the event. These were War Bonnet's own Dog Soldiers. Since Slocum was War Bonnet's friend and since there were no provisions in custom for a Blackfoot to fight a Sioux, Slocum would fight Squirrel as a Dog Soldier. This entailed certain obligations. Slocum objected.

"Owl Child," War Bonnet said with a touch of his usual grin, "these preparations are supposed to strengthen the warrior before a time of great trial and prepare his spirit for the shadow land if it comes to that. You may disbelieve if you wish, but the Dog Soldiers are very great warriors and it is what they do."

So Slocum said "All right" because he didn't want to insult his only friend.

On the upper reaches of Pumpkin Creek two sweat lodges were side by side above where the horses grazed and the women drew water. As he approached, in the midst of a bunch of chanting Dog Soldiers, Slocum recognized Snow Fox and the Cheyenne shaman outside the southernmost lodge. The Cheyenne was having some kind of argument with a Sioux shaman over the medicine needed.

Snow Fox glowered at the approaching mob of Dog Soldiers, and the Dog Soldiers returned the favor.

"What in the hell is this?" Slocum objected.

"We have a fine shaman," War Bonnet said, indicating a Sioux dressed for the part. "He has strong medicine."

Both men stripped. War Bonnet was openly curious about Slocum's body, reading it like a map of a dozen old battlefields. War Bonnet was broader through the chest than most Indians, sort of slab-sided. Like Slocum he had some fairly nasty wounds, healed long ago. He had been treated about as well. The worst was a lump where a broken rib had healed crooked, pushed out against the skin. With no embarrassment, War Bonnet touched the entry scar of a bullet that had nearly killed Slocum when he rode with Quantrill in Kansas. One of Quantrill's men had put that bullet through him. "Huh," War Bonnet grunted. The goose pimples stood up on Slocum's skin. He wasn't accustomed to being graded like a beef carcass and said so.

War Bonnet grinned. "If you have survived those wounds, you can survive more," he said.

"Thanks." The two men ducked into the sweat lodge. The lodge was shaped like an upside-down basket. A tiny vent at the roof peak and the flap of the doorway were the only openings. A crockery bowl was the lodge's centerpiece and some balsam branches its only household items. The roof of the sweat lodge was low and the big men were almost sitting on top of each other. A fire glowed, mostly coals now and stones the size of an apple, glowing red.

With iron tongs, War Bonnet dropped a couple of stones into the bowl of water and they whooshed as they lost their heat, and the steam cloud took Slocum's breath away. The lodge was very hot and already the sweat was running on Slocum's arms.

Outside, the Dog Soldiers started their chant, their "Ai, ai, ai, huh, huh." The Dog Soldier's shaman provided a running commentary above and beyond the chant. He spoke not of victory, not once, but only of courage. Victory could belong to the lucky. Valor belonged to the honorable. The shaman spoke of legendary Sioux heroes. He spoke of warriors who brought the lightning down from the sky and warriors who went into the underworld after the buffalo when they disappeared that time, a hundred generations ago, before the white man came. He spoke of men who were legends and of legends who may have been, at one time, men. He spoke of them familiarly, as if he'd known them all his life. The Dog Soldier's shaman didn't deny they were afraid. He spoke often of the coyote who runs to deceive and turns back to confuse his trail and laughs at the foolishness of the wolf, who can only fight and die. Many of the great Sioux warriors had doubts. None of them gave in to doubts. Some of the warriors were victorious. Others, like Roman Nose, died in their prime—killed by a fluke bullet.

John Slocum was dizzy. War Bonnet was chanting the same chant as the chorus outside. Like Slocum's, his body was glistening with sweat. With all that moisture in the air, Slocum's mouth shouldn't have been dry, but it was. Slocum imagined the sweat lodge next door. He imagined Squirrel was getting the same purification treatment, though the chants supplied to him would be Cheyenne stories—stories he only half understood— like the gossip in the family about remote cousins. Speaking of which, Slocum was thinking, Crazy Horse could have provided a real Sioux shaman for Squirrel if he'd wanted to—the best of the bunch—old Sitting Bull himself. Unless Sitting Bull was beyond this sort of thing these days.

War Bonnet waved a balsam wand and tapped Slocum's chest. It stung, though War Bonnet wasn't putting much force behind it. Slocum was surprised how easily rage came to the surface at those inconsequential stings. Slocum didn't know whether lungs could sweat but hoped so because his were being asked to. The chant outside had become background noise, a throb, and the shaman's stories echoed in Slocum's head as if he were whispering them to himself. The man sitting across from him, so close, became a blur in the mist except when he swatted Slocum's chest. His chest began to burn. War Bonnet wasn't just striking skin but the heart directly. Slocum was thinking about brave men, good and bad, and why they were. He'd ridden beside a few brave men. James Butler Hickok, in Missouri, when Slocum was a boy. Hell, Hickok had shown one dumb kid how to shoot a Colt and fight a war, and then it turned out old Hickok was a Yankee all the time. Bill had been a damn spy but he was brave enough for four men. Or Cole Younger. All Quantrill's bunch were crazy brave, indifferent to whether they lived or died, and Coleman Younger was the toughest of them all. Slocum found himself wondering what had happened to Cole after the war. He'd heard Coleman had been locked up somewhere. He and brother Bob and the James brothers had tried to rob some two-bit bank and been shot to pieces by irate citizens. Minnesota. Northfield, Minnesota, was where it was. Coleman wouldn't like prison too much, you could bet on that. The chanting was the sound of his own heartbeat. The scratches on his chest were the little buds of blood opening and closing inside his own heart, and he wondered, idly, why he couldn't see War Bonnet or the inside of the sweat lodge. His lungs took in the deep essence of the forest, so aromatic he could almost smell the scent of the mule deer and the fox under the shade trees. Slocum wondered how long he'd been blind and how it had happened. He wondered idly, as a man might wonder where and how he'd gotten the minor scratch he discovered in his bath.

Slocum had never had a medicine dream and never danced the sun dance. He'd sat in the Blackfoot sweat lodges a time or two. His body told him he had enough. Without willing, he got out of the sweat lodge, and outside he was struck by the sun right across the eyes, half a blow, half a benediction, and he ran to the edge of Pumpkin Creek and found himself suspended in the air above Pumpkin Creek in a dive. The creek was fed by icy springs but it was warm to him, like slipping his body into a warm glove. Puffing, blowing, John Slocum dived and surfaced, playing in that shallow creek as an otter plays: somersaulting, touching the gravel bottom with the flat of his hand, spewing water and steam from his lungs. The Dog Soldiers on shore were wordless, though a couple still shook bone rattles. When War Bonnet came out of the lodge, he didn't go into the water. From this point on the warrior was on his own. His guides had done what they could, but War Bonnet couldn't even enter the same water as John Slocum without altering the efficacy of the chant. He located a wooden whistle and blew on it, high and shrill: the call of the diving hawk. It was enough to set a man's teeth on edge, but John Slocum thought it was a perfectly natural and rather innocent sound.

When John Slocum came onto shore, he noticed he had a tremendous erection, and that seemed perfectly natural to him too. Slocum paid no attention to the second sweat lodge where Squirrel's Cheyenne was trying to work his magic. With the sweat already drying on his body, War Bonnet dipped briefly in the river.

Squirrel's shaman's chant had begun off-pace somehow, like a heart that squeaked, and it was a little unnerving, a little irritating, and when Squirrel dived into the creek he splashed like a fat trout thrown back because it is full of eggs and must be allowed to spawn.

A few seconds later, Snow Fox emerged from the lodge, his body glistening with sweat and his chest lacerated where he beat himself with the balsam wands. Odd.

Because it wouldn't be fair, War Bonnet climbed out of the water without a word to Squirrel, who was splashing around, clumsily, no natural swimmer.

Slocum climbed into his own pants again and his boots. War Bonnet looked his question. "My feet ain't tough as yours are, partner," Slocum said.

Preceded by four men with rattles and two with small drums, Slocum and War Bonnet made their way through the heart of the Sioux village. Everybody in the village knew of the challenge. The procession was slow and deliberate, and it made Slocum feel like a damn bride, purified before the altar. He walked as slow as his beaters, one long step after another, and neither acknowledged nor returned the hundreds of stares that followed the small band of slow-stepping warriors. Behind him War Bonnet walked shaking a bone rattle rapidly, making a sound like the whir of a timber rattler. In between whirs, he cried, "Owl Child is the greatest warrior of all the Blackfeet and has counted coup so many times he has forgotten the count. He has never run from an enemy and never deserted a friend. Come watch a brave man on a fine evening. Come watch how Loon people die." The procession was taking the long way about and passed directly in front of Crazy Horse's lodge, which certainly wasn't in the normal line of travel. Here the procession paused while War Bonnet shouted his boasts and even elaborated them a bit. In a while, the lodge flap fluttered and Crazy Horse himself came out and looked them over. He showed no particular emotion until War Bonnet got to the part about "how the Loon people die" and then he grinned. His teeth were sharp, short, and low in his gums, and it looked like a wolverine grinning at them. Crazy Horse walked around eying John Slocum from every angle. Slocum didn't give a damn. He was thinking about something else. Crazy Horse whistled softly. The procession moved off to War Bonnet's lodge.

Slocum sat cross-legged while War Bonnet's wives applied the warpaint. On each cheek, three broad diagonals: two red and one white. The broad strokes across his forehead were white as bone. One of War Bonnet's wives daubed his arms with a blue band like an arm bracelet, and another traced deep inverted V's above each breast in the same color.

Slocum wore his bowie on his left hip. Around his neck in a soft sheath he hung War Bonnet's fine Green River blade.

The chanting ceased. Their religious function finished, the Dog Soldiers were wagering with all comers. They were more than usually loyal, and many horses were offered up and many horses were wagered against them.

"Well, my friend," War Bonnet said at last. "Are you ready to fight Squirrel for this woman?"

That brought Slocum's eyes back from the nice place where they'd been. "For Opal? Me, fighting for Opal?" And he laughed then. He laughed very loud, and the watchers outside the lodge heard his laughter. It was like the bark of the solitary coyote across the plains at night, and one or two who were no less courageous than their fellows shuddered.

John Slocum passed through the square of light at the entrance of the lodge. A great many warriors voiced their murmur of approval. Slocum didn't pause long enough to hear the individual voices.

He strode toward the Stinking Springs, guided again by War Bonnet, who was hurried more than he thought proper. Slocum was like a locomotive hurtling toward an accident and looked neither to the left nor the right.

Squirrel waited for him. He was very tall—that was Slocum's first impression. His hands hung emptily at his sides. His eyes were very large and very brown. His warpaint was the same colors as Slocum's but instead of the Dog Soldier's V's and slashes, he wore a variety of circles, on his cheeks and chest and back. Both his knives were on his right hip, and Slocum thought that was a good sign. He couldn't have stood a chance against a two-handed fighter. Slocum let his eyes learn what they could from his enemy as he walked toward him. Squirrel didn't flinch. He was perhaps ten years younger than Slocum and in fine condition. Though he didn't carry Slocum's weight, he did have the reach. Slocum came at him like a stock dog approaching a bull, slow and easy, using his eyes every step of the way. The crowd that meant to watch this fight came hurrying behind him. The kids hurtling along pell-mell, hoping to get close enough before the grownups took all the best spots.

The combat was to be fought in a circle, fifty feet in diameter, just below the springs. The ground was grassless, black, and greasy.

All stopped. Both parties had to wait on the pleasure of the Sioux chiefs. Sitting Bull had declined to put in an appearance because, as he said, "Indian killing Indian is nothing I have not seen before. It will make the white men happy to hear of it."

Crazy Horse was under constraint to come because it was his kinsman fighting. Rain-in-the-Face came with him because he was fond of slaughter.

While they waited for Crazy Horse to arrive, the braves reexamined the two fighters. Once again, horses were wagered, and pelts, and weapons. Snow Fox wagered everything he owned on his son, all of the horses he had meant to give as Opal Duffy's bridal price.

Crazy Horse and Rain-in-the-Face took their places at the edge of the circle. War Bonnet and Snow Fox raised their arms to the heavens, and Slocum and Squirrel crossed the fifty-foot ring toward each other. Slocum's boots sunk in the soft ground, a good four inches at each step.

The strap that was to connect them had been specially woven of four rawhide thongs, each eight feet long, braided together for strength and elegance. Snow Fox handed one end to Squirrel. War Bonnet passed the other end to John Slocum, who took the rawhide between his teeth and clamped down on it like a vault door closing. He drew the bowie with his right hand but kept it point down.

Squirrel's teeth seized the rawhide and, with a complex move, his hands went to his right side, then his left, and back to his right. Both hands were very graceful, and a tingle found Slocum's spine. Squirrel's hands were a little too fluid for his tastes.

War Bonnet and Snow Fox backed away. At the edge of the circle they cried out, "Huh," and that was as good a signal as any.

Connected by the long thong, the two men circled each other, comfortably out of reach.

There's a gunfighter's move called the border shift. When the right-hand gun is empty, it's exchanged for the left-hand gun. It's an intricate play and only the best get it down right. Squirrel did a border shift with his matched knives. One second they were both in the air, then they settled again.

Slocum felt a touch of hot sweat along the back of his neck. He stayed low in his crouch, his left arm across his body to block.

Fast as a fencer, Squirrel struck, his right-hand knife going for Slocum's throat like a hurled thing.

Slocum's left arm swiveled like a latch, brushing the Squirrel's knife arm so that it passed behind him. In that instant his own knife came up and around, and if Squirrel hadn't retracted as quick as he'd struck, Slocum's bowie would have opened him like a book.

It went that way for a few minutes. Squirrel's attack, Slocum's block and riposte. Gradually Squirrel opened his arms and began to fight wide. The ground slowed them down. Though War Bonnet had meant the best for Slocum by specifying the muddy ground at Stinking Spring, he hadn't counted on Slocum's boots, which stuck in the clay mud more than Squirrel's unshod feet.

Squirrel got around better and he had the reach. As the fight continued, his knives came closer to Slocum's throat than the white's came to Squirrel's belly. The bettors were backing Squirrel now. War Bonnet's face was impassive, but he wasn't feeling too good. He felt as if the knife that would shortly lodge in his friend's belly had already lodged in his. The back of Slocum's arm was sore from deflecting Squirrel's lunges, and he had plenty of leg tension from forcing his balance, but otherwise he was doing all right. Squirrel jumped toward him—frog-jumped, landing wide open with a knife in each hand, and Slocum dropped to one knee in the mud as Squirrel's left-hand blade cut out a path through the air where his belly had been just a second ago. Slocum hoped Squirrel would overbalance from the swing but he didn't, and the right-hand knife came back like a windmill, only aimed lower. Slocum lunged up like a cocked spring to meet it and heave the slighter man on his back, but the mud ruined him. His leg slipped and the two of them embraced and went into the mud. As they fell, each of them was going for the other's knife hand. Slocum landed on the side of his face and the damn rawhide nearly jerked his teeth out.

Slocum turned loose of his bowie and his hands were claws as he scrabbled for the slighter man's back. He brought his knee under the other man's chin and lifted Squirrel right off the ground. Squirrel landed on his back with the rawhide between his teeth and mud in his eyes and over his knife blades.

Slocum's hand sped to the knife dangling from his neck, and the fine steel of the Green River knife flashed in the sun. His blade found unprotected flesh. Slocum dealt him the worst blow he could. The Green River knife slipped into the thin skin behind Squirrel's muddy heel and Slocum slashed up, hamstringing the man. Squirrel's right foot flopped around like a loose extra. Squirrel could not walk. He got to his knees, though, his knives in front of him.

Suddenly, John Slocum felt vulnerable; he was so much taller than his enemy.

Squirrel began singing his death song. Without dropping the leather strap from his teeth or lowering the Green River knife in his hand, John Slocum gave his crippled opponent time to make his peace. The words of the death song were simple and repeated over with slight rhythmic and melodic variations. "Old Fathers, I am coming home to you now," that was what Squirrel sang. His father, Snow Fox, hadn't seen the thrust that hamstrung his son and only knew that he rested on his knees like a woman at the laundry rock and sang his death song. Tears ran down his father's face as he shouted, "Rise and fight! It will be time to sing your death song when he has killed you! You are no son of mine! You are no Loon warrior!" Slocum waited, knife ready.

Squirrel sang the death song through once and again. Without ceasing his song he invited John Slocum to come.

John Slocum got to his knees and waddled toward

his opponent. A gasp arose from the assembled warriors. To give away such an advantage as Slocum had! The two men circled, neither able to do much in the mud, on the points of their knees. They shuffled like old men, clockwise, then counterclockwise, tied together by the leather thong. Slocum saw Squirrel working his one good leg and read the sign of attack. Crabwise, they moved, and each time Squirrel's good leg was in a position to thrust, it trembled and his hand trembled too.

Squirrel sprang. He launched himself toward John Slocum with two knives in his fists and a scream on his lips. Arms raised, he bowled the white man onto his back and obscured him from everybody's sight. No one could tell who'd scored because of the mud splash. Squirrel's skin tented up, just behind his right kidney. The mud-covered skin tented up and a knife gleamed briefly as it came out his back.

Snow Fox said, "Ohhh!"

Several of the Loon people groaned out loud.

When John Slocum rolled out from under the man he'd killed, he was smeared and daubed with mud. He had mud in his hair and his face was muddy—quite obscuring the war paint. He glowered at the assemblage of warriors.

War Bonnet said, "Hoo-hah!" in a voice that spoke his triumph. Slocum's bettors started collecting. Slocum bent and rolled the dead Indian onto his back. Only the haft of the Green River knife was visible where he'd impaled himself with his last leap. When Slocum pulled the blade out, a spout of blood shot two feet into the air. Just the one spout, no more.

"I am honored by Squirrel's death," Slocum shouted. "I am honored by his courage. It is an honor to kill such a great warrior as he was!"

Snow Fox's face was stone. He shrugged off his supporter's arm and stared impassively at his son's dead body. John Slocum knelt in the mud beside the dead body, and with the same razor-sharp Green River knife he set the tip under the edge of Squirrel's hair and tore his scalp loose, braid and all. He was a Blackfoot warrior, Owl Child, and he had killed.

Snow Fox twitched as if he meant to come forward. The Cheyenne shaman shook his rattle. He was the first to step into the fighting circle where each skid and slide was indelibly marked and where the last of Squirrel's blood lay like oil on the mud.

The scalp dangling from John Slocum's hand was muddy. Squirrel's skull was bone white and trickling blood.

Slocum lay down in the back of War Bonnet's lodge for a rest. No, he didn't want anything to eat and he didn't want any herb tea either. Maybe he should have had the tea, because when he woke up a couple of hours later, his mouth was bone dry and his head felt like popskull liquor. When he sat up, it was worse. War Bonnet's first wife handed him a bowl of tea. The smell of it was enough to make Slocum heave on the spot, but it wasn't so bad once he got some of it past his tastebuds, and it landed on the sickness in his stomach like a warm poultice. He took a deep breath. His headache lightened some, though it'd rest behind his eyes for a couple of hours. He blinked and drank more tea. He spoke his thanks, and War Bonnet's first wife offered him more.

"No, ma'am," he said. "This foul brew is just about enough, if you don't mind." She shrugged. His affair. She called his attention to the rack by the fire where a pair of braids hung, suspended over a wooden crosspiece.

Slocum remembered. "Oh, Jesus," he said. His headache returned. The heat from the drying fire was ruffling the tips of the braids and they swung as if they were still alive. Slocum looked away.

War Bonnet burst back into the lodge. "Ah, sleepy warrior. No wonder you are called Owl Child—because you sleep during the daylight hours. Six horses!"

"Six horses!"

"I have won six horses. Four of them are poor

horses," he admitted judiciously, "but two are fine spotted ponies!"

Slocum didn't feel up to the elaborate courtesies that were required, but the braids twitched again in the warmth from the fire and he had to give it a try. "Only a great warrior can help another great warrior," he began.

War Bonnet preened. He beamed.

"And it was your knife that killed my enemy," Slocum went on. "I would have been lost without it."

War Bonnet was pleased as a cat in the sun.

"I must give you a great gift," Slocum continued.

War Bonnet didn't refuse. "One great warrior can give."

The headache was throbbing. He gestured toward the drying scalp.

War Bonnet's face was shocked. He cocked his head as though he hadn't heard the offer quite right. Then his nostrils flared. His eyebrows drew close together. "We have been friends," he said very slowly and very deliberately. "We have been friends and you are a great warrior."

Slocum started to ask, "What the hell?" but War Bonnet flagged away his objections. "Do you offer the scalp of a Sioux warrior to a Sioux warrior?" he hissed. He was very upset. He stood up. He paced back and forth before the fire. "I have Blackfoot scalps," he said. "I have Seizer scalps. Would I honor you by offering them?"

Slocum bowed his head. That damn headache. "You are my brother," Slocum began.

"You have been my brother," War Bonnet corrected him. "In the morning, you will sleep in some other lodge or with your white women. We are brothers no more."

Slocum saw no more of War Bonnet until that evening when the Dog Soldiers gathered at the medicine lodge to honor Owl Child, successful warrior. They honored him as a Blackfoot or Sioux would have been honored, with the recital of all their deeds from the least famous among them to the very great warriors. Generally, the beginners just touched on the high points of their careers, but the more famous warriors were allowed a little more latitude, taking five or ten minutes each to detail the raids they'd been on, the horses they had stolen, the coup they had counted, the famous warriors they had killed. When War Bonnet's turn came, just before the guest of honor, War Bonnet became unaccountably modest. Since the evening of boasting built quite naturally to the peak story of the man who was to be honored, War Bonnet's sudden aversion caused attention.

"I'm a great warrior," he began. "I have killed so many Sioux enemies I have forgotten them." He laid a lot of emphasis on that word *Sioux* and sat down as soon as his brief speech was done. It created silence. The Dog Soldier's shaman was as puzzled as any of them at War Bonnet's rectitude, but it was his job to keep the show moving, so he boomed out, "We ask Owl Child to tell his story."

He meant for Slocum to recount the fight that afternoon as he alone had seen it. Indian courtesy would punctuate the tale with ohh's and ahh's of admiration.

Slocum's head was pounding, and each time he looked at War Bonnet, he felt sick. "The knife of War Bonnet. . . ." The lodgepoles seemed to rotate around him. Standing, the smoke from the musty fire was bad, and it was hard to catch his breath. "The knife of my friend, War Bonnet, killed Squirrel," he said. And sat down.

The murmurs that traveled the room were puzzled and fairly annoyed. Slocum had ended the party in his honor with this brief speech and War Bonnet hadn't encouraged general hilarity either. The men shook their heads and shrugged. The shaman was half angry but got back to his feet. If a warrior did not wish the honor due him, that was his right.

The lodge door flap opened for the Loon people to file in. Technically, the medicine lodge was for everyone. In practice, the chiefs and big shamans used it unless a warrior wanted to meet all together, like to-night. Ordinarily, the Loons wouldn't have been expected to attend, and a few hands went to weapons as the nine members of Squirrel's band filed in, followed by Snow Fox and, finally, Crazy Horse.

Slocum got up. He wasn't sure why these men were here, but he had something to do with it.

It was tense—the two warrior societies face to face and not enough room between them for peaceable intentions. Crazy Horse, with a few gestures, made the gestures a polite man would have made on the outside of the lodge before crashing in. "All honor to the Dog Soldiers of the Sioux nation," he said with one hand in the hail of peaceful intentions.

The Dog Soldier shaman replied in kind. "All honor to the great warriors of the Loon Society."

"Of the Sioux nation," Crazy Horse added softly.

"Of the Sioux nation, yes," the shaman repeated, puzzled.

Crazy Horse seemed to have gotten what he wanted because he turned to Slocum then and greeted him with the sort of smile a hungry man extends to a thick steak.

Slocum didn't like the look of things. "The Dog Soldiers are great warriors of the Sioux," Crazy Horse repeated.

Not to be outdone, the Dog Soldier shaman murmured some phrases about the great warriors of the Loon people and that Crazy Horse was the greatest of any of them.

Crazy Horse modestly admitted that truth. He noted his cousin, the brave who'd been killed that very afternoon by a Blackfoot warrior.

"First time I ever heard you claim kin," Slocum muttered under his breath. He was still dressed Indian fashion, with one knife at his side and the other in a sheath around his neck. He wished he had a couple of Colts. The medicine circle wasn't twenty feet across. A couple of Colts could do a lot of damage in that little space. Well, he'd have to do the best he could with the hog stickers. He probably could tag a couple anyway. They'd get in each other's way trying to get to him.

"The Loons claim their due," Crazy Horse said, pointing at Slocum.

"You already tried once," Slocum said. "You could always try again. If you're such red-hot warriors as you claim, maybe you could take me on one at a time." Slocum didn't have a hope of setting conditions, but he thought he'd try.

The Dog Soldier shaman gave him his only chance. "War Bonnet. I have heard you say this Owl Child is your brother."

War Bonnet's brow furrowed deep and he glared at his feet. "How can a Sioux have a Blackfoot for a brother?" he asked.

Wordlessly, Slocum withdrew the Green River knife and tossed it and the sheath in the dust at War Bonnet's feet. It was so quiet everybody heard it hit.

"The Loon Society seeks satisfaction," Snow Fox said. There was a hint of great stubborness in his voice. "Crazy Horse advised us."

"Then why don't me and him meet," Slocum snapped.

Crazy Horse gave him that same hungry smile. "I would enjoy that," he said. "You would not."

"No," Snow Fox explained. "It is we who are directly injured. We have lost a son and many, many horses. Crazy Horse has given us his horses to do what we must do."

Slocum kept mum. It didn't sound like they were going to kill him in the next ten minutes. That was the best he'd do.

Snow Fox continued his explanation. He spoke like any man who'd lost his only son. "The honor of the Loon family . . ." he began. "It was marriage that would restore our family honor."

"Squirrel is dead," the Dog Soldier replied.

"But the white women are alive," Snow Fox replied. "They are friends of the Seizers. The Loon Society will kill them."

Slocum snarled, "What honor is there in killing women?"

Crazy Horse just smiled.

"None," Snow Fox said, speaking to Slocum. "You are a great warrior, and if the Dog Soldiers are not your people, these women are your people."

"I see. Well, come ahead." Slocum drew his remaining knife and wished he hadn't been so generous with the other one.

The warriors in the medicine lodge reacted to the knife with shock and horror. No man drew steel on another in the medicine lodge. It was defilement.

Only Crazy Horse was unfazed. "No. You will leave our village at once. We will give you a start, Owl Child, before Loon warriors follow. Make your run."

8

Laura Duffy stabbed her fork into a mess of bully beef and pulled it to her mouth. She didn't taste a thing. Literally, not a thing.

As was their habit, they ate dinner shortly after sunset and went to bed not more than an hour later. They said it was to make the most of the daylight.

"Where is Mr. Slocum?" Opal asked. She made a mound of bully beef and skidded it around her plate.

"Stop that," Laura said. "Mr. Slocum has gone to negotiate with the Indians. He means to convince them you will one day take a—" She coughed. Something caught in her throat. "A husband of your own race."

"I don't want a husband."

"You will. Eat your bully beef."

The girl took a taste and looked revolted. "Why do we have to eat this all the time? For supper and dinner every day. Every single day!"

"It is what we have."

"If Mr. Slocum was here, he could shoot us something and we'd have something besides canned stuff to eat. I'm sick of canned meat."

"I'm sure Mr. Slocum would eat what was put before him," her mother said serenely.

The girl put her chin in her hands. "I wonder what it's like to be married to a Sioux Indian."

Her mother shuddered.

"I'll bet it would be exciting. We'd get up on our horses and ride like the wind. We'd swim in high waterfalls and we'd go to places where white men have never been before. Maybe I'd be famous. I'd do for an article in *Godey's Ladies Book*." The girl traced the outline of that publication with her hands, 'My Life

166

Among the Hostiles,' that's what I'd call it. There'd be a picture of me in my Sioux jewels."

Though she hadn't taken more than three bites of dinner, Laura returned her plate to the dry sink, where she scraped it clean. The dry sink faced a closed shutter. Though it looked like a wall, it was much thinner than a wall and she could hear more through it than she wanted to. A horse nickering. Another horse nickering. Probably her own poor horses. She said, "You'd marry Squirrel? I don't believe I've seen a neck that long on a man before, though I believe they're quite common on the African giraffe."

Her daughter giggled. "Oh, him. Well, if I had to marry a Sioux I wouldn't pick him. I'd pick some big chief like Sitting Bull."

Her mother shuddered again. "I saw him once at Fort Tullock, when the commissioners were trying to get him to sign the treaty. You know what he looked like? A moth-eaten buffalo."

Her daughter put her hand over her mouth and giggled. "It would be like sleeping under a great old buffalo robe," she ventured.

Laura Duffy was half shocked. Her daughter was becoming a woman and had no one else to confide to and had an ordinary healthy interest in sex. That's what she told herself, though the color went right to the tip of her ears. She looked away.

Some owl was hooting outside. Laura said, "Why don't you go get my shawl. I feel a chill." Opal whined, but obeyed. Laura scraped her daughter's plate. Tomorrow, like every morning in the past six months, she'd take their uneaten food down to the meadow and dig a modest hole and bury it. It had been something she'd figured out by herself. The edge of that meadow was cratered, like the surface of the moon.

Opal startled her, she came in so quietly. Laura snapped, "Don't you ever do that!"

The owl hooted its mournful hoot, the searching, hunting sound.

Laura took the shawl and wrapped her shoulders.

"What about Mr. Slocum, Ma?"

"I venture to say we'll be hearing from him any day. I do believe he will be successful and we shall take a short holiday from our labors here."

"Fort Pierre?"

"Perhaps St. Louis. Without your father's guidance . . ."

"Is Daddy really dead?"

Laura's mouth was hard as the mouth of General Grant's statue in St. Louis's main square. "Mr. Slocum spoke with Thomas before he passed away," she said.

"How do we know Slocum wasn't lyin'?" Opal whined.

"Why would he do a thing like that?" Laura hoped the horses settled down soon because she didn't want to go outside tonight when there might be a rattle snake among them.

"Maybe he wanted to get us on the trail alone to ravage us and rob us."

"You look like you'd enjoy that," her mother commented.

The girl's face turned from her mother. "Maybe I would, at that!"

"Opal!"

"I thought we were going to stay right here," Opal said stubbornly. "You told Mr. Slocum. I remember."

Laura was calm as a white swan. "That was before I'd thought, dear," she said. "Although we have a great deal invested here, we need the army's protection." Laura didn't tell her daughter about the nights she lay awake, her joints so stiff with terror she feared they'd lock and she'd never walk again. Laura didn't tell her daughter how frequently she slept with her hand in her mouth lest she scream. How many times the howling had sounded like a Sioux warrior creeping up on them. Rape would be the least of it. They would be raped many times and tortured and killed. Laura Duffy knew what awaited them at the hands of the Sioux. She'd go back to St. Louis.

"Will we return?"

"Of course, dear." She hadn't the slightest notion.

"I don't care if we ever come back," Opal said. "I hate it here."

The owl called a third time, nearer now. Laura's "Yes, dear" was mere sound, devoid of meaning.

Laura and Opal and her husband had painted the thick pine shutters green as a finishing touch. Something shiny pushed its way through the shutters. Right through the crack between the second and third board. At first the shiny thing came in silently, but swelled toward the base and squeaked. She watched it, dumbfounded. The shiny thing wiggled. The knife blade was twelve inches long and had plunged right through the shutter of her house, and it moved as if it was searching. She gasped.

The girl couldn't see what her mother saw but didn't like that gasp, and when she got to her feet, she knocked over her chair and didn't bother to right it. "Oh, no."

The knife blade was intelligent. It had a will of its own. It slid up the shutter until it met the top cross-piece and then down again until it cut into the bottom cross-piece. It wiggled. It wiggled around until it could whittle a long strip from the edge of the boards, and it did so. Laura put her hand over her mouth. The knife made noise: *scree, scree, scree.*

A crash at their front door released them from their terror.

"It's Indians," Laura said, though why she spoke was hard to tell. Some instinct to get everything right. "Opal, to the storeroom!"

The Sioux worked the front door of the roadhouse, smashing the heavy panels out with war axes of Hudson's Bay steel. Though the door was stout, no door will stand up long to that kind of treatment.

The brave at the kitchen window sought the latch with his knife tip but wasn't finding it. He heard the women scream and was glad to hear it. They'd followed the white Blackfoot from the camp on Pumpkin Creek, only two hours after he pulled out himself.

Crazy Horse said to wait until morning, but Snow Fox and the rest of the Loon people were very angry and told Crazy Horse that he could speak for himself.

Crazy Horse gave them horses from his own band. Two horses each for the nine warriors who meant to ride the Blackfoot down.

"He will go directly to his women," Crazy Horse had advised them. Although Crazy Horse was not going along, he was a famous warrior and they needed his advice.

"Why would he go to the women?" Snow Fox had asked.

"Because he is too brave," Crazy Horse replied. "That is how you can kill him if you will. Remember that he is too brave."

Of the Loon Society band, only Snow Fox believed Crazy Horse's words, and he was so tormented by grief for his dead son, Squirrel, that he was almost incoherent. The Cheyenne shaman was in charge of the band until the old man recovered, and he gave the orders to ride out. Snow Fox was mumbling something about reclaiming his son's hair so he would not be shamed going through the shadow land. War Bonnet was the only brave in that camp who knew Squirrel's scalp was in his own lodge right then. Since he didn't mean to tangle with the entire Loon people, he didn't say a word but vowed he'd toss the damn thing down a prairie dog hole first thing in the morning.

Nine warriors rode out behind the Cheyenne shaman. They had Crazy Horse's finest horses, six repeating rifles: three Spencers, two Henrys, and one 73 Winchester, for a wonder. It was the newest rifle in the Sioux camp.

Three men had good stout bows, and one of them carried a Hudson's Bay musket.

The man who owned the musket also owned the long sharp skinning knife that was probing through the shutter. He hadn't heard Owl Child's voice inside and presumed that he had tricked them and gone the other way. The white women feared they would be raped by the Sioux. The man working the boards apart thought their fear was very funny. "A man could also fuck a maggot," that's what the Sioux said about braves who went with white women. They were bad medicine and Squirrel hadn't understood that, and that's why the young chief lay on his litter tonight with sightless eyes and his other wives were gashing their arms and slitting their noses and wailing. There was no honor counting coup on women, so these warriors meant to kill, then fire the roadhouse and ride. There wasn't enough moon tonight for tracking Owl Child, but there'd be plenty of time to pick up his sign as soon as the first light.

His long skinning knife split one of the planks apart. He heard a scream inside. This brave knew Crazy Horse was wrong for once, that the white man had ridden past this roadhouse like a thief in the night.

The brave broke the plank inward. Three axes smashed against the front door.

The shutter swung outward, a perfect rectangle in the night. It was bright inside from the whites' oil lamps. The brave got one knee over the window sill.

The Sioux didn't usually fight at night because a man killed then would get lost in the shadow land and not be able to join those who had gone on before. If they'd seen Slocum's horses in the corral, the Loon people would have waited until morning.

The front door looked like a bone a dog has been working on, split top to bottom. Now the Sioux were kicking the planks loose at the bottom. Other Sioux waited outside in the corral, silently facing the house. Killing these two white women was beneath these men's dignity, so they dealt themselves out. The first warrior squeezed just inside. The guest parlor was black as the ace of spades. There were no lamps and all the shutters were drawn, and when the gun flashed, the whole room lit up. The gun flashed again and the Indian was hurled against the wall, where he hit a sack of wet laundry, his life hammered out of him.

The flash was visible inside and out, and the sound

of a Colt's bark was distinct. The two warriors who'd reduced the door to kindling stood stock still, unable to make up their minds. The brave who'd gone inside hadn't said one word before he died. One of the braves at the door stuck the muzzle of his Spencer carbine inside the door crack, fully intending to search the room with bullets. His rifle came alive. It twisted suddenly in his grasp and away. A moment later he stared as his Spencer disappeared into the blackness. He made a startled grab as the walnut stock and steel butt plate vanished, but was too late. It was as if the gun had never been.

That did it for the two of them. They jumped back from the doorway with a hell of a yell and ran for their horses at the hitchrail.

When the brave in the kitchen heard the gun blast in the front of the house, he was thrilled. What had been a duty slaughter without honor became a chance to kill the warrior who had slain his kinsman, Squirrel. The brave had been inspecting the storeroom door (fastened from within), but at the shot he wheeled and, with his knife held low, stalked toward the front of the house. He made no noise.

The Sioux slipped down a hallway festooned with empty coat hooks. He moved silent as a ghost, heel to toe. Though there wasn't much light in that interior hall—mostly from the kitchen behind him—his eyes took in what there was and used every bit of it.

He was young—not yet twenty summers and in his prime. He'd killed three men, two in single combat, and the death of this Blackfoot, Owl Child, would honor him. His nostrils whiffed as he stepped through the far door, ready to jump left or right, slightly bent, his legs cocked. The smell of the scorched black powder was very strong. It made his eyes water and he squinted against it. Another smell too. The familiar rich stink of fresh-shed human blood.

"Bound for glory," John Slocum remarked ruefully before he dropped the hammer. He stood in the far corner of the room, screened by the fireplace, and his Colt was extended like a duelist's weapon. His voice had warned the brave and he started his move. Didn't get far. Like a rising quail, he jumped right into the bullet that took his life. He rose for another foot or so, but he tipped over one of the benches and lost control of his bowels, bladder, and knife.

John Slocum stepped over his body and started to the back of the house as the Indians outside jumped their horses and rode out. Some warriors were cranking rounds at the house and every one of them had a threat to make, but their blood wasn't up and Slocum thought that'd be the end of this play.

He worked the broken shutter closed and relatched it. He took one of the kerosene lamps from the wall sconces and, lamp in hand, searched the house carefully because he'd known a few men who'd lie doggo to reach an enemy's unprotected back. He set the lamp down and rapped sharply on the storehouse door with the butt of his pistol. "Don't shoot, ma'am," he yelled. "It's me, John Slocum." He reloaded his Colt.

While he was popping new caps into the Colt, the door swung open wide enough to reveal frightened eyes. Opal preceded her mother.

"Well, now, Mr. Slocum," Laura said.

"You came back! You came back!"

Slocum slid a fresh charge into the cylinder. "Yes, ma'am," he said to either or both.

"The Indians. . . ." Laura shuddered and the shudder shook her whole light body. "They meant to . . . rape us."

Slocum didn't think so, but it wouldn't do them any harm to believe that.

Opal eyed the dark hallway as if it were forbidden fruit. She stepped cautiously in the darkness.

Laura was saying something.

"Excuse me," Slocum said. "Hardest thing about a gunfight indoors is the damn racket. I can't hardly hear a thing except my own ears ringin', and if you want to say something, you are going to have to shout."

She shouted, "What now, Mr. Slocum?"

"Yes. I suppose that's about the truth of it."

"Mama. They're dead!" The girl's voice broke into a scream.

Slocum winced.

Laura started toward the front but stopped herself. "Yes, and a good thing they are, my dear. Is either of them your lover?"

"Wha . . . ?"

"Squirrel? Is any of them that Squirrel?"

"Mrs. Duffy, Squirrel met up with some bad luck."

"He's hurt? Injured?" Her smile said she wished he were.

"Worse luck than that," Slocum said.

"Good." She clapped her hands. "You can't kill too many redskins to suit me."

The girl came into the kitchen, hands held out before her. They were covered with blood and she wouldn't look at them. "Please pump me some water." She was one step this side of hysterical. The pump squealed and she had Slocum pump more water when her hands were as clean as they'd ever get. "They're both dead," she said.

Slocum gave her a funny look. If this girl was as squeamish as she seemed, she was living on the wrong side of the Missouri. "You'll have one hour to pack," Slocum said. "I mean to ride out of here tonight."

"Tonight? Why so quickly?"

"Because the Sioux won't be expecting it, and if we wait until morning, it's open season."

"But can't you kill them?"

Slocum grinned and scratched his head. "Or vice versa," he said.

"You brought this attack on us—is that true?"

"I suppose you could say that."

"You practically invited them to come into this house. You led them right here and then you hid. Sir, you are reckless."

"I suppose you could look at it that way if you had a mind to. But all I wanted was those Indians' horses.

Wait'll you see what is tied outside at the hitchrail. You won't mind those dead Indians then."

Laura's nose was high enough to spear a passing cloud. "I doubt that, sir. I doubt that very much."

She went to her woodstove and opened the grate and rattled the embers into something a little hotter. "Camomile tea. My stomach is delicate, sir."

"Fine. You just brew your tea while you ready to go."

"Must you always play the brute?"

"Mrs. Duffy. Opal. In one hour I'm ridin' out of here. You can come or go as you elect. I can pack provisions for one easier than three, and I imagine the traveling will be faster too."

Laura Duffy had her back up. "Well, sir, if that is how . . ."

"Ma! For once don't be so pigheaded."

Her daughter had never spoken so harshly or directly before, and she only knew she didn't like it. "Opal!"

Opal put her hands on her hips, "Ma, if you ain't goin' with him, I am. You heard. In the morning the Indians will be at us again. If you need remindin', take a walk into the parlor."

That took the wind out of her sails. She put her head in her hands. "This is our home . . ." she said softly.

Her daughter relented and patted her mother's arm. "It's okay, Ma. You just rest a spell. I'll help Mr. Slocum load provisions."

So Slocum and the girl sorted out goods from the cases in the storeroom while Laura Duffy sat quietly at the kitchen table. When her water boiled, her daughter put a spoon of tea into the pot to steep.

Slocum passed goods to the girl, who made room for them in the pack saddles. Slocum kept up a running commentary. "Soap? Well, we can wash our dishes in sand, so two bars ought to serve us. . . . Beans are always welcome. We'll skip the beef. . . ."

The pack saddles bulged with goods and he took

them outside one at a time. The dead Indians' ponies were still tied up. They weren't especially happy to see him and didn't get happier when he turned them into pack animals.

Slocum figured the Sioux were watching his every move. He didn't care.

He saddled his Morgan for the mother and an ex-cavalry horse for the girl. "Warm clothes," he said. "Some warm wrap and your stoutest shoes. Heavy socks if you have them, and if you own boots it would be better. Dress for the high passes."

He gave his final instructions, speaking soft and low. "I don't believe they'll try and keep us from leavin'. Snow Fox has two warriors lost in the shadow land tonight and won't want to lose any more. They'll figure to track us and kill us tomorrow."

"Mr. Slocum?" It was the girl, Opal. "If I'm to be captured, will you, will you . . ."

"Kill you? You'll have to get your mother to do that," Slocum said harshly. "I don't figure you own anything more precious than your life."

Opal looked like she was going to cry, but she gave her horse a kick in the ribs anyway and the small party moved out.

The clouds skidded across the narrow moon and the night changed from brightness to darkness every few seconds. Slocum moved into the lead. The Sioux would sure as hell fight if they rode right over them. He picked an angle that'd carry them wide of the best sentry positions.

He kept his reins between his teeth and a Colt in each hand. He kept both hands below silhouette level because he didn't want to provoke something if he could help it. He rode at a slow walk, giving the Sioux plenty of time to get out of the way. He hoped he'd read it right. The odds were seven to three, and these Loon soldiers were fine fighters. His horse crossed the patches of moonlight beside Mizpah Creek. Slocum holstered one Colt and kneed his horse into a canter. The two women and the packhorse picked up the pace.

Slocum rode down the riverbank, leaving plenty of sign for the Sioux to find in the morning. Twenty minutes downstream from Mizpah Creek he drew rein and waited for his companions to come alongside. They could see the flash of his teeth in the dark, but the rest of his face was shadowed. "So far, so good," he said.

Mrs. Duffy pointed across the river. "That way lies the line of forts and civilization and home."

"Yes, ma'am."

"And the river before us is shallow and the enemy are behind."

"Yes, ma'am."

A note of gaiety in her voice: "Well, then, sir, shall I take the lead?"

"No." When he adjusted his hat, his eyes flickered at her like distant lights. "We ain't goin' that way."

She cocked her head like a sparrow, questioning him, because that was how she had always questioned Mr. Duffy, God rest him. But the strange rider was too rude to heed her unspoken query.

Swiftly he dismounted to check lashings on the packhorse. One good hard tug satisfied him. His uptilted face was like a shiny plate in the moonlight. "Now we're gonna need a lot of luck. You just follow me and my horse. I'll try to pick a route without too many holes in it. Don't let your horse get all nervy and don't go to talkin' between yourselves. If you know any good prayers, now's the time to pray them." Without further ado, he rode his horse into the shallow stream and the Indian packhorse followed, tied behind. The two women rode side by side.

A shallow gravel bar provided fairly good footing for the animals. Though Slocum eyed the banks suspiciously, he saw none of the signs of a quicksand. The bar wavered from one bank to another. On the bar the water was only two feet deep, but it shoaled on either side and Slocum followed the thin ribbon of the bar, twisting like a milk snake under the water.

They went upstream. Back the way they came. The

moon skidded through the clouds like a polo pony.
The light went from bright to dark, and the cloud
shadows hurried across the river. Slocum kept his
Winchester in the scabbard. Out here they were sitting ducks and he didn't want to think about a gunfight. His horse stepped off the bar into a hole and
went to its withers, thrashing. Slocum urged it, and
the horse found better footing. The water pattered below the horse's belly and the legs made their steady
swoosh through the water. The horse didn't like it.
Slocum's own animals were high-spirited, and the two
women weren't the world's most skillful riders. His own
horse was unused to him and unhappy about going
where a boat should have gone, and Slocum kept his
head down and a firm hand on the reins. From time
to time he leaned over beside the horse's neck and
muttered. Getting acquainted.

The western shoreline was a mottle of blacks and
grays. Sometimes Slocum saw a beach; more often
trees came right down to the waterline. The moonlight
on the river was brighter than shore and Slocum felt
like they were on a stage: an execution stage.

He heard Mizpah Creek before he saw it, just a
faint babble, a higher-pitched sound than the river
made. He reined up and waited for the women. When
they were at his stirrup he leaned so his mouth wasn't
more than two inches from Laura's Duffy's ear. "Keep
the horses quiet. If they let the Sioux know we're here,
we're done." Then he dismounted, knee deep in the
chilly water. His animals were more likely to signal
to their old buddies than the other horses, and he
wanted to be where he could clamp their nostrils when
he had to.

The Sioux were somewhere on shore. Maybe the
Sioux had gone into the deserted roadhouse by now.
Maybe they were asleep or already following the trail
Slocum had laid to the river. He hoped like blazes
none had a notion for a moonlight swim.

There wasn't much wind and he was thankful for
that. No telling what the Sioux horses would do if

they got a whiff. Indian ponies weren't faulted for kicking up a ruckus at odd smells or noises either. He kept his hand on the packhorse's bridle across the bridge of its nose and walked slower. The hair on the back of his neck was prickling and he felt that old familiar weight in his stomach, as if his dinner had congealed into stone. The girl, Opal, was far the better rider of the two women and rode ahead, seeking for the elusive bar. The water was more turbulent at the mouth of the creek and Opal lost the bar and made a bad guess and her horse went into deep water. It splashed up on its front hooves, churning the water like a side-wheeler. The slight young girl sawed the reins to the side and leaned at a tremendous angle to give her more leverage. Slocum could see the muscles bulging in the horse's neck and its hooves splashing the water like ten beavers panicking in unison. She got back to the bar and flashed Slocum a look of apology and despair. He raised his hand to stop and the three of them waited in the middle of the river for a full five minutes. The only sound was the water drops spattering off their horses' bellies and the cheery, foolish babble of Mizpah Creek. Slocum raised his hand again and they resumed their journey. Slocum's legs were awful damn heavy and his pants were full of water; he'd been a damn fool not to take them off. That was a gentleman's mistake, and hell, he was no kind of a gentleman. That's what he was thinking as they rounded the bend and the sound of Mizpah Creek faded behind them.

Slocum held them to the center of the river for another quarter-mile before he pointed at a nice gravel beach and the horses climbed out of the Powder River with real relief. Slocum felt it too. The stone in his stomach was gone. Once he was on shore, he took the time to go through his saddlebags for dry pants. He got into them with only his horse screening him from the ladies. He was fairly annoyed at himself. He made plenty of mistakes of his own without making the other man's too.

When the three rode away from the Powder River,

John Slocum held to a course slightly south of west. He'd want to give the big village at Pumpkin Creek a wide berth. The three rode in silence for a couple of hours before Slocum called a halt.

"Grain your horse, loosen the cinches, but don't unsaddle. My own animals won't stray during the night, but I expect the Indian ponies will need to be tethered."

"Mr. Slocum." Laura Duffy swung stiffly from the saddle. "Since there is moonlight yet, why don't we continue riding?"

"Ma'am. If one horse steps in a prairie dog hole, then we'll have no packhorse. If two horses step in prairie dog holes, one of us is gonna have to walk." John Slocum was already spreading his soogans. As he bent to pull one boot, a wave of dizziness hit him, strong. He was damn near tired enough to fall and he sat down to remove his boot. "What did you say?" he asked.

"Opal and I will sleep together on the far side of the horses. Decency . . ."

"Sure." He tossed his boots where his head would lie. They'd make a dandy pillow. He was thinking that as his head hit them, and then he was asleep.

The next morning the Cheyenne shaman rose from his blanket feeling better than he had in days, as if strength was flowing directly from the fat sun to his body. He stretched and stroked his masculinity with a sense of wonder at how young and hard he was. He tied his loincloth and leggings. The Loon people were camped in a loose circle behind the roadhouse. The shaman stretched, casting a long shadow over the sleeping bundles of men. A couple of the bundles moved because the presence of a man was enough to wake them. He strutted to the bank of Mizpah Creek and after drinking he took a piss in the water. Haw! He felt fine! He felt like the victor in a long fight—not like a man recently defeated. Not even the sight of Snow

Fox's face back at the circle dispelled all his enthusiasm, though he restrained it as much as he could.

Snow Fox blamed the Cheyenne shaman for his son's death. The shaman's magic was too weak and the white man's knife had found Squirrel's life, and the shaman owed him, Snow Fox, his life. Snow Fox hated the shaman, but a man uses the tools he has at hand, and the Loon people had no shaman of their own. This was their fight, not every Sioux's, so they couldn't use one of the Dog Soldiers' medicine men. Snow Fox's eyes were bleak when he looked at this Cheyenne. He saw a young, short man with tremendous power through his torso and arms. The shaman's name was Deer Wrestler because in his medicine dream he saw himself throwing a fawn over his knee and breaking its back. The Cheyenne's name was known perfectly well, but Snow Fox referred to him always as the Cheyenne.

The Cheyenne nodded his greeting and Snow Fox replied to it with a nod short enough to be insulting. Snow Fox had three sons, and all three had died as warriors. Squirrel, the youngest, was the last to die. Snow Fox had had great honor from his three sons, but he would find no campfire to take him in and warm his bones when he got old. The green-eyed man called Owl Child had taken his only chance for the time when he would be too old to fend for himself.

The Cheyenne noticed the new lines in Snow Fox's forehead and the sad gray cast to his face, and though he seemed to remember the older man having many laugh lines, he couldn't see them now. "Good morning. The sun blesses us this morning."

Tight-lipped: "We shall see."

Without orders a couple of braves had already disappeared from the circle to search the roadhouse for trifles.

"Two women to slow him and us with the finest horses Crazy Horse has!" The more Snow Fox disapproved, the more the Cheyenne wanted to show him the brighter side.

"Yes. Two of those horses were ridden by Loon people, yesterday. We mourn them today."

"Perhaps we can mourn Owl Child too."

The old chief shrugged. "Perhaps." He walked away from the Cheyenne. He extracted a chunk of pemmican from his parfleche. It was his breakfast, this hard blend of dried berries, nuts, and venison. He chewed on it thoughtfully, looking off into space.

The Cheyenne had been dismissed like a child. The Cheyenne cared. His own life had been a struggle to achieve the kind of visions and insight that comes to other shamans very readily. Often mere warriors, like Crazy Horse, seem to have better medicine than he had. His father had been a famous Cheyenne seer named Walking Dog, and as a boy, when other Cheyenne were hunting rabbits or playing at warfare, the Cheyenne was working charms and forming amulets. Each man's medicine is his secret name.

When the first dustings of hair appeared at his groin, the Cheyenne went through the coming-of-age ceremony with three other young men. The three were purified for several days. A medicine man whispered knowledge into the boy's ears. The Cheyenne's own father had whispered to the boy, and since he was such a great shaman, this was considered an important gift.

For two weeks the Cheyenne fasted in the wilderness, alone, naked on a high rock shelf in the Crazy Woman Mountains. Near the end of his stay he had his dream —the dream of the fawn—and when he returned to the camp and told his dream, he was named. With his own hands, his father fashioned the medicine bag that he'd wear around his neck for the rest of his life. His father took a tail of a fresh-killed fawn and some dry leaves from the healing plant and the fingerbone of an enemy and put them into the little buckskin bag. That was his medicine bag, his name, his future, and his best chance. At the battle of the Greasy Grass he took a brass cartridge that lay beside the rifle of one of the dead Seizers because it glistened like the foolish

metal white men seek. He added this cartridge to his
medicine bag, the first addition he'd made to it since
his father gave it to him. It felt wrong, and he'd been
happy to get rid of the brass case with the magic he
used against John Slocum. Slocum turned the tables
and the Cheyenne blamed himself. He was afraid he
ruined his medicine by adding to it with the brass
cartridge. Otherwise, how could Slocum have bested
him? Otherwise, how could his chants have been in-
effective to protect Squirrel from the white man's
knife? Like everything else in the world, medicine
can change, and the Cheyenne prayed it would change
for the better. When Slocum's scalp hung from the
end of his lance, his medicine would improve again and
he would be the man he'd been.

In two or three days they would ride the whites
down. It was a journey of two weeks to Fort Pierre
and the Sioux would overtake them before they reached
safety. The Cheyenne figured they'd catch up to them
close to the spot he'd tried buffalo-skull magic on
Slocum. Somewhere near there.

Tumult at the roadhouse. Three or four of the Loon
braves had gotten into Laura's clothing. One had her
carefully preserved wedding dress hanging from his
shoulders like a cape. Another was real proud of the
bright red pillbox hat he wore. Whenever the veil
flopped down over his face, he brushed it away.

A single shot sounded inside the kitchen, muffled by
the shutters. The Duffys had made them rich and very
happy. They cavorted around the corral in finery, firing
shots in the air.

Like the Cheyenne, John Slocum felt pretty good
that morning. Both the women were already awake,
shivering under a single blanket. Between clenched
teeth, Laura Duffy complained, "In the future we must
have a decent heating fire."

"No. Make sure your horses are fed and then eat
some of this damn hardtack. It ain't fit for hogs, but
this morning we ain't so particular as they are."

When Slocum swallowed the last of the brittle rye

cracker, he said, "Ladies, let's ride. Every mile we put between them and us is a chance of life."

Delicately, Laura dabbed at her lips. "But surely, sir, we're traveling the wrong way." She pointed east. "Fort Pierre is that way."

"Yes, ma'am. Fort Bozeman is west of here and there's soldier boys still in residence. That's where we're riding."

"But, Mr. Slocum, I wish to go to Fort Pierre."

He shrugged. "Suit yourself. If you get to the Missouri, bear right and you'll run into it directly." His horse started walking and the two women had to hurry to catch up to him.

A half-hour later he heard the shots. Unconsciously, John Slocum picked up the pace. The Loon Society would be riding after them now, and it was an awful long damn way to the safety of Fort Bozeman.

If the Sioux rode all day and late into the evening, they might overtake the whites—particularly if they'd been unlucky and lamed a horse with night riding. Once the dancing and hollering had gone on for a while, the Cheyenne approached Snow Fox. "Will you tell your warriors to mount? The whites are farther away with every instant."

Snow Fox watched his warriors dance. "Leave them be," he said. "This is their first victory."

The Cheyenne sulked and made his horse ready for travel, but he waited until Snow Fox gave the word. Men torched the women's clothing and set it against flammable walls and doors. They left bodies of their dead comrades inside the burning building. Flames are not a bad way to travel to shadow land. The fire got hot and pushed the shutters open. The cans and bottles in the storeroom began to explode, followed by some ammunition. Finally, the twenty-gallon kerosene keg went up with a hollow boom.

Then Snow Fox gave his orders for the braves to ride. They were still terribly excited, and when they rode out of what had been Duffy's Roadhouse they were hollering and shouting.

With no difficulty they followed the trail the whites had made last night. A column with Snow Fox and the Cheyenne in the lead and outriders fifty yards to the left and the right. They hit the water where Slocum had entered, full tilt, throwing up a tremendous splash of water, ki-yi-ing their way across. Every Sioux knows there are two ways to search when an enemy uses a stream to cover his tracks. Either you send careful men up and downstream to find the spot where he has emerged and pick up the trail there or, if you're feeling lucky, you guess what he has in mind and ride accordingly.

Here's what the Cheyenne knew. And the Cheyenne was important because until he was totally discredited, he was in charge of this hunt. The Cheyenne knew that the white Blackfoot traveled with four horses, two of them unfamiliar, and two women who were not great riders and couldn't stand a hard pace.

The Cheyenne knew that the nearest fort was Fort Lincoln, abandoned since one moon ago. The next nearest was Fort Pierre, downriver. There might be army patrols on the Missouri, sidewheelers perhaps, and the whites might try to connect with those. The fastest route to Fort Pierre or the Missouri was southeastern. Downstream from the spot Slocum's party entered the water. Slocum might have tried to throw them off the track by going upstream and proceeding east, but the Cheyenne knew—he knew—Slocum hadn't.

When the Loon people pelted out of the water, the Cheyenne shouted and waved his hands, signaling for them to ride left, downstream toward the Yellowstone. The riders yipped and yelled as they swung. Automatically, the outriders spread out farther and a third outrider joined them. They'd be unlikely to miss the whites' tracks no matter how carefully disguised.

Their horses were fresh and the braves were hot for blood, and they tore away down the riverbank like banshees. They didn't bother to ride quiet. They were the Loon people. God spare those who crossed their path, because the Loon people surely wouldn't. The sun climbed up and dried the water clinging to the horses' tails and manes. The outriders hung on the sides of their ponies, closer to the rushing ground.

The Cheyenne began to feel bad. He caught himself. They wouldn't have come out of the river so soon.

The Sioux thundered downstream, their horses eating up miles. The lead horses were shiny with sweat and still they galloped. The Cheyenne was putting himself in the white Blackfoot's place. The white Blackfoot would have ridden all night just to throw them off, hoping the Sioux would turn back before the place where the whites came out of the river. All night in the river. You couldn't ride a fast walk through the water, and it'd be awful hard on the horses, but Owl Child—it was just the sort of thing he might try. The Cheyenne thought of the red wolf who waits outside a prairie dog's burrow for hours, motionless. The prey appears and then the sky goes black. That was how Owl Child fought. The Cheyenne started picking out landmarks ahead, saying to himself, "They must have come out by the big rock." Or "They couldn't have gotten so far as those alders." The Cheyenne began to feel worse, and none of the Loon people were hollering anymore. Snow Fox slowed the pace to a trot. No sense ruining their horses. The Cheyenne's pony had a gallop smooth as butter, but all its slower gaits were rough and the animal commenced to jolting him. The Sioux continued downstream for another half-hour before, reluctantly, the Cheyenne raised his hand and halted them. He spoke to the chief loudly enough so others would hear. "They cannot be farther downstream," he said. "We have covered more than the distance the whites could have. Either they came out upstream or we missed their tracks from fast riding. I think we missed their tracks because that is the kind of cunning this white Blackfoot shows." His face was set in very stubborn lines and the outriders' angry protests didn't change matters. They said they would have seen any such tracks. The whites must have gone upstream.

"Why would they put more days between them and safety?" the Cheyenne said reasonably enough.

There was no reading Snow Fox's expression. "Huh," he said. "We will find their tracks."

Thus ordered, the band reversed direction, moving very slowly back upstream. They spread themselves out. There are many tricks to cover a man's passage, and the Sioux knew every one of them. Knew about tying brush behind your hoof marks to brush them over. Knew about hopping from rock to rock or hard slab to hard slab. They looked for brush marks. They searched for the marks of steel hooves on rocks. Two riders stayed very close to the river looking for rocks that had been upset by an emerging rider.

Now the sweat dried on their horses. Now the sweat dried on their bodies. Now their eyes narrowed into squints because they rode into the eye of the sun, where tiny shadows could deceive them. They were very, very thorough because they were ashamed at having missed the tracks, and often a man would dismount and inspect the ground with his fingertips when he saw something unusual. They found plenty of tracks. Buffalo tracks, fresh and old mule deer tracks, the tracks of a bobcat family and one cougar. They found their own tracks, and in a soft spot under an alder tree they found tracks of a shod hoof. The soil was moist and it would hold the outline of a horse's hoof for a very long time. They finally decided this single track had been left by a wild donkey because they found no others and nothing passes through the world without leaving sign of its passage.

At noon they had worked their way back up to the mouth of Mizpah Creek.

Snow Fox pointed angrily across the river. "We have made no progress toward these whites," he announced.

That was perfectly obvious. The Cheyenne's face

was gloomy, and a vein was jumping in his temple. Some of the braves stopped to let their animals water, and that angered the Cheyenne because he hadn't given an order that anybody should water his horse. "They are upstream!" the Cheyenne said. "He has tricked us. He is cunning and a devil, this white who killed Squirrel!"

Snow Fox winced. He had meant to take some pemmican nourishment but suddenly had no appetite. "Six hours," he said. "Six hours' lead they have."

"We are getting no closer," the Cheyenne said.

Snow Fox gave the order and the band struck out upstream, spread out searching for tracks. No more hollering or shouting. The men kept their eyes on the ground and dismounted whenever they saw anything out of the ordinary. The idea of disguised tracks had become an obsession, so they rode even slower. They were slow but certain. As the miles wore on and they approached the badlands, the old chief's spine got stiffer and stiffer and the color mounted to his neck. They rode ten miles upstream. When he was satisfied the whites hadn't come this way either, Snow Fox drew up. The Loon people were tired and disgruntled and their eyes weren't too good. "They came out on the west side of the river."

"Perhaps they mean to circle around us."

Snow Fox didn't dignify the speculation. He snorted and jerked his pony's head around so fast the animal's eyeballs clicked. "Hyah!" Angrily the Loon chief went into the river. He didn't look for a ford and his horse's belly crashed a great flurry of water and the others followed him. He was an old man. Yesterday he had lost his son and today he'd lost today. His horse was scrambling up the cutbank. He hated the Cheyenne shaman. He would kill the shaman. Though the Cheyenne was younger than he and had great strength, Snow Fox had no doubt he could kill him. He would not count coup. That would be too great an honor. The sky was clouding over and tonight or tomorrow it would rain. He kept his horse at a canter, husbanding strength but covering ground too. Once more they rode back the way they came, though now the sun was a good deal lower.

Slocum hadn't made any particular effort to conceal where they came out of the river. Because of a jog in the river, it wasn't more than three hundred yards from where the Sioux had camped last night.

The marks were unmistakable, and Snow Fox came off his horse directly on top of the sign. He studied. Four horses walking due west. No signs of weariness in their stride. Two of the horses were shod, two unshod.

Snow Fox felt some of the heart go out of him.

John Slocum, Laura Duffy, Opal Duffy, one Appaloosa, one half Morgan, one standard bred, and one grulla mustang rode from dawn until dark, traveling across the plains straight as a die. They dismounted every two hours to lead their horses. Slocum kept his eyes on the country around him. They also crossed one sign of a smallish hunting party, not more than four hours old. Slocum said nothing, though he dismounted to test the firmness of the dirt around the hunting party's hoof marks to time their passage.

Opal saw the tracks. Her mother was too miserable to notice anything except her own pain. She was no rider and never had been. Her horse's saddle chafed her legs and her thighs felt permanently sprung apart. The horse's back slapped her tailbone, and when she stood in the stirrups for a change, her horse took that as a signal to pick up the tempo, and the saddle punched her.

The first time they dismounted, her legs felt wobbly and she was curiously euphoric, curiously weak. The next time she dismounted, she'd lost the euphoria.

The sun came up hotter in the sky and she squinted against it. Her daughter had some sort of cap, but she did not. The sweat ran off her forehead, stinging her eyes until she rode with them squeezed shut. She wanted to last until lunch. It was all she could think of. She wasn't hungry, but she'd lie down while the others ate. She'd gather strength for the afternoon.

They crossed Pumpkin Creek a good two hours south of the Sioux camp. Slocum let the horses drink their fill. He threw one glance at the girl and another at her mother. Dropping his own reins, he went to the packhorse and opened a pannikin. He was very careful to fasten the hasp again before he went to Laura Duffy. He helped her down.

"Thank you, Mr. Slocum," she said through parched lips. Her tongue moistened them. "I didn't know you were such a gentleman."

"Yeah. Lie down. Girl, get a pailful of water."

Her shock was slow traveling. "Sir!"

"Lie down under that alder there, in the shade. Girl, ain't you got that damn water yet?"

The girl Opal found herself hurrying with the bucket splashing her legs and hands. It felt fine.

"You gonna lie down or am I gonna knock you down?"

Laura Duffy sat as bidden, like a woman who can't avoid the fate worse than death. She closed her eyes.

She heard a splashing and felt a tremendous shock and opened her eyes inside rough cloth. "Now you take ths cold cloth and hold it to the back of your neck. Honestly, woman, ain't you got no damn sense at all?"

She was very dizzy and the cloth felt so cold it was burning her skin. Her breath was short. Opal removed the cloth and dipped it in the cold water again. John Slocum was hunkered by the stream, resting on his heels. He was thinking that Pumpkin Creek flowed through a wide, beautiful valley that'd hold a good many cows once the land was wrested from the Indians. He was thinking that was what it was about: two sets of folks in love with the same land.

When he went back to the two women, the older was looking better and the younger was tougher than she looked. She hadn't faded, though it had been a hard ride. He opened a couple of tins of tomatoes and plucked one for himself before he handed the cans over. "Eat something. Get something into your stomach besides the water."

Mrs. Duffy was daubing her own face in a nervous, sparrowlike manner.

"Ladies, if you ain't gonna eat them tomato fruits, then hand one of those cans back. I'll oblige them."

As if he'd caught the two of them out, the two women hastily took some juice. It left a red smudge on Mrs. Duffy's chin. She swallowed with an effort.

Carefully, she unbuttoned the very top button of her blouse. Slocum's eyes held no particular interest, but she was painfully embarrassed anyway. "The Indians, Mr. Slocum?"

"Oh, they're behind us, I reckon."

"But surely if you hadn't fooled them they would have been upon us by now."

"Ma'am, I only know one thing about Indians. Don't count on them to do what you would."

When he tugged at his horse's lead, the horse came away from the water readily, so he swung aboard. "That rag you're cleaning your face with is a red kerchief," he said. "It won't do the work of a J. B. Stetson, but if you ain't wearin' some sort of head cover, you'll fall off your horse before dark tonight. And if you fall off your horse, I plan to ride on without you because we are playing a game where each of us has just one chance and I figure I almost used up mine."

On the far side of Pumpkin Creek they began to see the far mountain range the Crows call Chetish and the white man Wolf Mountains. Laura Duffy forgot her pains as they rode down into a vast sea of buffalo grass interrupted only by the slash of small streams. This river valley had been a favorite stop for the buffalo on their annual migration, but because of hunters off the Missouri, the migration had shifted a hundred miles to the east, just on the far side of the Chetish. Now the grass was overlush and so thick it slowed the horses' passage and so rich they ate their fill within two hours. Periodically, Slocum dismounted and led the horses. They startled a band of pronghorns, which bounded away into the distance like golden kangaroos in the green grass. A couple of times the grass bent down to one side for the wake of small animal, though they couldn't see it. The wet bandanna dried and Laura unscrewed the canteen top and soaked it again.

All afternoon they rode without encountering Sioux sign. Slocum wondered what the hunting bands would make of the tracks they'd laid. When the news of shod horses got back to Crazy Horse, would he laugh?

The clouds darkened over the Chetish and Slocum felt a few twinges of real hope. *Gullywasher* was the word in the back of his throat like a prayer. A real rain that'd flatten this grass and make his path impossible to follow. All day long he'd been heading toward the north end of the Chetish. Deliberately he turned slightly more south. He'd cross the Chetish in the Tongue River Canyon. If it rained a real gullywasher. . . .

At dusk clouds of midges and mosquitoes lifted from the tall grass, and plenty of them found Mrs. Duffy's face. Her tired daughter flopped her hat before her face with the slow, monotonous movement of a pendulum. Tick. Tick. Tick. The sun put on its evening show and the clouds above the Chetish were black billowing things, towering like battlements. The sun backlit the tallest of the towers. That sunset darkened the plain early. Laura Duffy nudged her horse forward beside Slocum. Her right hand was raw where she'd gripped the rein. The skin was peeling over her thighs and her head had been snapped around on her neck all day by her horse's motion, and now her face was puffy from bites. "When we stop?" she asked from between swollen lips.

Slocum had his eyes on the shape of the mountain range ahead. His horse was going through the buffalo grass like a boat, parting the deep grass as it passed. Those mountains—they could reach the Tongue River Canyon by noon tomorrow without taking too much out of the horses. If the Sioux rode their animals to death, they might catch them then. If it didn't rain. If it rained, that would be a different story. Slocum squinted. Those thunderheads made the air somewhat electric, and the mountains stood out like they sometimes do. Still, it'd be a real ride to catch them tomorrow by midday. He could see the cut of the Tongue River exit.

"We'll ride until we risk the horses," Slocum said. The woman looked like hell. He wondered if he hoped she made it.

If there was a next life, Slocum figured Warrant Officer Duffy had a few things to answer for. Death followed his greedy foolishness like a scent. First all the Indians he'd murdered and now his own wife. For a moment Slocum had a mental picture of what her life had been like waiting on Mizpah Creek. Waiting. He put the thought away because it would distract him.

"Drink a little water," he said, more kindly. "Ask your daughter to daub some of that sweat and blood off your face. There'll be a cooling breeze along directly."

The moon came up. For a long time it hung on the eastern edge of the world, coy as a schoolgirl, but it lit up the the sky and though Slocum slowed the horses, he didn't stop. He was right about the wind. After a while it started up, fairly gentle but thoroughly washing the day's stink off them and their horses. When Slocum changed his seat he felt his wet shirt cooling on his back. Clouds stretched across the western half of the sky, but above them it was flat blue with stars. The moon wasn't too much smaller than the night before. The thunderheads slid toward them. A man could see them move if he had a mind to, and Slocum kept his eyes on those thunderheads, not on the ground ahead, which was a dark, fuzzy jungle. His horse stumbled. The Appaloosa was a high-stepping horse and recovered right away, but she had stumbled. Slocum turned in his saddle. "We can stop here," he said. He tapped Laura Duffy's leg as she sat swaying in the saddle. "Ma'am? Oh, damn." Tapped her again. "You just come down off there, I'll help you."

She was light in his arms and smelled bad. He left her in her daughter's care while he trampled down a circle of grass for a camp. He wished he could risk a fire. There were plenty of deer beds that might have burned real well. When he came back, the girl had spread a couple of saddle blankets for her mother, who lay with her hand over her eyes. "Take some more blankets," Slocum said. "The thunder's heading our way and the weather's likely to get rough."

Twenty miles behind them the Sioux warriors were watching the thunderheads. They'd made a few more miles than their quarry that day, but they'd pushed their horses hard. They hadn't dismounted since they first set out at dawn, except once when they hauled up long enough to water their animals. When every animal had had its fill, Snow Fox jumped his horse and the others followed like a hive swarming.

First Snow Fox, then his six Loon warriors, and finally the Cheyenne shaman, who rode behind the others. Each man had two horses and each man's horse had been fresh two days ago, and they changed saddles when their mounts tired. The Cheyenne had changed horses three times because he was heavier than most and wore his mustangs out faster.

Several animals got damaged. One mustang cut its hoof slightly. Another swelled up in the hip muscles. One slightly asthmatic young brave began to show the harshness with clearly audible breathing. When Snow Fox heard the boy's awful gasps, his face set harder.

Like Slocum, they rode into the sunset. When the sun's edge finally disappeared, Snow Fox changed back to his original horse, settling harder than he'd meant to. As the light collapsed, Snow Fox was thinking about growing old: childless and dishonored. If he were to slay the Cheyenne shaman, that wouldn't remove any shame but would still his rage.

He wondered if he should try to make more sons. Take himself a young wife. He remembered he had no horses of his own. He would not find another nubile young woman to warm his furs at night. He had no horses. He had no sons. He had shame and two old wives and one female daughter aged about six. The light was gone. One day his life would be gone too. If he met the Seizers, he could die like a man. Perhaps this white Blackfoot. . . . He put the heels to his horse. Far in the rear the Cheyenne shaman kicked his horse when he saw the band pulling away from him and yelled the cry of the Cheyenne when they hunt, a cry like a hawk yodeling.

They rode with no regard for their horses. They rode when the moon came up and when it started its long tour. They rode until the moon dipped under the clouds, winked, and was gone. They could no longer see their enemy's track. They made camp in a dry ravine. One of the braves dug under an alder bush for water. Patiently he waited beside his hole. In an hour the sand had darkened but no more. He put the cool sand on his face. "This feels like my wife's touch," he said. His voice was yearning.

Another said, "Why should the mountain lion follow the teachings of the wolf?" That question hung in everybody's mind for a while.

"You follow me," Snow Fox answered it.

This close to Pumpkin Creek and the big camp, they weren't especially cautious, and one brave gathered sticks for a fire. This brave had a prairie chicken in his parfleche. Snow Fox kicked the pyramid of sticks with his foot. The brave's eyes flashed hot but he didn't do anything about it. That night the Loon people ate pemmican that was cold or cold venison jerky and, in one case, cold prairie chicken.

Slocum thought a beetle had hit his slicker. One of those big black beetles, undertaker beetles. Sometimes they flew around at night. Or maybe it was a moth diving into his warmth. Just the tiniest pat at his shoulder, that was all.

He'd been dreaming hard. In his dream he was riding mowing hay at Slocum's Stand. His daddy was sitting up on the horse-drawn mower and his brother was at the head of the horse and the grass was tumbling in the swath and the sound was bees and the chatter of the sickle bar. Any rain that fell on this hay would dry right with the grass itself and it wouldn't make trouble, but they hurried because they all felt the pressure in their chests from the approaching storm. Slocum walked behind his father watching the fall of the green-headed grass. He had a lead line in his hand, attached behind. It was Bird-Calling, up on his brown and white Appaloosa.

Her face was grave and reserved as if her thoughts were elsewhere, and their daughter was in the crook of one arm, wrapped in the little beaded garment Bird-Calling had made to carry her. Bird-Calling's grave eyes—he'd never noticed their color before, how truly black they were. He knew they were black but didn't know how black.

The tap on his shoulder woke him. The dream faded before his eyes as if it had been painted with clouds. His eyes were wide open. He felt the stiffness of the boot tops under his head and the familiar shape of the pistol butt. Another tap, on his cheek. The thing that hit him ran down his cheek and he knew it was water. He blinked when another raindrop hit him in the eyes and he sat up. His rubberized poncho was proof against this, but nothing else he had was waterproof. Some part of his mind was still thinking about Bird-Calling and the color of her eyes. He wondered why he'd never noticed their color when he'd married her and she'd been his wife. Slocum blinked. Lit by the gray filtered moon, five hundred yards to the west the storm was rushing toward them. Ahead of the main sheet of water the coils of vapor lifted and spiraled and lunged like they were anxious to escape. A tenuous outreach of storm moved past Slocum's right not forty yards beyond, and its passage made the air damp. Already Slocum's cheeks were glistening. He put on his hat and stood up. He was buckling his belt when the wave of water hit and drenched him to the skin. He danced around for a second, fumbling his boots, and wrapped his scabbarded Winchester and Colt in the slicker. The only part of him that was dry was his forehead just under his hat brim, and he was glad he remembered where the women had bedded down because he surely couldn't see much now, not with the rain sheeting so bad. The two women were sitting up, huddled in a mound of drenched blankets. Their hair was soaked and stringy. They were about the same size. The tall grass waved and went flat as the cross-currents of rain knocked into it.

Slocum had the women stand. He unfolded the wettest blanket from their shoulders and made a pad for the three of them to sit on. Laura Duffy's knuckles were white.

"Excuse me, ladies," Slocum said as he unfolded his slicker. "Now, if we wrap this hellacious big piece of rubber canvas about our shoulders, we'll sit this out, snug as church mice. It won't quite make a tent, but it's the next best thing." Laura Duffy didn't seem to hear, but the girl's eyes were bright and she took the other end of the slicker.

"Now, not in no damn lineup. We ain't brass monkeys, you know."

The girl didn't understand and the words escaped Slocum right then, and the water was running down his neck in a torrent and washing the girl's face clear of all personality. She became merely planes and angles; surfaces that repelled water. Slocum took her arms and sat her down facing their back trail. "Here, ma'am, you just sit like this." He flipped the blankets over them and then the slicker to make their little hillock waterproof. That's how they sat, facing out like a threepointed star, resting their backs and heads together. John Slocum had the openings folded across his knees. So long as they kept their knees tucked up, they stayed dry. The saddle blankets were wool. Though they were wet, they'd be good for some heat. "A sudden chill will kill a man quick as a bullet." Slocum said that, though it was already beginning to get warm in their tent. His hat kept the water from splashing his face.

The slicker was tight around their bodies. Slocum tried to make his thoughts return to the color of Bird-Calling's eyes, but he couldn't really remember the color and he felt a mild panic that he would lose her more than he already had. He grunted once, as a man will when he's been struck.

"Sit on a stone, Mr. Slocum?" the girl asked. Somewhere she found a merry tone for her question. Slocum felt her skull against the back of his. He let his head slump forward on his chest. He told his right hand to clutch the blankets tight even while he slept. His guns were beside him too and the powder dry. He felt a buzz through his body. One of the women was asleep a second before he was.

Nobody slept well. Their little pyramid depended on cooperation. During the night Laura Duffy straightened her legs and got soaked and cold. She wanted to lie over on her side and she couldn't because that'd expose her two partners. Opal Duffy's leg cramped and shot out from cover and she twisted around trying to straighten. Her head rang against Slocum's own and he blinked awake long enough to say, "Goddamnit."

The rain fell through the night—sometimes soft, sometimes hard. It was a sleep of drifting images. They each felt the others' bodies, the grumble of the empty guts, the twisting of abused muscles, the tiny moves to ease or change position. The night wore on. Buttocks and legs got sore.

They slept in a miasma of their own farts and stinks and the smell of horse sweat from the blankets. The stink was warm and nobody objected to it.

Just before dawn Slocum fell into his deepest sleep and his head settled like a dead man's.

The sun was full up when his eyes opened, and the fear hit his heart. They should have been traveling two hours ago—as soon as there was light for the horses.

The back of his neck felt as if somebody had clipped him, and his buttocks felt like he'd been trying to hatch a roadbed of sharp gravel. His right hand was shut as if in rigor mortis. He willed it to release its grip and the blankets simply fell apart. His gray whipcord pants were black with moisture and stuck to his legs like skin. His flannel shirt hung out and the sleeves were rolled up over the wrists and the shirt was soaked clean through too. The slicker fell away from his shoulders and off Laura Duffy's own arm. "Mumbug," she said.

Slocum's legs and knees were awful damn stiff, and when he stood up a sharp pain in his lower back told of that bone's objection to mishandling. He shook his head sideways and his hat fell off and his wet hair flapped around. When he stretched, his unbuttoned pants gaped open and a little air tickled his belly, and that felt okay.

"Goddamn," he said, and it was more of a prayer of thanksgiving than a curse. The world was beautiful.

Everywhere he looked around him the storm had beaten the grass flat, snapped the stems, broken the thin blades, and the surface of the grass looked like an extraordinary heap of jackstraws. The night before, their track through this grass was a progress of broken stems and mashed grass—broad and obvious as a roadway. It didn't take a tracker to follow them across the plains; a child could have done it. But now the grass lay down across their track and their passage was covered completely by the passage of the storm. "Goddamn," Slocum said again.

The Chetish Mountains shone in the pale morning light. Their slopes were bare on this side, but maybe they were wooded on top or the far side. In daylight Slocum could see more of the mouth of the Tongue River Canyon. By noon they'd be inside that canyon. The track the Sioux followed pointed irreducibly to the shortest way past the Chetish—the north pass, fifty miles north. Slocum stripped off his soggy shirt and stepped past the horses to take a leak. The horses were a little hangdog but their skins steamed as sun dried them, and they all looked at Slocum when he explained that this was the most beautiful morning in this part of God's Creation. Neatly rolled up in the bottom of his pack he found a clean shirt and a pair of clean gray whipcords. When he took out the shirt, he got a puff of dust, but the shirt looked pretty nice—a Saturday-night going-to-town shirt—blue with pearl buttons at the sleeves. Hell, he shouldn't wear it, but he sure would.

The woman and the girl were up too. When he came around the horse, he gave it a pat on the rump and said, "Good mornin', ladies. Ain't it good to be alive?"

The girl was stretching, but her mother was still wrapped in the blankets of last night. Slocum's voice lost some heartiness. "She all right?"

Opal Duffy had sharp young breasts and her gingham dress was soaked through. She knew he was looking and continued her stretch maybe a mite longer than was strictly necessary. She eyed his broad chest and his tight pants and she blushed and collapsed out of her stretch. "She's better, I think. She said she had to rest."

Slocum nodded. "When you got to answer the call, go downwind of the horses." He pointed.

He faced away from her then and got out of his boots and stripped off his pants and put the dry ones on. The wet clothes had been chafing him pretty bad, but the dry trousers felt like talcum powder on his skin. And they were completely warm.

While he fed the horses, Opal got her mother to swallow some beef jerky. The older woman's gums were bleeding and the girl was alarmed but couldn't see what to do about it.

The horses were fine. At a reasonable rate these same animals could take them well past Fort Bozeman, all the way to the Rockies, and Slocum meant to spare them. The Sioux couldn't track them across the storm-damaged plain, and he felt fifty pounds lighter than yesterday. Still, he took the little oilcloth case out of his saddlebag and spent fifteen minutes checking and oiling his guns. His Colt had a tiny tick of rust at the muzzle, but that was all the damage he found.

Maybe the horses shared his mood. They were pretty cheerful about the day and swished their tails, and

Opal's horse got so frisky she had to bat it between the ears with the reins.

They padded Laura Duffy's saddle. Though she had some color back, she was still poorly and moved like someone who'd been stretched on a rack the day before.

The two women changed clothes behind the horses. Slocum repacked his saddlebags while they changed. The older woman had heavy, short thighs and her ass looked like a satchel. The girl turned around as he fooled with the pack and walked straight to him, and when she got there she looked him right in the eye and said, "I don't suppose you have a pair of dry socks I could wear." Her breasts were young and high and set far apart. She had nipples as big as pencils, and they were taut. She had goose pimples on her upper arms. Slocum deliberately let his gaze travel down her body. "I got socks, but they might be big for you."

"We'll never know until we try," she said.

"I suppose that's true. Dress your mother warm."

"Sure." When she walked away she gave him a nice twitch of her buttocks.

Like their quarry, the Sioux were caught by the gullywasher. When they rode out of the big camp on Pumpkin Creek they'd hadn't thought to be gone for more than a couple of days. They brought blankets for their horses and nothing to make a lodge. That night, Snow Fox and several other Loon people sheltered under the alder bush. Snow Fox had a fur saddle blanket that kept his shoulders warm, but his leather breechcloth turned black and the water glistened on his knees and feet. Without seeing if his eyes were open, a man couldn't have told whether he was awake or asleep. Several of the Loon people had tatty saddle blankets and were the coldest during the night. The warmest found a mass of cottonwood roots undercut by floods in the spring, and it made a roof for two men so long as they didn't move too much.

Nobody wondered where the Cheyenne shaman slept. He appeared in the morning with his two horses. He wrapped his bow string around his arm and stretched it and loosened it so it wouldn't shorten when it dried.

Because they'd left so fast, they hadn't carried much pemmican. Half the Loon people had finished their last at dinner. They'd been traveling too fast to hunt. The only man who looked full that morning was the man who'd gotten the prairie chicken.

It was a cold gray dawn but nobody felt like waiting around until the sun was up. They were under no illusions.

Snow Fox's voice had gone hoarse during the night. He pointed west. "Today we ride them down. For are we not Loon people? Are we not great warriors?"

A couple of braves cheered this sentiment, and maybe it was a trick of sound but their cheers sounded like jeers.

The Cheyenne's glance was angry. For the first time Snow Fox felt approval, and he gave the shaman a stiff nod.

This morning they spread out very quickly. It wasn't fifteen minutes before they lost Slocum's trail. Wherever the trail crossed open ground, the horse's imprints had been washed out. Though Slocum had made no particular attempt to disguise his tracks this side of Pumpkin Creek, the rain had washed them out, and since the Sioux didn't know if he meant to turn back and circle for Fort Pierre, they spread out. And so scarce were the rock patches in this land that they rode for a half-hour at a steady walk before the shaman found a good sign again—a hoof print protected from the rain by the greasewood leaves.

The shaman hollered and yelled. The horse practically jumped. He was eager to go, and it felt good to have the wind rushing past him again and the sun just coming up now, heating his body.

Within an hour they'd lost the trail. Once more they spread out in a line.

The Sioux horses moved ahead at that same slow funereal speed, and their riders leaned off one side or the other or lay against their animal's length searching for marks of passage.

A brave shouted at the north end of the line and the party came to him like a whip coiling. A youth was pointing at a scratch on a slab of travertine rock. The shaman dismounted and walked up and down, casting like a hunting dog.

"It is a scratch made by an iron hoof," the youth said. "I have found it."

The shaman came back to the rock and knelt and put his face right on the surface of the cool, flat rock. He snorted. He held up something white in his hand. "White Bear has found moss," he snorted before remounting.

The youth flushed and said, "No Cheyenne has the right to mock a Sioux warrior."

Snow Fox said, "Hold your tongue. You waste more time," and set the pace by galloping his own horse back to the farthest end of the line.

Snow Fox found slide marks where the packhorse had skidded its way to the bottom of a steep coulee. On the far side they petered out again.

They rode slow enough to please their horses. The sun was clear and hot and baked the moisture out of the horses and the Sioux warriors alike. Snow Fox's belly was grumbling, and he'd been farting pretty bad for the last hour. The horses they'd pushed the night before were showing the wear.

In the afternoon the sun was godawful hot. For every mile the Indians went forward, they wove two miles side to side. The trail disappeared, maddeningly, every half-hour or so. The Indians got down now to check what their eyes had told them, because their eyes were weary now.

The day got older and the ground climbed. Three miles from Pumpkin Creek they ran into the buffalo grass. The grass was whorled flat. Though the resilient plants were trying to stand, it'd be two or three days before they amounted to anything, and meanwhile they concealed every vestige of a trail. Snow Fox leaned forward on his horse. He waved his men together. When his irritated band had assembled, he said, "Ahead lies Pumpkin Creek. Its banks are soft and we will find where they crossed."

One man objected. "They are making two times our speed. While we search for an invisible trail, they escape us."

Snow Fox said, "They will not escape us if fools don't mistake sign for moss." He kicked at his animal.

The Indian ponies didn't care to hurry, and their gait, stiffened all day, was rough as a cob. The blood thundering in their ears gave them a dull sense of purpose.

At Pumpkin Creek they split up. Half the band went downstream under the shaman and half followed Snow Fox upstream. It was dusk and the mosquitoes, by the slow-flowing water, were particularly bad. Snow Fox found where the whites had crossed. He waited for half an hour, hollering. From time to time others in his band added their shouts to his, but the echoes came back empty.

The Cheyenne rode back alone. He drew up to Snow Fox and glanced at the evidence of the whites' passage. "You have found the scent," he said.

"Where are the other Loon people?" Snow Fox asked. "Those who rode with you?"

"They are very great warriors," the Cheyenne said. "They are too great to follow a Cheyenne. This they have told me and held the muzzles of their rifles pointing at me as they said this brave thing."

A tiredness washed across Snow Fox's eyes. "They would not follow you?"

Pumpkin Creek gurgled placidly. Just twenty miles downstream was the encampment. A man's family would be there. And plenty of fresh game hanging on the rack.

"They would not follow me." The Cheyenne looked at the old chief with something hot and untamed in his eyes. "I believe they fear Owl Child's magic."

Snow Fox nodded. For a second he closed his eyes.

"They said they had to mourn. They said Squirrel and the others Owl Child killed have gone unmourned."

One of Snow Fox's people stirred into wakefulness. The mosquitoes were out for blood. A man could make the Pumpkin Creek encampment in a few hours.

One warrior took up the theme. Neither Squirrel nor the other dead had been mourned according to the traditions of the Loon people.

Snow Fox's mouth got hard. He would not argue. He said, "My son is scalped before my eyes and two of your brothers are dead." He pointed at the dead men's next of kin. They stirred restlessly under his gaze.

If he'd been satisfied he might have held them. Though they were hungry and weary, they'd been hungrier and wearier. The Cheyenne knew enough to keep silent, but not Snow Fox.

"He has killed and . . . and . . . the honor of the Loon people has been dirtied. Crazy Horse first dirtied it."

Since these men were riding Crazy Horse's ponies and since they hadn't anything to show for the hunt and since Pumpkin Creek seemed like an arrow pointed straight for home, a few of the older braves said that they thought old Crazy Horse was not such a bad sort after all, and if a man wants to take his wife back, then that's his business. At least Crazy Horse kills Seizers.

Snow Fox got pretty hot. He asked if they were no longer accepting him as a chief.

The braves said that as a matter of fact they might like to elect another chief and they'd ask their cousins and second cousins about it. Meanwhile they shouldn't stand too close to a man with such bad medicine as Snow Fox had because they might get struck during his next spell of bad luck. They added that Squirrel's medicine hadn't been too hot either. For desiring a puny white woman who didn't work, he probably deserved what he got.

Snow Fox never looked haughtier. "Then it will be my magic against Owl Child's," he said.

"Will you return with us to the camp on Pumpkin Creek?"

"I will ride after the murderer of my son," Snow Fox said between his teeth. Nudging his horse forward, he began to make good on his word.

Only the Cheyenne followed.

The two riders never turned around as the rest of their band hurried off down Pumpkin Creek. Snow Fox rode on ahead. They rode across the flattened grass. The grass was like a soft carpet as far as they could see. They each had two horses, the finest of Crazy Horse's animals. In a bit the Cheyenne drew up beside Snow Fox. The moon laid a path to the southeast. They rode toward the north, toward the north pass of the Chetish Mountains that gleamed so fine far ahead of them. That was the way the tracks had led. They rode silently for a half-hour before the Cheyenne began to get uneasy. He stole a glance at his older companion's stern face. For a moment, Snow Fox looked the way his own father had looked. "We are in his power," the Cheyenne said. "The white Blackfoot has tricked us. I can tell it. See my horse's ear—it is laying flat, and this horse has had both ears pointed at this Blackfoot's trail since we began."

Snow Fox didn't say a word, but he did look at the horse's ears.

"We are off the trail," the Cheyenne said, his skin tingling with the growing certainty.

"I see no trail," Snow Fox said, sniffing.

"Because we are off the trail." Suddenly the Cheyenne reached behind his saddle where he kept his wrapped-up horn bow and his rifle. In a single motion he offered the rifle to the moon, then his hand flashed at the lever and the unexploded cartridges were ejected up and formed, for one instant, a magic arc.

"Pugh," the Cheyenne grunted in disgust and cried, "Seizers' filth!" He hurled his rifle onto the flattened grass, where it vanished without a trace.

A real ringing silence. Snow Fox grunted—this time a grunt of approval. He unwrapped his own rifle and discarded it. He rubbed the reassuring length of his bow under his hands, polished it as he had a hundred thousand times. Their horses had turned, pawing for shorter grass. The horses faced one direction, a different direction from the one they'd traveled.

"They will not go north of the Chetish," the Cheyenne said with utter conviction in his voice. "They will cross through the canyon of the Tongue."

Though Snow Fox had been plagued by a few disasters which he blamed this shaman for, there was no denying that the one man willing to ride with him into the dark and unfriendly night was this same shaman. He said, "Yes," and they turned their horses toward the Tongue.

The walls of the Tongue River Canyon were almost sheer. A few pine trees clung to the sides of the walls, though a burro surely couldn't. The river was shallow but clean and cold. It eddied around Slocum's horse's hoofs. The horse liked standing in the water to drink. They were far enough inside the canyon mouth to risk a fire, and it looked pretty damn cheerful with the first real camp they'd known on this run. The fire was set against the back wall of the canyon, and it turned the rock golden for twenty feet. The slab threw back plenty of heat. Laura was lying propped up against a couple of smallish logs that her daughter had dragged over for a makeshift back rest. She was covered with blankets. She hadn't waited for dinner, though the first hot meal in days was cooking in Slocum's billy. He had pulled a couple of good-sized trout out of the Tongue and they were sizzling in the skillet. The girl had a coffeepot boiling on the fire and Slocum could smell the rich aroma from the riverbank a hundred yards away.

The girl sat by the fire, her arms around her legs. Slocum took a place beside her. He poured a cup of whiskey and held it in his hands to warm.

The girl eyed him curiously. "You a drinkin' man, Mr. Slocum?"

"Yep."

"And I suppose you're a gambling man too."

"I've passed the time that way."

She meant to ask another question but thought better of it. She preened. "Mr. Slocum, I shall not wish to marry."

"Uh-huh." He took a sip of whiskey. Her mother snored.

"But I could marry anybody if I wanted to, couldn't I?"

He remembered how she'd looked that morning. It had been another long ride to the entrance of these mountains and it had put years on her ma but not a scratch on the girl. Slocum thought Opal's nipples would be a tremendous amount of fun. He thought about telling her so. He thought about saying she could marry most anyone she wanted to. He said, "Squirrel wanted to make you his youngest wife. I suppose that's something to brag on."

"Ha, ha."

Laura Duffy groaned in her sleep. Slocum turned to look her over. Plenty of bone close to the surface. Her skin was puffy and discolored. He sighed.

"She's bad, ain't she?" the girl asked.

"She's weak. She must have loved your father."

"Oh, she did. She was blind for him. Anything he wanted that was hers to give."

Slocum said, "That's a hell of a way to be." He drank his whiskey.

She said, "Let me have some of that."

He handed her the bottle and she took a healthy slug and coughed and gagged and sputtered. She set the bottle down between them. After a while she said, "Good. Good."

"If it was any better, you'd have puked?" he asked.

She made a face. Deliberately, she moved closer. He could feel the heat of her hips through his clothes. Felt okay. Together they watched the trout fry like it was the most interesting thing in the world. When the meat was ready to pick it off the bones, it fairly disintegrated. She gave the fire a poke with her cooking stick and said, critically, "Reckon that's done. Will you help me with Ma?"

"Sure."

The girl shook her mother until she forced a glimmer of recognition from the half-open eyes. Slocum moved her like a sack of grain while her daughter stacked short, thick logs for a back rest. She could sit that way, still warmed by her blankets, feet almost in the fire.

"Come on, Ma. You're gonna have to wake up and eat some of this."

Laura Duffy's tongue moistened her lips. "I told him. I told him, you know. That we wouldn't get customers. We were too far out of the way to get travelers. He just laughed in that bluff way he has. Laughed at me. Well, he wasn't the one had to sit there day after day waitin' for the business to come to our door. He wasn't the one used to be afraid to look at the ground every morning for fear she'd see marks of them damn Indian ponies. It was me."

"Sure, Ma. Now you shush and eat some of this."

She spooned her mother's dinner into her mouth. She took her time and dabbed her lips whenever anything spilled. Slocum rolled a quirly and watched the fire. Over the whoosh and crackle of the flames he could hear the girl's voice saying all the kind things she could think of.

A faint spot of color returned to her mother's cheeks and the girl decided she'd had enough. "That's all right now, Ma. Here, I'll just pull you around and lay you down beside the fire."

Laura Duffy said she was cold.

"Sure you are. I'll just wrap you with another blanket."

The woman muttered something. Slocum didn't say anything, though he noticed that left him only his slicker for warmth. He poured himself another cup of whiskey. When he leaned back, he could see the dim red sparks trying to imitate the cold stars.

"It's a nice fire," she said.

"Uh-huh." He nudged a clinker with his boot tip.

"She's out. She'll sleep like a log." Slocum sensed, rather than saw, the girl's thumb jerk.

"Uh-huh."

Slocum felt warmth at his hip again when she sat.

"I'm eighteen years and six months old," she said firmly. "I'm a woman growed."

"I noticed that this morning," Slocum said slowly. He straightened one leg because it was painful sitting the way he was.

"John?" she spoke in a whisper. "John?"

If his head turned, his lips would meet hers. He stared into the fire. He listened to the sound of the fire and their breathing. He felt bad. The whiskey he swallowed didn't help. "I think I'll have me some fish," he said. And was as good as his word. She said she'd eat later.

He tried to taste the trout, but after one bite decided he didn't want any either. He faced her, eye to eye, dinner forgotten. "I'd like to lie with you," he said. "But I can't."

She'd been hurt by his refusal, her eyes showed that. Like a half-tamed animal that'd just been kicked. Her eyes widened with hope because any kind of explanation was better than the ones she'd been tormenting herself with. She'd been telling herself that she wasn't good-looking enough for a man to want even when she climbed practically naked into his lap. She was saying she was malformed, so ugly a strong man wouldn't want her after days on the trail. She thought she was ugly and horrible and unlovable and not like other women.

John Slocum told her her father had been a murderer and had murdered his wife and daughter. Slocum said it made bad blood between them.

There're as many ways to die as there are horses. When Snow Fox and the Cheyenne broke off from the rest of their discouraged party, it was already dusk. It got darker. Both men had one tall brown cavalry horse, and a mustang too, broad-shouldered, short-haunched, and wiry. Mustangs that could weave through a buffalo herd like a polo pony. The cavalry horses were taller than the mustangs and almost identically colored. Cavalry brown—almost a roan color. These animals had been bred to carry a full-armed trooper and his thirty-pound pack and his ten-pound rifle and his forty-pound saddle and eight-pound canteen across rough country. These horses had been trained to lie down to serve as forts behind which their masters could return fire. They were young: neither of them more than four. One of Snow Fox's mustangs was eight and the Cheyenne's mustang had long, long teeth.

The Chetish Mountains swam in the moonlight above the broad plain like a theatrical backdrop. They seemed flat as the pictographs painted on buffalo skin.

The buffalo grass was trying to spring back upright where the sun could do it some good. Here and there beaten grass pushed itself back into tufts and bushes and hummocks. It was impossible to tell what these odd-looking clumps were, tufts or boulder outcroppings. The prairie dog villages were easy to spot because they were bare of grass and the moon glared on bare ground like it was white and cancerous.

Snow Fox weighed a hundred fifty pounds, and the heavy-chested Cheyenne probably weighed twenty pounds more. It was less weight than the cavalry horses had been bred to carry, and the mustangs carried nothing at all.

The Cheyenne knew how far back they were, and Snow Fox knew too. It had been mental exercise during the long, aggravating day—calculating how rapidly their quarry was drawing away from here.

Snow Fox knew this part of the country. He'd hunted here many times. He kept the lead because he knew the shortest route between here and the Tongue. In white man's measurements, about twenty miles.

The broken grass lay like shiny, intricate roadways through the night. Snow Fox rode pretty straight ahead and pretty hard too, not veering much left or right.

At his side, slightly behind, rode the Cheyenne. From time to time Snow Fox shot a glance at him or gave him an encouraging grin. He caught the younger Indian studying him instead of looking where he was going, which made Snow Fox mutter something about "a damn fool who doesn't watch his horse's footing." But he really wasn't too displeased.

What they did was insane. At every step, one of their horses might lose it. The horses pounded through the grass mat to ground they couldn't see. Snow Fox was feeling so good he let off a series of high-pitched yelps. Way off on the plains, some coyote took him up on his boast, barking its own salute to the night and the moon. He'd fooled it. The Cheyenne's teeth flashed because coyotes weren't often the butt of any man's joke.

Nothing but the moon and the night and the stars and the wind rushing past their shoulders and their horses. They floated along with their animals. Orion was high in the sky, and the tipsy moon was careening toward home when the Cheyenne fell.

It wasn't just the gopher hole. It was the neighborhood this gopher elected to call home. Like his fellows, he'd bored his hole at an angle under a rock slab. The rock wasn't more than five inches thick and a strong man could have jiggled it; in fact, the horse did jar it loose when his hoof shot into the hole and locked between the hole and the rock, which didn't move far enough or soon enough either. The horse was moving at half gallop and broke the cannon bone as clean as if some surgeon had done it with an ax. Except for the gristle and tendons, which were flexible enough to stretch half their normal length, the horse would have left six inches of leg in that hole instead of dragging it behind him as he did. Deprived of one foot, the horse dropped his shoulder and kind of curled over on his right side.

The Cheyenne was welded to his animal and to his animal's pain and knew when the horse lost his luck and when his balance went. If he'd ridden the horse down, the falling animal would have smashed him flat as a lizard on a rock, but he turned loose of his grip and sailed into the air. The horse's rump missed his head by three inches. No more.

The Cheyenne lost his wind when he hit, but thanks to the carpet of collapsed grass he wasn't hurt any worse. When he got to his feet he still had spring in him. Snow Fox was circling back at a trot. He'd already grabbed hold of the Cheyenne's other pony.

They cut the army horse's throat with Snow Fox's scalping knife. The knife blade was thin and delicate like a fileting knife, and they had to saw to get through the thick muscle. Snow Fox cupped his hands and drank some of the horse's black, hot blood, and the Cheyenne followed his example.

With the Cheyenne up on his mustang, they rode toward the opening they could see in the Chetish. The opening looked like a smudge. Just a smudge. That was a trick of the sky, which had gone pretty dark.

Snow Fox's horse lost his gait. First thing Snow Fox noticed was the tiny click of the horse's front hooves, which were just touching his rear hooves as he ran. It put a tiny hitch in his stride. This hitch expanded until every few minutes the stride would fall to pieces and the hooves would strike each other, and the ride was like an overbalanced man running down a too-steep hill. Snow Fox's mustang hadn't carried his share of the load that morning and still had bottom. The Cheyenne's pony was running well. There was the slightest hint of more light in the east. The wind was cool coming off the grass and Snow Fox thought he smelled some moisture. Maybe the Tongue River. His horse's breathing was getting very bad. Snow Fox leaned quickly and felt the horse's nostrils. The horse nearly dropped from the weight shift, as if his front legs couldn't carry one more ounce. The Cheyenne touched his cheek with his wet hand and what he felt was blood, not mucus.

Snow Fox went over to the mustang's back. Freed of his burden, the army horse made a fast dash to show his gallant heels before he broke up completely, slowing and stopping. He stood, splay-footed, head down.

The Cheyenne hung a few feet off the ground, study-ing the flat grasses like a scholar. In a second Snow Fox followed his lead because he wasn't too old to be a great warrior and a great rider too. He spotted what the Cheyenne was excited about. The tracks of four horses were not very old; perhaps they were made just late last night. That smell was certainly the Tongue River, and the tracks swerved to the left to parallel the river as it pointed at the canyon through the Chetish. The cold air was rolling down off those mountains like a silent avalanche and leaving dew on the mashed grasses. It got so wet the mustang's hooves kicked up a steady spray of near-freezing water, chilling Snow Fox's skin. These horses had several more hours of running left in them.

The Cheyenne slowed to a canter, then a trot. His horse changed gaits awkwardly like its blood was thick and sticky.

The sky behind them was dead gray. The dewy grass looked as black as dried blood. The slopes of the Chetish were cold and white like dirty snow. The river was dark and mysterious, and as they neared the canyon mouth they felt the wind that had started on the other side of the mountains, twenty miles away.

Carried in that cold wind they could also smell the smell of honey clover, though it was very faint, like perfume.

A few miles ahead, John Slocum smelled that same perfume. To him it smelled like a promise. Like things might get better somehow. Tired as he'd been, he'd slept fitfully, tormented by dreams of Bird-Calling. In his dreams she appeared sometimes as his lover and sometimes as a monster who meant to drag him into her grave. He woke up sweating. He'd let the girl have the slicker last night because it was the least he could do. She'd been hit pretty hard when he told her about Quartermaster Duffy. She opened her mouth a couple of times because maybe she wanted to say "I'm sorry," but she didn't because she didn't feel worthy enough for that small contact. She took the slicker and lay wrapped against the cold like a stiff mummy. Slocum covered himself with dirty shirts and sat next to the fire with a couple of log reflectors. It got too low to warm him and he sat up, drawing the shirts close, shivering. He poked the fire. His eyes were gluey and crusted. The last thing he'd seen in his dream was Bird-Calling, weeping and waving a brave farewell just like she'd waved when he set out on the hunting trip that was to be his last hunt as a Blackfoot. He rubbed his eyes. He wondered if he'd ever dream about her again and decided he would but that it'd be different because she was dead in a second way. He thought she'd die again and again in his mind, and each time her dying would seem easier to bear.

He'd hurt that girl last night. He hadn't wished to—or maybe he had. Wasn't it better she knew the truth?

The clover smell. He knew the valley it came from on the far side of the Chetish and not ten days' ride from Fort Bozeman. There might be some bands of Indians, but most of the Sioux were on Pumpkin Creek and ordinary care should see them through to the fort.

He wondered what he'd do then. He put a couple of sticks on the gray ashes and blew the fire to life.

In the gray morning light he went to the river and washed his face in the steaming cold water. His Appaloosa nickered.

"Good morning, horse," Slocum said, but the Appaloosa wasn't listening.

Slocum filled the coffeepot and set it at the back of the coals where it'd be hot when the ladies woke up. No sense waking them before the sun warmed things up.

Until the golden light found its way into the canyon tinting the high stone walls in a line, he sat by the fire. He felt loose and relaxed and he decided that maybe he'd get into a few poker games at Fort Bozeman. He'd been lone-wolfing it too much lately.

"Jesus! You startled me."

The woman pushed at his shoulders so he'd make a place beside the fire. She sat herself down. Under the blankets her legs were naked and blue like some streams he'd seen. She smelled awful—like a piece of machinery that hasn't been oiled right and burns itself out. She put her hands to the fire. Her hands were raw. "I heard you," she said. Her voice was the voice of a eighty-year-old crone.

"Oh?" He reached for the coffeepot, poured a little whiskey in the cup, and filled it with hot black coffee. He offered the cup wreathed with its fruitful aroma.

"You want to get me drunk?" She struck out at the cup with the side of her hand and upset the scalding stuff. It splashed Slocum's leg and he jumped up to hold the hot cloth away from his flesh. "What the hell?"

"I heard you," she repeated stubbornly. "You and my daughter. You thought I was asleep, but I woke."

Slocum's horse nickered again. Across the river a thrush started singing its heart out. Slocum enjoyed listening to that damn bird. Reluctantly he listened to what the woman was saying. Something about how Slocum had lied. He'd lied about Duffy and lied about

Duffy's death. She said it had all been a lie from beginning to end, meant to decoy them out of the safety of the roadhouse, which he wanted because he knew the railroad was coming through just at the spot on Mizpah Creek. She said the stage was going to make Mizpah Creek one of its regular stops. She said her husband had told her so.

"Sure," Slocum said. He'd been thinking about making up some breakfast but lost his appetite.

With her slicker still wrapped around her, Opal came over to the fire. "Ma?" she said softly, touching her shoulder.

"Get away from me," her mother said. "You damn slattern. You shame your father. You shame me. Takin' up with him." She jabbed one angry finger at Slocum. Her eyes looked like someone had moved into a vacant house and was peeking timidly through the window.

"I guess I'll feed the horses," Slocum said. "She didn't want any coffee."

"I'll take nothing from your hands," she said, haughty as a queen.

"Sure."

"I'll see to her," Opal said softly.

She meant to feed her mother some gruel or some of the leftover trout. She hoped to get her dressed and into her clothes. She hoped to move her into the sun when it finally struck this side of the river. Her mother got up real suddenly, off balance, and took a step and bumped into Slocum. The arrow took her precisely through the throat. Thuck. It sounded like an arrow that strikes a tree. For a second, Opal saw the fletching of the arrow, two trimmed brown chicken-hawk feathers and the reddish feather from a woodpecker's tail. A brooch appeared at the undefended hollow of her mother's throat. Her mother put her hands to her neck, wondering. Her eyes lost some of their madness—some of her crazy fear. Her eyes softened. Her eyes got thoughtful and brave and intelligent. Her eyes recognized her daughter and tried to make amends. Her eyes got sad at the impending loss. Briefly they were scared. Her fingers fluttered around the arrow feathers, flicking them nervously. Her mouth opened and the blood ran out, a gusher.

"Ma!"

Slocum was going for the ground, his hand crossing his body for his Colt. Because he was off balance he hit the ground awkwardly on his left chest and lost a little air, though that didn't bother him as much as the ringing in his ears. The Colt was out from under his body by then anyway. His fingers clamped the ebony grip like talons, and his callused thumb swept back, catching the hammer and drawing it to full cock even as the muzzle sniffed for its target like a birddog. His hand shot out straight. In the alders at the water's edge he saw a shape that shouldn't be there. He fired. The bloom of smoke from his Colt. The jerk as it jumped in his hand. The burn of hot powder on the side of his hand.

"Ma! Oh, my God!"

"Drop, girl!"

He didn't hear the sound that meant she'd done as he said. The sound of heavy straining. The blurred figure in the alders hadn't budged an inch.

Her mother's body got very heavy and Opal swayed with the effort to hold it upright. The body slid out of her grasp though she cried, "Help me. God. Please!"

The figure was still blurred. Slocum blinked. The figure came into the open and it was still unclear, and its voice boomed in his ears.

"Your bullet cannot touch me, Owl Child. I am proof against your weapons and your cunning. Your medicine is weak and my medicine is stronger." Slocum lifted his Colt and the Colt barrel was vague and furry too. He must have taken a harder rap than he thought. As Laura Duffy crumpled to the ground, he heard the sounds of death, her bowels voiding and the thick gurgle of her blood.

"I have killed one horse to reach here," the Cheyenne bragged as he stepped out into the open fifty feet from the huddled whites. "And a second great horse is foundered and will never be of use. That is how my magic brought me here. My medicine is made up of two strong horses and the honor of a friend. What is your medicine, Blackfoot? Is your magic the bullet that misses—the old woman who bleeds? Are those your dreams? Do you dream of Seizers?" The Cheyenne kept his bow in his right hand, string undrawn.

Slocum wished he could see him. He cocked and loosed off another round. The pistol created a hell of a fog. It covered the already blurred figure with a cloud.

"I can kill you as I wish," the Cheyenne boasted. His boast wasn't very loud—just a calm man stating a pleasant fact.

The blast of the shot echoed down the tall, narrow canyon for miles, scaring a covey of partridge aloft.

John Slocum got to his feet. His knees were dirty. The horses made the little snuffling sounds of horses who smell blood, and quite suddenly Slocum was angry with them for carrying on that way. They'd smelled blood before.

The band of gold on the north wall of the canyon had dropped down and became a wide golden band, thick enough for a heavy bracelet or belt. The rimrock trees were a brighter green than the blue-black trees in the shade.

John Slocum felt every single one of his thirty-two years. His knees hurt and he had an ache in his chest.

Still screened by the brush, Snow Fox waited still. His horse's head was low and its ribs heaved, but it wasn't foundered or windbroke. It had given and given of its heart and still had heart to give. Snow Fox waited, his bare legs clamped to the barrel of his horse and the single rein laid across his arm. In his right hand he held his coup stick. Snow Fox's coup stick was a length of deer bone—the small bone that connects the haunch to the hooves. It was twelve inches long and narrowed to less than an inch. Eagle feathers were tied to its haft.

The girl was huddled over her mother, shaking with sobs. Snow Fox felt sadness for her. It expanded him, being able to feel something for his white enemy. Slocum had gotten too fat and too careless. Like any great warrior he was brought to this state by his own arrogance.

Opal Duffy's tears were crystals and she saw a dozen Indians walking toward them. The Cheyenne's red medicine bag which hung from his neck looked very much like the blood-red muscle, the heart. He wore a sweatband that was purely white. The bow that hung from his right hand seemed to pulse with the beating of her heart. Releasing her mother's head, she stood beside John Slocum. Nearer his shoulder, she could see the Cheyenne as he was, a proud, happy warrior strutting toward them with a wild grin laid across his face. But out of the shadow of Slocum's shoulder, she saw twelve of him. She put her arm through Slocum's.

That move broke the spell. The Cheyenne extended his arms with the bow at full stretch and Slocum put a bullet between his eyes. The black spot in his skull wasn't very big, but the impact jerked his head back though it didn't affect the rest of his body at all.

The Cheyenne imagined snapping a fawn's spine over his knee. He had the most vivid image of that fawn. His lights went out.

His arrow cut through the space between Slocum and Opal. Slocum blinked. He let the gun fall to the end of his hand.

Some of the partridge who'd settled again jumped up a second time that morning, calling querulously to each other. The thunder rang against the cliffs and turned and rolled. It sounded louder than one pistol shot.

Snow Fox's horse threw up its head like the warhorse it was. It snorted.

Three, four, five steps. John Slocum knelt beside the Cheyenne brave in the blood-smeared grass.

Opal saw Snow Fox coming. Above his head a two-hundred-foot golden band on the canyon walls. His black and gray braids streaming out behind him. He had no son, so he was young again. He was without hope except for the wild surge of his heart. His heart beat as a young man's as he jumped across the clearing toward Owl Child, bent over the shaman whose magic had failed him at last.

Opal screamed at the top of her lungs.

Snow Fox saw the slow, slow turn of his enemy's face. He saw the pistol lying uselessly beside him in the grass. Snow Fox stood up on his horse, swelling into a giant, like a chief of old.

With his coup stick, he struck John Slocum across the face.

The light piece of bone barely tapped his cheek, but it had come out of nowhere. He had not seen the man rushing down on him. The blow seared his flesh and he felt like a man branded.

The woman ran toward him. Seemed she moved awful damn slow. Slocum's cheek felt like the lightning had marked it. The Colt lay in the grass beside him. It was already cocked. How many bullets had he fired at the Cheyenne—was it two or three? He couldn't take his eyes off the Cheyenne. Snow Fox reined his horse back down and the animal went back on its haunches as it turned. The chief raised the mustang up, hooves in the air, and him riding the horse at the shoulders, coup stick raised high. He stayed up for a second.

Opal gasped.

Slocum felt somewhat older.

Snow Fox let his horse's hooves come down and when he touched earth again, the horse was weary, played out, and its rider was just an old Indian past his prime. Without a single backward glance, the old Indian and his horse made their way downstream. They rode very slowly, slower than a man walks, and they were in range of Slocum's guns for a couple of minutes. The old man rode with a sour grace. Slocum wondered if he'd go back to the big village on Pumpkin Creek. There wouldn't be much waiting for him when he did.

When he was quite out of sight behind the pines, Opal put her hand on Slocum's shoulder. "Are you hurt?" she whispered.

"Not so much as I was."

"What did that Indian do?"

"He counted coup on his bravest enemy. He is a very great warrior, that old man."

"Counted coup?"

"He struck an armed man in the face and turned his back and rode away. He insulted a man he feared."

"You could have killed him."

"Maybe not."

Epilogue

Just ten days later, on the 18th of August 1876, John Slocum and Opal Duffy rode through the gates of Fort Bozeman. The sentry who first spotted them at first thought Opal was a boy because she was dressed in Slocum's oversize clothing except for the red kerchief on her head.

Their horses were fat from grass. Opal's face was tanned and soft. John Slocum's gun butt was dull flat black.

They were the first riders to reach Fort Bozeman from the east since June.